Beyond Belief in the Land of Rhythm

Lesley Ann Eden

Strategic Book Group

Strategic Book Group
P.O. Box 333
Durham CT 06422
www.StrategicBookClub.com

ISBN: 978-1-61204-113-1

Printed in the United States of America

Book Design: Suzanne Kelly

Dedication

For my children Sarah, Nina, Benjamin, and Gemma,
and their children, and their children's children
who journey on this earth. Wherever they roam,
I will sing them to my heart and when they call,
I will dance them to my door.

Author's Note

Do we ever have forever? Is always only a myth? Do we exist beyond the beyond and out past the beginning? So many questions with too few answers! I do not have the answers, for I only peeped through a crack in the universe and glimpsed a splinter of knowledge from the great universal tree. An artist friend said, "You should write your life—but no one would ever believe you!"

So I have. At the risk of being ridiculed and disbelieved, I have recorded amazing and incredible events which question reality and contest belief beyond belief.

After my extraordinary expedition through Central America, whilst embroiled in a poisoned fever in Playa del Carmen, I was contacted by a spirit who made me memorise a message, enticing me to chase its meaning across Cuba, leading me to far-out places, searching worn-out traces of the spirit's heroic life. The journey unravelled more than I expected, hoisting me back to a time and place shrouded in mystery, to a palace where history still questions its obscure existence. To a time when Knossos Palace was a thriving, magnificent monument set deep in the heart of Minoan Society, to seek a child in the last sighs of her brief existence. Unexpectedly, and as absurd as it seems, I was pushed back through time to find myself inside her body to witness her horrific ordeal. I do not know how or why it happened. I can only relate the truth as it occurred and record the little girl's life as my own. Living inside her mind, I became her. I believe reliving her story and sharing her grief will bring comfort and peace to her troubled soul.

Lesley Ann Eden

If we have travelled together before, you will know that nothing is fabricated, with the exception of people's names in order to protect their identity. In most cases my encounters can be verified by others who witnessed many strange events and have been part of my story.

Please dare to accompany me once again into unknown territory outside imagination, past the confines of your understanding, to partake of my paranormal happenings that are, as my friend said, "beyond belief."

Chapters

CHAPTER I

Message

"I am as strong as the person I am inside."

Words, words, and more words tumble from nowhere and are planted on my lips from an unseen presence standing by my bed. In and out of a fever I twist and turn. I wake as I memorise the words, but drop back into broiling confusion.

Where am I?

Mexico, Playa del Carmen. Memory creeps back as the infection beats a path through my intestines, invades my body, and attacks my sanity. I recall the night on the tiny Caribbean Island of Caye Caulker when the sickness struck after my being poisoned by a girl who detested me for befriending a man, a Masai basketball player. I am fearful of the next day's long journey through Belize and Guatemala, crossing seven borders into Mexico, pounding uneven terrain on local buses, barely conscious, travelling in a wretched semi-coma, waking only when helped from terminal to terminal by my fellow travellers before finally arriving in Playa.

I half open my eyes. Towering whitewashed walls, shaded under a dark thatched canopy, encase me in a cool barn, a haven from the heat: heat outside, heat inside my head. Under the white sheets my body oozes a yellow, waxy sweat, staining

1

the linen from the poisoned orange juice the jealous girl on the island slipped me and now bubble, babble, garble, words form in the front of my mouth not from my brain; they are not my words. They are masculine in essence. I feel his energy but cannot see him. He makes me repeat the lines over and over again but the words fall out of time with my rhythm. Words, hold still. I need to tame you and make order out of your confusion. I need peace, but his spirit is restless after being held captive for so long with his ideas fermenting in yeasty silence. I yearn to make sense out of the chaos. Words garble, rabble on, bubble out, leak over the edge of reason in this endless fight while I burn and twist, struggling to dig up a meaning. I claw my way out of the madness, climbing upwards into the breaking light of morning, where the shadow of a single palm branch waves playfully over a white tablecloth. I slowly sit up. My head clears as I repeat the words:

> *My head is as heavy as a revolution.*
> *My body is as weak as a soldier's bayonet after battle,*
> *But I am strong as the person I am inside.*

On returning to my cottage in North Yorkshire after my expedition through Mexico, Guatemala, Antigua, and Belize, flying from Cancun, battling a hurricane in Miami with huge delays of flights, trains, and buses, I stood in the hallowed quiet of my small garden. I looked very different from the person who thought she was ready to challenge the universe, with my unkempt straggly hair and my long, hand-woven poncho, appearing a stranger in my garden, peering at the rambling disarray through bronzed face and careworn eyes. I had lost weight through illness and my jeans were slack around my waist and hips. I was the traveller, back from unimaginable places, bearing worn-out traces of dust and dirt between fingers and blue toes dyed from my shoes in the wet rainforest. The grass had grown long wild tufts and the weeds had taken over the rockery, but I was happy to be back, content to have completed my journey across Central America, relieved to open the door and not to be blown to smithereens by a gas leak that threatened two hours before I left.

A mountain of mail jeered a welcome. I was afraid of opening the brown envelopes. For a glorious time I avoided my worries and fears about my tax investigation and now I was forced to face them head on. I read everything, including the junk mail, but left the two brown envelopes staring, daring me to open them. On that Sunday evening in early September the thought of school in the morning made me nervous. The beginning of a new school year is always daunting and having survived my first year back in the frontline firing zone of the classroom, after the freedom and excitement of choreographing shows across four different countries, I felt anxious about my new classes and how I would cope with the tedium and the discipline.

The house was quiet and empty. My footsteps echoed across the hall. On the one hand I felt happy to be back and have some peace but, on the other, I secretly missed my travelling companions. I plucked up the courage to take the brown envelopes and sit in my conservatory pondering my incredible trip, having escaped the mundane chores and the worries of the tax investigation that haunted me for nearly two years, accruing more penalty payment the longer it was dragged out by the investigator. Travelling allowed me to forget, but back in my routine zone the worry returned and the loneliness crept back through the cracks in my defence mechanisms. It is true I kept money back and did not declare it, but with my being alone with four children and financing my son's education, it was a necessary evil. I am sorry, but I do not regret it. I would do it again for his sake.

The September evening was like the closing of a show after the final curtain call. It was glorious but sad, for soon the flowers would fade, the nights darken and the days grow dismal. My trip would be a distant memory, my companions becoming vague shadows of people who once shared a journey of a lifetime. Although I had their addresses I knew I would not contact them; to revisit what was is never a good idea. Sipping purple wine I revelled in the moment, enjoying the decadent glory of freedom before stepping into the harness of my working life. I opened the envelopes and read the contents with dread. Miss Mohannen, the chief investigator, planned to scrutinize six years back tax and required all the relevant bank information. My salary was never great, but to suggest that I owed in the region of £80,000 was ludicrous. I didn't know what to do. The light faded and evening tints of lilac and purple seeped through the day's edge, disappearing with the sun beyond the horizon. Summer was definitely over.

The next day at school I learned I had been given a horrible class to teach English. They were awarded the nickname of "Darts Team" because they would dart off anywhere, any time they chose. I called them my "monsters," the dreaded class from hell. The lesson was a minefield, a battleground between them and me where I fought to inject tiny snippets of knowledge into their barricaded brains, but they hurled everything back at me, throwing their work onto the floor, tearing up paper, throwing things at each other, whispering in corners, seedily sharing the latest porn photos on their mobiles. I recoiled when a voice shouted from the back of the classroom: "Do ya wanna see this, Miss? It's a man gerrin' his head cut off with a knife! Look at him screamin,' Miss!"

I was appalled that the students were bandying around such disgusting violence, and sickened to the core by their zest for gore. I demanded the mobile from the miscreant but he refused. Unable to wrestle with an obstinate fifteen-year-old boy, I sent him out but he stormed into the corridor, slammed the door, and disappeared. I had to call for help to deal with him. Papa Nics came to my aid. I stood back in admiration as he summoned up a magnificent, booming voice which echoed around the quad and bounded back, lashing the insolent boy into submission. I envied this tool and tried to emulate his warrior war cry but my feeble attempts fell, strangled in a splutter, and I was relieved when the bell shrieked and the other monsters darted out wildly, throwing bits of paper onto the floor like dirty confetti. My head ached. I sat down at my desk, pining to be liberated. Words drifted into my mind, words which a ghostly someone made me remember: *"My head is as heavy as a revolution."*

I am always glad when the end of the school day hangs heavily in the air after the shouting, the scrimmage, and the tug of war fade into the late afternoon, when the sighs have died, leaving the creaking vacant desks mocking the moment. I muster up more energy inside to embrace the pupils in my performing arts school where striving for excellence is the goal, where learning is a joy. I would be happy just to teach them, but being single I have a hefty mortgage and need both the day and night job to pay my way. Following the Mexico expedition my knee injury had worsened and I bore constant discomfort; even in my sleep I fitfully awakened to stabbing pain. I was afraid to go to the doctor in case he were to tell me I could not dance. I could not afford the time in hospital. Dance (apart from my children) is my life and I could not let it go.

Returning home late in the evening, it was a chore to resume the routine of preparing my own meals and eating alone. I missed the Mexican food and the freshly prepared salsa. I switched on the radio and the Buena Vista Social Club pulsed through the hallway. The music incited me to cha-cha-cha my way toward the cupboards to explore herbs to spice up my mincemeat. Cuban rhythm enticed my feet to slink across the floor, shimmying my shoulders toward the fridge where I had stored a bottle of Cava. I love the moment when the bubbles gush up my nose. I gasped, inhaling the cool effervescence that glided down the back of my throat. Disappointed when the intoxicating Cubanismo beat drifted into nothing, I yearned for more and tracked down a CD from my music library. Che Guevara stared from the CD cover and I paused to look at the man who was my iconic hero during my late teens. Words echoed through a tunnel: *"I am as strong as the person I am inside."*

I smiled at his handsome face. I watched the golden bubbles rise to the top of the champagne glass where they break and fizz, recalling the first time I saw his picture. As a young university student in London with very little money I used to walk down Kensington High Street admiring the small boutiques. It was early October when the term had just begun, and pausing by an army shop that sold belts made out of empty bullet cases and all kinds of military gear, I noticed a man's eyes staring at me in the bright lights of the early evening. His dark, enigmatic, rugged features enchanted me. The word "Che" boldly inscribed across the tee shirt embossed in red branded my heart. It was a college-girl crush, which only faded, never died. Something strange happened as I stood gazing up into his face. It was as though we were communicating on a level far away from the earth. We were meeting through the stars, across the cosmos.

Drifting out of the dream, with the little money I had left for food I bought the tee shirt and a cartridge belt, emulating a guerrilla fighter. I walked along the street feeling part of his cause, hoping one day I might meet him. Suddenly, a young man in a rush carelessly ran in front of a car, and his life was taken in a second. Blood trickled along the pavement. I slumped down next to a bus stop and retched in the gutter, fighting dizziness. As I lifted my head, I saw a dark grey shape rise out of the man's body. It was a wedge of energy released from his physical shell. It hovered over the gathering crowd before it floated over the edge of Derry and Tom's store, then disappeared above the lights of the city. The rising soul did not shock me; I was used to it. Since I could remember I could see and hear spirits, entities, and energies that others couldn't even comprehend. I lived my life in two worlds: reality and something beyond. I was used to communicating with other beings not of the earth.

Around the age of four years I realized that I could rise out of my body. Instinctively I knew the method of lifting out. It was easy. Hovering above, I was all of myself but without my shell, light as the air around me. I could clearly see the little girl lying under the pink eiderdown. I watched myself breathing but never stayed out too long in case I couldn't return. I was anchored to my body by a long silver umbilical cord and all it took to be back was the desire to return. Living in two worlds at the same time was confusing and, to make matters worse, I was plagued by what the grown-ups called my "nightmares." I often heard voices in my head but bedtime was the worst—the sounds increased and multiplied like the tweaking of a wireless set struggling to make sense of conversations, with strands of music cutting in and garbled foreign vibrations fighting all at once for air space in my brain. Disembodied hands would menacingly form in the half-light, as fingers tugged and pummelled the bed covers. From my hideout under the blankets I sometimes had the courage to peer at the shadow of a person standing over my bed with his curly hair outlined against my tiny rosebud wallpaper. I tried to stop breathing as the sound of each breath magnified in the silence, until a scream formed in my throat, rising and rising until it shot out like a caged cockerel screeching in the early morning. "It's those nightmares again!" they always said. No one ever believed what I tried to tell them.

I was too young to understand that our house was built on an ancient Druid burial ground. I had constant dreams of walking in a swamp, avoiding stepping on heads and faces concealed in the ground. Half-dead people buried up to their necks rolled their rotting eyes at me with open mouths miming silent, suffocated shrieks locked in caverns below my bed, where cold blood from the past seeped through my floorboards, feeding nightly on my fear. Dread of their terror beleaguered me. Sometimes I used a game to entertain myself. We did not have a television so I didn't know what one looked like, but lying in my bed in the dark I could muster a large screen in the air which appeared through a swirling mass of colours, changing from microscopic pink, lilac, and purple molecules into a fluorescent flat monitor, where visages appeared at random. Sometimes the image would be horrible with glaring eyes and I would dare myself to stare back for as long as I could before blinking, whereupon it would automatically disappear. Other times the faces appeared softer, sometimes sad, and on rare occasions comical. The Druid connection was strange—my grandparents owned a pub in the main town called The Druid's Arms and I often felt shadows from the past lurking in its murky corridors alongside the smell of stale beer and boiled fish that tainted the gloomy saloon where old men stared and spit into sawdust buckets.

Witnessing the young man's spirit leaving his body that evening in the high street had not been a shock; it was, rather, the anguish of a life snatched harshly which made me feel weak. What is the meaning of weak? Letters appeared from another sphere, forming words across my white kitchen wall: *"I am as*

7

weak as a soldier's bayonet after battle." I pondered the layers of meaning. After battle a bayonet is smeared with blood, defiled, de-energised. A man like Che would know. I tingled as a strange realisation caught me off balance. Could I dare to think that the message was from Che? Could I dare to dare to think that?

Vague feelings from Playa del Carmen strayed through my mind. I stared at the face I had admired for many years and sat down to eat my chili. Surely it couldn't be him? Perhaps it was just a fanciful notion, but the incident in Mexico was very real. My fever was real and so was the person urging me to remember the words. If the message was from him, then what was the purpose and why? Many people who have left earth have spoken to me across the great cosmos, but the idea of Che choosing me seemed too fantastic.

I needed to know more about his life and Cuba, so after rushing my supper I flicked through the catalogue from the company who had organised my last adventure through Central America. I found a dance and music course offering students the chance to travel across Cuba studying the music of the people, staying in local houses whilst learning indigenous percussion instruments and dance. The trip seemed tailored for me. The only drawback was my leg injury but that was a minor detail! Perhaps travelling to Cuba I would unravel a meaning behind the message and, if not, making a pilgrimage to Che's resting place at Santa Clara where the course terminated would be very special. It was good to have a goal at the end of an adventure. Planning for the end before the beginning was like a good piece of choreography—like in the precarious dance of life, we must always have one eye on the exit.

As the Cava took me into a floating sphere where the idea of Cuba was a relief, an adventure, and an anxiety, I was on the verge of crying but couldn't find the tears. I was hypnotised by the translucent bubbles rising to the surface racing swiftly in rigid lines before breaking effervescently into nothing. My cracked voice echoed across the kitchen, shouting at the cupboards, "I've lost my song. How did I lose it? When did it die?" The fluorescent pink street lamps glinted on the tiny mirrors dangling in my ancient cherry tree and sent tiny bright lights dancing across my white ceiling. Alone in the dying evening, the rainforest in Guatemala called where I fleetingly unearthed a forgotten melody which sang briefly in exotic places, leaving spaces of hot sighs and forbidden caresses outcast on a desert island, but it drifted away to a back file in an empty cabinet, where it waits to be rediscovered, perhaps in a dusty folksong somewhere in rural England, or maybe coaxed by the sensuous Cuban rhythms. The night closed in and I locked out the day's turmoil, and drifted back to the heat and the sand, the ocean and the music, that I missed so much.

The next morning in the staff room a few stray laughs relieved the tension of the new term, with bright teachers fresh from college nervously waiting for the bell to sweep them off into their assigned classrooms. The seagulls swooped over the playing field in the September gloom. I envied their freedom. I longed to be in faraway places where Education is honoured, unlike here, with the dull, dismal faces of the unenthusiastic teenagers who amble to their lessons, detesting every minute of their schooling. The day wore on, dragging its feet through untimely bells punctuating the daily ritual. Let me go home now? A dark butterfly flitted past the window as the autumn sunshine broke through the shadows and drew a stray ray across the back of my neck. I recalled lazy days on a tiny Caribbean island, where in the hazy heat I meandered through traces of worn-out places, shacks and tin huts, to find a blatant sign of "Betta no Litta" displayed under a heap of rotting rubbish in that less than idyllic paradise.

I tidied away the memory and prepared to face my monsters, the dreaded class from hell, endeavouring to coax them with the tantalising curriculum of Shakespeare, modern poets, and general English skills—which is difficult, as they have barely mastered the spelling of their own names, for during their fifteen years on the planet they have learnt so well how not to learn, how to prevent information from seeping into their brains. It was only a small group of twelve, nine boys and three girls, and the next lesson was in one of the worst classrooms for miscreants: the pottery room. I am always terrified they will destroy the tiny vases, the delicate pots that other classes have so lovingly made. They waited like hungry animals outside the classroom door. I pretended to be in control, spying dangerous weapons in their hands with which they challenged each other before the class begins. The boys ambled in, throwing their bags haphazardly across the room and just missing a fine display of newly kilned ashtrays. The girls giggled shyly having lavished their shared lip gloss over their pouting mouths. I sent the boys out to file in again and they did so, muttering abuse beneath their breath. I made a mental note to myself:

RECIPE TO SURVIVE THE MONSTERS

Preparation
Before the lesson begins I will confiscate the following ingredients:
1. A sharp knife stolen from the Design and Tech department.
2. A pair of scissors snatched from the teacher's desk at break.
3. A broken shard of glass stolen from a girl's compact mirror.
4. A bent fork stolen from the canteen at lunch.
5. A large needle stolen from the sewing room.

Method
Collect items together, even though owners adamantly object and call you names. Display items on teacher's desk clearly for all to see. Baste the class with threats of multiple detentions and relevant reports, adding the full amount of forceful hand gestures, until emotion is brought to the boil. Keep at boiling point for a few moments while class responds with reverent silence. Leave to simmer, displaying another fitful warning before collecting items up off the desk to show to appropriate authority, whilst allowing class to cool down before being served their next lesson.

When the bell rang they charged out and I was left exhausted. My seasons were out of time. I still felt in the summer of my life, yet chronologically I was in the autumn. After the battering of the monsters I craved company and yearned to be caressed by a summer breeze. I had decided to join a dating agency but was told that men in general do not want to date an older woman, and although I still felt in the sunshine of my youth and wanted to be bathed in golden light and sent dizzy by the heady perfume of orange lilies, I was discouragingly warned that I must be grateful to be kissed by the winter sun when it deems to shine through the dark empty branches of the stark trees, taking comfort in the artificial scent of hothouse plants displayed in the supermarkets before Christmas.

Back at my cottage, I felt a failure at relationships, considering the two divorces and countless boyfriends. I signed the papers to join an exclusive dating agency, embarrassed to be in that position but the prospect of my new adventure travelling across Cuba in August, even with the threat of hurricanes and torrential tropical rainfall, did not dampen my enthusiasm.

I gazed down at my bare feet, which were still pale blue, after being dyed darkest blue from my open sandals in continuous wet weather in the rainforest. I missed those times. The children in my dance school were shocked and amazed when they saw my bright blue feet! Unfortunately in the humid heat I caught an infection in my little toe just before I travelled back home. After a few nights home, the skin split open like a peapod shell. Ripe, ready to burst, it ruptured, spilling blood and gore across the bedsheets. Such is the price of adventure! Routine robs us of our chance to know ourselves beyond our deepest roots, and the price of such knowledge cannot be counted. I bandaged my toe, ready to dance the next morning, accepting my situation, knowing that I would venture out again to discover new challenges because, after all, it was only a toe!

Back home, Che's face peered down from my bookshelf, giving me strength to plan my Cuba trip, plying me with a sense of hope to get me through tough days, the drudgery of school, and my financial difficulties. I comforted myself with the thought that not long before I had stood on top of a temple in the jungle of Guatemala and watched a new day dawn, feeling the greatness of the universe unravelling its beauty for everyone. I heard it whisper a warning:

> It is certain, there is no certain certainty, which will guarantee anyone anything other than their final breath. The breath of the sea, the breath of the jungle, is one and the same as the breath in our being and will be so until the sun and the moon fade into each other and that is for certain.

The wall of skulls by the jungle temples reinforced the message, staring at today through empty orbs from yesterday, silently screaming: *"I was once as you are when I was only a man, I was only a woman."*

From somewhere in the universal memory bank, I plucked a filed recollection of a man facing death; a great man who on the verge of execution reminded his executioner not to be hesitant: *"Shoot me for I am only a man!"*

I stared out of the window at the failing light, recalling a magical occurrence when I was ten years old; a time when I had been removed from my lovely village school where the sun shone through the windows to a cold, dark, dismal Catholic building. Our concrete playground was at the back of a garage and to get to it we had to walk past the priests' house where we were uniformly made to turn our heads to the right so as not to look into their living quarters. It was a merciless regime where children were beaten for not knowing the catechism, where we had to recite unfamiliar prayers. Coiled in fear and loneliness, I hated my existence. I detested the living cell where cruelty watched every move, ready to pounce with a stick on small people. I remembered the night I lay in bed with the walls crashing in on my world. I wanted to die. Ten years old and I longed to quit life.

I shouted to the universe, "Take me away from here… please…please." A child's cry out to the cosmos was heard and I suddenly found myself standing on rough, damp grass feeling the cold night earth between my toes, with my long white night dress billowing in the bleak wind under the watchful gaze of my keeper, the moon, as she lit my pathway up the steep hill. I recognised the terrain. Near where I lived was a nature reserve with an outcrop of rocks. I had no idea why I was climbing up the Beacon Rise but I knew to wait by the ledge. I wasn't afraid. It seemed quite natural. It was not a dream. I did not know the story of *The Lion, the Witch and the Wardrobe* and so when over the top of the rise strolled the total embodiment of majesty, the king of the jungle with gentle eyes cocooning the whole world in liquid golden orbs of energy that spilt over the ground as he walked, transforming the rough spiky grass into a soft verdant carpet, I simply accepted his presence and power. His supremacy, strength, kindness was everything a child could love and trust. I put my small hand into a thick mass of silky warm fur by the side of his ear.

Telepathically, he relayed his name: Aslan. I had never heard the name before but the sound of it was comforting. I walked with him up the hill feeling the earth beneath my bare feet change from a coarse, stony path to a smooth, comforting, spongy texture. I never let go of his fur, all the time feeling his padded feet rhythmically drumming as we strolled into an amazing meadow, in a land buzzing with vibrant colours, brimming with light somersaulting across a perfect sky. All my senses were blasted into a dimension more alive than alive, more acute than is imaginable. The flowers were colours beyond colour so rich, so hot, that they melted sound and singed the air with perfume and scents so delicious and sharp that I could taste the delicate flavours wafting from flower to flower. The valley was a sumptuous haven. We hovered over the soft ground, feet hardly touching base as we floated by the mountains. They were perfection in glorious luminescent purples, blues, magenta, and lilac. It seemed possible to pull the colours around me like a cloak and disappear into their glory.

We walked and talked, immersed in the total harmonious forest, breathing in strange melodies, until I could feel the air cooling and the gentle breeze depart, taking with it the delicious smells and tastes of the heavenly paradise. Beneath my feet the soft grass began to grow coarse and cold as we approached the Beacon mound where Aslan had collected me. I clung to his fur and begged him not to send me back. His soft, kind eyes smiled with gentle authority as he whispered in my mind, "You have to go back. One day you will understand that you have special work to complete. As a gift you will always remember our short time together. You will find me again in words, for I am universal; you will teach other children about me and they too will come to know and love me. Be at peace. You must go back; learn to live as you must."

His words stuck and became embedded in my brain. I tried to cling to him as he disappeared through the mist but I was reluctantly transported back to the little world of my village, my small bedroom, my cage. I flung off the covers ready to make haste for the day and stared at my feet in wonder. The previous night was bath night and I had gone to bed squeaky clean, powdered in a freshly laundered nightdress. Now it was crumpled, dirty, and stained with mud. My feet were black, dusty, and grimy with green grass stains under my soles. My heart leapt as I investigated the crushed leaf blotches. Aslan had left me evidence of our adventure together. It wasn't a dream and I hadn't imagined it. I crept to the bathroom before anyone was awake and reluctantly washed my feet knowing that I would always remember that world beyond the world. Aslan had left a gift of the memory deep inside my being which I would hold for the rest of my life, not realizing that eight years later I would again find him.

As a student teacher, I had to study the book *The Lion, the Witch and the Wardrobe* in preparation for my first teaching practice. When I opened the book for the first time I was shocked, overjoyed, and amazed, for there staring up from the pages was Aslan. I realised the message from my childhood was to pass on the power of his numinous energy. Forty years on I find myself in a darkened classroom watching the magic of Aslan through the amazing film, sharing the enchantment of the story with the students as they become engrossed in the supernatural elements, whilst secretly rejoicing in my heart, reminiscing the real Aslan who took me for a walk one night.

CHAPTER 2

Escape

*Love is the music and the dance of
the universe, so let us love until our song
is a distant echo among the stars and
our steps run dry in the fading earth.*

Halloween was in the air as I walked the streets of medieval York. The quaint shops in the Shambles heaved with witches on broomsticks, black spiders, and pumpkin lanterns. At the cottage there was a scent of winter wood smoke and dank mushrooms. I had made a pact with myself not to turn on the heating until November but I was not sure that I could keep it— I shivered in the cold entrance hall as I pick up the mail looking for my first date from the agency. I scoured the details of a suitable candidate and arranged to meet him that coming weekend. I was nervous, having been out of the dating zone for some time, and I felt a mixture of emotions. I recalled my last night in Mexico when I met a wonderful man but it was only fleeting. I had that romantic memory—which was a gift—but I needed to move on. Uncertainty lurked around the corner and I was nervous to meet a date for the first time: What if I didn't like him or he me? What do we say, how do we progress, what are the rules of the game? My daughter, home from university for the weekend, was amused by our role reversal. She chose my dress and my hairstyle, did my makeup, and waved goodbye at the garden gate enquiring what time would I be home?

I walked into the restaurant apprehensively and was shown to a table where a man—almost resembling his photograph—waited patiently, drinking a glass of water. As I sat down, he smiled and I believed he liked me. As he passed the menu, I noticed that he had one arm. I asked him about his accident and he told me his sad story. I liked his face and his manner and felt sorry that he had only one eye. I wanted to escape, not because of his disability, but because the whole setup was false and I didn't want to play the game. He spared no expense on the meal and had bought me beautiful flowers but I went home knowing we wouldn't meet again. My daughter smiled affectionately as I put the flowers in water and arranged them carefully, shrugging off my disappointment. "Next time will be better," she assured me as we settled down to watch television.

By early November the trees had not yet lost all their leaves. That time of year is usually stark but the meteorologists informed us that we were six weeks behind the traditional seasons. I was myself out of season, spaced in the wrong time-zone, school-zone, want-to-go-home -zone. I was locked in blocks taking daily shocks of constant battles, banter, ranting, raving, whilst craving sanity among the quiet books and the lazy pencils of a normal class. Instead, the monsters remained undeterred in their goal to cheat the system. There was a new scheme in the school that rewarded their deviance with treats every Friday: a new project to give the deviants a chance to feel special. They are special! Spending most weekends in prison made them very special and every Monday they boasted about their special exploits.

I am out of my season when reason defines I should date men of my own age but they are so boring, locked in their lifestyles of comfort, containment, and careful hobbies. After my first agency date another followed. I was set to meet a man whose photograph clearly portrayed a full head of hair and his own teeth, but when a small, insignificant bald man—whose false teeth clattered as he spoke—was the reality, I felt embarrassed. "Oh, I'm sorry, I've only got time for a quick drink," I heard myself lie from afar. He understood, as did the following dates, also bearing no resemblance to their agency photographs, having lost their youthful smiles to careworn lines and wrinkles somewhere along the journey to the pub.

"Light does not grow old," I read in a science magazine left haphazardly in the staff room amidst piles of unmarked books and detention pink slips. "What's this? The English department interested in the unfathomable mysteries of light?" teased Mr. Grimble from the Science department. I hand him the magazine smiling sarcastically; little did he know of my unfathomable, strange dealings with "light." Waiting for the bell, my mind drifted to a time when a strange light came to my rescue.

I was the vice principal of a dance college and had to attend a Christmas staff presentation. I hated driving at night but, living in a remote village, had no choice. I wasn't well and was suffering with a painful tooth abscess that threatened to burst. During the evening my toothache grew worse as the abscess pulsed underneath the gum. I absented myself early from the celebrations, feeling nervous about driving through a busy city. After a few wrong turns, I was eventually out on the motorway heading home. My jaw throbbed, making it difficult to concentrate as the fog descended. The road seemed endless. I spied a sign which I didn't recognise and realised I had missed my turning. Thick mist squalled around the car, impenetrable as a woollen blanket, making me slow to a snail's pace. Trapped inside swirling fog I was unable to detect whether I was in the middle of the road or driving on the other side. I stopped and got out into the eerie stillness. I couldn't believe that I had driven into an open field through a narrow gate! I was afraid, stranded, imprisoned inside a suffocating white vapour. My jaw twanged as the abscess burst, releasing putrid toxins down the back of my throat, plunging my body into a cold sweat. My clothes clung to my cold, damp body while my fevered head struggled to think my way to safety. Logically, I knew I had to turn the car around and drive back through the gate but it wasn't easy manoeuvring through dense cloud. I felt dizzy, almost on the verge of losing consciousness. I was scared and pleaded with the Great Ones for help.

Shaking, clutching the wheel with cold, wet palms, I begged to be shown a way out. As I sat staring into the white curtain, shaking and frightened, two tiny red lights appeared from nowhere: red rear lights of a car that glinted like small beacons through the bleak mist. I knew if I followed closely they would guide me somewhere, anywhere, perhaps to a main road, any road, it didn't matter. Through the density I was lead by the rear lights as we wound our way up and down farmyard tracks until we came to the solid road of a nearby village. Just as we rounded a corner, the veil lifted and the road was clear but the car vanished. The road was wide and long so it could not have turned off or sped ahead without being seen. I was shocked but felt strangely humbled, for the mysterious light had saved me.

Another bell, another class drained enthusiasm from my tired mind. I wanted to flee the humdrum cycle of work and sleep. My Cuba trip in August seemed a million years away. Outside the staff room window I spied the Darts team preparing for their gardening session with the Deputy Head, which was another scheme to try to give them extra-curricular activities that might take their minds off the other extra-curricular activities that usually lead to police intervention. The Deputy Head with his frail, straggling grey hair and long, thin beard looked like Noah leading his animals two by two out of the school gates. New tools and equipment had been specially purchased for the project, but already I noticed one of the boys attempting to stab a girl with his shiny fork, and another boy pretending to chop a boy's head off with a glistening pair of shears. The class assistant looked on with dread, knowing they were not going to take the session seriously. Unfortunately she was right—half an hour later the police were called in to break up a fight that had broken out within the happy band of gardeners. The poor Deputy shook his head dispiritedly.

Later, as I was in full swing with a drama class teaching them to throw their voices across the hall, the clatter of paint tins and buckets dragged across the wooden stage interrupted the flow of our lesson. The Deputy Head somewhat apologetically appeared, accompanied by the Darts team who were about to be engaged in painting and decorating the green room at the back. I could already detect an air of mischief within the group as they made rude gestures at my class with their new paintbrushes. I waited until they were well out of sight to pick up the pieces of our interrupted class to master our stage-fighting techniques of hair-pulling and face-slapping. Moments later, two of the Darts boys bounded on the stage, sword fighting with smeared paintbrushes, oozing lime green emulsion all over themselves and the floor. A patient Deputy Head intervened and marched them and the rest of the gang back to the classroom, abandoning their new training as painters and decorators.

At lunchtime I was relieved to close my classroom door to block out the mayhem whilst researching information about Che from the Web, but always the same stories spring up about his arrogance, his anti-social behaviour, his lack of personal hygiene—it is reported he wore only one shirt a week and his friends referred to him as "the Pig"—and the account about the time when his father took him to stay for the weekend at his rich friend's house and he defecated on their grand piano. His *Motorcycle Diaries* shows a young man's quest for adventure, but there was nothing that led me toward answers concerning the message. I checked the time, dreading the next lesson with the monsters. Just as I closed down the computer, I heard a voice in the back of my head: *"That lifetime was not for living, but fighting."*

I questioned the statement but there came no reply. The words did not slip from my mind but entered from outside my sphere of thinking. I stopped my internal dialogue and listened to see if another comment pushed through, but all was silent before the monsters arrived to defile the peace. As I watched them stroll in disdainfully, I mused how each one is like an animal. Lyle is a short, fat, ginger hamster with puffed-out freckled cheeks. Carson is a white-haired silver fox with a silly, cunning, inane grin. Dane is a Disney-type warthog dipping his pitted face down on his chest, never venturing to speak but prone to fits of uncontrolled anger. Jake is a mild-natured, ginger jackass who likes skateboarding, can't write, but likes art. Martin is a tall, dark-haired goat, with a deceitful, stupid nature. Seamus is a round-faced piggy with a sweet smile but harbours a mean, perverted streak, feeding the other boys pornographic pictures from his mobile. Carter is an orang-utan, with long dangling arms swaying by his side which he skilfully employs to jump onto desks, window ledges, and cabinets. The other boys are wolves and the girls are sweet, woolly sheep.

Before I began the lesson I had to discipline individuals who were engaged in various counter activities. The orang-utan was bouncing a ball at the back of the class and attempting to jump from one desk to the next; the sly fox was throwing pencils across the room; the fat pig was leering at something underneath the desk; the hamster was twanging a ruler against the radiator; the warthog was upset and sat at the back of the room hiding his face. The girls, unperturbed by any of the disturbance around them, checked their makeup in the half-broken compact mirror that the goat cracked the previous day. I had prepared a poetry lesson from the set anthology, which was not at all suitable for the class, but it is part of the curriculum that has to be taught. I turned on my outraged programme, threatening higher intervention, detentions, and letters home until quiet descended. To grab their attention, I chose a poem beginning "Sweetheart bastard," but instead of churning up their interest it incited them to accuse me of swearing and another ten minutes ensued while I settled them down. They preferred to draw pictures rather than study words they will never have to utter, so I gave in, watching the clock and urging the seconds to whiz by. *Set me free, I want to break free*, my mind screamed, while outwardly I sauntered calmly around the class admiring the Romeo and Juliet posters they have acquiesced to design. The orang-utan tore up his poster as I peered at his work but I did not respond. I watched him proceed to wipe dust off the window ledge and smear it around his eye. I wondered what game he was playing but refused to be drawn into his antics. At last the bell set us all free and they dashed out, fighting for the door, all except the orang-utan who sauntered past my desk and paused to say, "Does this look good, Miss?"

"What do you mean?" I questioned.

"Does it look like I've got a black eye?"

"Er…it does a bit."

"Good, then I'm gonna tell them you bashed my head in the door an' I'll get let off me next lesson!" he laughed, pounding his fist into the wall.

"You just do that," I retorted, hurt by his ingenious, deceitful plot. As the door slammed, I was relieved to have survived another session with the monsters, and glad to have something to look forward to at the weekend—another agency date!

At the weekend I arrived at the designated hotel. I was surprised to find the car park full, with two large coaches stationed near the entrance. Standing on guard near large glass doors a doorman waited in evening dress, complete with a top hat which he tipped as I passed. I mused whether my black leather coat and designer jeans were suitable for the occasion. As I sailed through the entrance, the clatter, chatter, and glass-clinking ceased as a wedding party with bride, groom, and all their guests arrayed in a semicircle faced me, glaring in curious silence. Equally shocked, I locked in a frozen second of uncertainty, pausing in front of them like a thief caught in the act of stealing, feeling awkward, wondering if they thought I was gate crashing. The fragmented silence was broken by a voice in the crowd that hailed my name like a white surrender flag, signalling the party to continue their celebration amidst roars of laughter and chinking of champagne glasses. A tall man carrying drinks emerged from the din.

"Are you my blind date?" he enquired jovially.

Embarrassed, I forced a smile, replying, "You didn't tell me we were invited to a wedding party!"

"We're not. I just happen to know the local couple getting married and as we agreed to meet here I had to tell them I was waiting for a blind date."

"Oh, no! You didn't, did you?"

"Yes. They asked me what you looked like and I told them that you are small and blonde, so when you entered they knew it was you!"

I felt the whole room eating into my privacy, judging me as a man-hunter and I wished to vanish quietly into oblivion. He was good enough to take me elsewhere for a drink but we both knew we were not for each other. My friends questioned, "Why go through all the humiliation when you could use your psychic gift to help you?"

"That's just it!" I smiled to them. "It's a gift but not to be used for myself!"

In late November I was in school with the toothache. On my birthday I felt downhearted. I felt depressed but I know that like the earth's diurnal round we turn, turn and turn again, and as day turns to night, our agony becomes our ecstasy. We turn, turn, and turn again. Time changes everything and time will heal the broken morning, for tomorrow will mingle our agony and ecstasy into a new form.

Outside there was nothing to see under the grey, steel-lidded sky. The sun could not melt through the barrier. Only the ploughed fields held hope of bright yellow rape flowers, flooding the field rudely in spring. A desolate sense of empti-ness echoed down the corridors like a vacant theatre when the audience has left, scattering their warmth, laughter, litter, and tickets on a rich red carpet. I sighed in the gaping space and, despite accepting what happened, I knew that nature continues her diurnal round, the seas continue to rise and fall, day turn to night whether asleep or awake, for all we have is what we are. I drove back home as the watery winter sky drenched the slip-pery tarmac, blinding my view of the car in front as the spray streamed off its back wheels.

I did not celebrate my birthday. Back home I opened cards from my children and felt aware that time had slipped some-where out beyond where it began, knowing that I had lost some of my words; they had abandoned me. I searched to remember, to recall the sense, but the words hid from me. I needed to regain them and ensnare the past, to re-locate the shape of the phrases so that I could understand the present. A few months before, I stood in the jungle rainforest of Central America feeling warm rain washing away my fear, hoisting me forwards to begin a new journey, preparing me to capture words which I have remembered to forget, making me ready to forget what I have remembered without regret and free the text from within, which has danced its way through my being.

After a few days off school I returned to find that two of my boys had been expelled. The orang-utan and the piggy attempted to rape a young girl in my classroom. I was shocked and dismayed at the news but relieved that the school had taken firm action against them. The class was slowly dwindling: one of the girls never attends and the boys took it in turns skiving off school to fix underhanded deals and steal bicycles. I prepared the coloured paper ready for the monsters to make their Christmas cards using the theme of Charles Dickens' *A Christmas Carol* which is part of their set reading, but the text was too difficult for them to understand and I resorted to showing them the video, but they preferred to watch the Muppets' film of the story. As they filed in they were anxious to tell me the gory details of their classmates' crime, revelling in the details without realizing the severity of the assault. I ask them not to talk about it, and refuse to listen.

Christmas hovered in mounting expectation for the pupils, but not for me. I have come to detest the false sentiments, especially since my children have left; I prefer not to celebrate commercially but quietly alone. The previous New Year my wish came true to have all my children and their families back with me for a champagne celebration, which was the best present ever. The year ahead promised adventure and I was happy to wait, planning, anticipating my escape. Watching the game of hide and seek behind the cloudy shadows, the moon smiled and I was reminded of a different new year when we lived in a small house that had been built on the site of a leper colony established in the 1800s.

My son and youngest daughter often heard voices, unusual things, and sometimes witnessed strange events. A friend who had come around to fix my bathroom light turned off the electricity to remove the bulb, but when he did so a torrent of light shot out as we stood back on the stairs. Amazed, we were dazzled by an explosion of multi-coloured energy flowing above our heads, projecting onto the white wall behind us, displaying a brilliant show of radiance, dancing, whirling like a tornado sucked into a white hole.

My friend, an engineer, had never experienced anything that even remotely deviated from the norm. He was not content to admit that it was a paranormal demonstration. He checked all the electrical sockets and connections but found nothing. He didn't stay long, and made excuses to go, but as he stood under my hall lamp about to open the front door, the bulb exploded around his head, smashing and splintering inside the glass lampshade without harming him. He escaped devoid of a single scratch and when he examined the light casing, it had imploded in such a way that it was impossible for the bulb to have maintained its inner coil. In his scientific approach to his life and work he was stupefied, but after many other incidents has learnt to simply accept that there are things which happen which are totally beyond our comprehension.

My children had sometimes heard a young girl crying in the dead of night but never saw anyone. I had seen a vision of a young girl lying over my doorstep curled in a once lavish, ornate cloak which had become dirty and stained. I gleaned she was from an aristocratic family and had been left alone in the leper colony to die. The Little Sisters of Clare down the road ministered to the diseased people, feeding them and taking care of their burial needs. I saw a lovely young girl ravaged by leprosy, crying out her lonely last gasps. She threw her name to me as though casting a last lifeline to a distant land. It was Emma, the breeze sighed through the open windows as the sun left golden trails of dust falling slowly on the windowsills; Emma, the autumn leaves swirled playfully at my doorstep; Emma, sparkled the frost, the day after bonfire night when the air was crisp and new. Emma never wavered, always waiting to be released.

My children had grown up with strange and unusual paranormal happenings and were used to me performing burial rites for the undead, so they were not surprised when I suggested we initiated a special funeral for Emma. As it was nearing New Year, the best energy would be just after midnight. I prepared everything and as my son came down the stairs in the candlelight, the main lights flashed on and off, flicking switches with an invisible force, rattling the door handles, shaking the fabric of the house. I was not deterred from my task and I lit a special candle for Emma. As I chanted and invoked help, the rattling grew to a crescendo and then died, leaving an eerie, watchful silence.

When my son and I opened our front door, celebrations echoed from the houses around the miniature park while the moon kept guard directly over our house. Emma was there but so were many others. My son stood behind me as I welcomed the congregation of spirits. We were blessed by higher presences which engulfed all gathered, swaddling the lost souls in cleansing, healing energy, and coaxing limbo spirits to pass through the barrier that had imprisoned them in a goal of their own devising. As each one prepared to pass on, they flew through me, using my body as a portal to beyond, creating a vision of a playful wind ruffling my hair, rippling my dress, and wafting my face with warm caresses. My son watched, spellbound by the vision. I was supremely happy as each one flowed into the cosmos. The ceremony lasted for about half an hour but as soon as the last spirit departed, the whole park burst alive with people pouring out of their doors, singing and dancing into the square, carrying bottles of wine to sit on the benches and carouse until the dawn welcomed in the New Year.

A few days later I was with a friend in my sitting room having a drink and while she was commenting on all my theatrical paraphernalia festooned everywhere, an artefact fell with an almighty crash at the foot of the stairs. We got up immediately to find a belt from the Middle East made out of coins and semi-precious stones torn from its position at the top of the stair rail and thrown down with great force. Puzzled, I stooped to pick it up and saw something laying under the belt. I picked up a tainted silver ring in the shape of a musical treble clef, recognising it as the one I had bought twenty years previously but had thrown away because its design was dangerous—I had nearly lost my finger when the ring got caught in a door handle. Finding it again after all those years was a miracle, but even more so was the way it transformed itself under our watchful gaze from a tainted brown, old ring, to a polished, shiny, silver new one. In my hand it shone and glistened in the light, magically restored. I thought that Emma might have given it back to me as a gift for her release—there didn't seem to be any other explanation.

As the New Year excitement faded, a new school term began and I made a resolution not to meet any more blind dates, preferring to meet someone by chance, so I was back in the work-sleep-work mode. The tedium was happily shattered by an amazing phone call asking me to choreograph the Temple Dance from *Aida* for a major international opera company. The request was a great honour and I was allowed to choose ten dancers and one soloist. We had only two weeks to learn, polish, and perfect the routine. I arrived early outside the theatre where two huge transport giants paused to be unloaded with a myriad of small Russian men scurrying like worker bees building an extravagant Egyptian set. There were forty-three musicians standing nonchalantly outside, smoking or talking in their unfamiliar dialect. One hundred and twenty professional singers streamed out of buses, forming an endless line to backstage like a string of Russian paper dolls.

I was excited and nervous waiting for my girls who duly arrived sparkling clean and wide-eyed with anticipation. A small woman, with typical eastern European flat cheekbones, appeared through the congestion introducing herself as Olga, the stage manager, and she led us through the parade of performers streaming into the dressing rooms. The bright red and gold womb-like cocoon of the auditorium welcomed us as we sat in awe of the magnificent stage set that magically transformed the whole theatre into the hallowed sanctum of an

Egyptian temple, complete with an upper ornate balcony, huge columns, and marble floor.

We didn't have long to wait before being called onto the stage to rehearse. It was strange being on set with the famous singers wearing their casual clothes in the ancient setting. The conductor of the orchestra waited for my commands as the costume ladies buzzed around us like two cross hornets. We had one more dancer than they had anticipated and they argued in Russian, shaking their heads, but I made it quite clear that all the girls had to dance and it was their responsibility to find costumes for everyone. They understood my position and went away to find a set; meanwhile, the company watched with professional respect as my dancers rehearsed their steps. I had been sent a DVD of the dance but it was too simplistic and not of the genre, so I devised something different. Everyone watched with delight, enjoying the new interpretation. The stage manager was charmed by their performance and gave my girls extra scenes.

Soon the low buzz of showbiz preparation began to grow, vibrating through the whole building. Lights flashed chasing set sequences; tuning of instruments filled the orchestra pit; voices gliding up and down scales echoed from dressing rooms; the smell of makeup and dusty wigs cloyed the corridors; while endless last minute touches were added to swords, coconut shell lights, and wax flower garlands. Trying on the costumes was exciting, and my girls were transformed into exotic Temple virgins. Our dressing room was a bar over the other side of the theatre, across the top of the gods, up and down myriads of steps and stairs, and my poor injured leg pained me but I loved every minute being back with an international company, taking part in a spartakiad of music and voices, preparing for the first moment when the curtain rises and we all jump together into the secret, magical realm of make-believe.

Sitting on the stairs just minutes before the curtain went up I was thrown down a time tunnel: sometimes when the vibration of the moment flicks a switch inside my brain, I unconsciously travel into a past zone where time is now, has been, always will be. The still night was hot and the smell of rich, perfumed oils mingled with goat-fat torches wafting down dim, private corridors of the queen's ancient chambers. I was back in a scene I had known many lifetimes before. The endless parade of the authentic-seeming Egyptian costumes striding past transported me to a palace not in Egypt but in Crete, Knossos. I shut my eyes and was sucked into brilliant scenes of dancers and bulls leaping out of the darkness, as servants quietly tended their duties, but I was quickly brought back as the signal for the opera to begin wailed over the speakers.

My girls' eyes glistened excitedly. Their big moment was coming. Hobbling, I escorted them onto the side of the stage where we could spy the action. The whole company was on the set, their voices swelling into grand crescendos bound in pure harmony, compelling, uplifting, energising, and transcending the moment into emotion beyond emotion. Wrapped in the thrilling ecstasy of the quivering cadences, I could see the chequered floor of the great hall at Knossos Palace, and remembered a time of happiness before the entrapment of evil crept into the bones and blood of close ones poisoned by Her, the new queen, my stepmother…eons of lifetimes ago.

My stomach felt severed from my chest as I was brought back quickly into the present of the performance as my girls elegantly took their places. Pride welled as they glided through their steps with graceful ease, charming the audience and the singers. It was awesome, as though we were witnessing an historic, private, ritualistic scene from the past under the golden lights, with the shimmering gilded costumes, the flickering of the fire-lit torches, and the magic of the voices harnessed to the dance. As they turned and balanced, sliding nimbly to the floor and leaping effortlessly, I danced every step with them and they for me, totally submitting to the moment. The minutes spiralled too quickly as the thunderous applause swept through the auditorium signalling my girls to take their places for their next piece. The male voices chanted hauntingly behind the set, while Aida's pure soprano melody curled to the gods, hurling me unwittingly back to the inner chambers of the king's suite at Knossos…

The distant past swept forward, swirling and circling through a vast tunnel with stars exploding and coiling beyond the cosmos. Momentarily I glimpsed the palace and a great hall but the light faded and the moment recoiled back to the present. I was watching my lovely little dancers on stage leading a procession accompanied by the orchestra blasting out the famous Aida march. The next section was purely unrehearsed. They had to stand still on stage holding coconut shell lamps for over seven minutes while the chorus triumphantly wailed in their ears, with clashing swords and fighting next to their faces without flinching, like trained soldiers standing to attention as the battle raged around them with lights pulsing and lightning bolts cracking over their heads. Without warning, explosions tore across the stage with an amazing display of pyrotechnics, culminating in a glittering shower of golden raindrops falling triumphantly overhead, landing in their hair, eyes, and costumes and still they never budged. The curtain fell to a roar from the audience and thunderous applause as they ran off the stage to greet me, flushed with their brilliant success.

After the highlight of the opera it was difficult to resume my normal routine, especially after experiencing my return to Knossos. It had been many years since I was drawn back to that time and I knew in the future I would have to face those events which held mysteries and intrigues that I had been previously prevented from discovering. I was not sure whether I was ready to face the demons lurking in the past and I tried to lose myself in the school tedium. The drag of the days before the end of term palled out hourly paces of daily traces of drill, marked by clocks, electric bells, break time confusion, silence in the hall in the season of exams, the dinner hour, the endless marking and recording of school reports—and, of course, my monsters. I lost a few more class members along the rough road through the year due to their weekend criminal activities, the school having no option but to expel them. After nearly a year of constant battling the other members grew to understand me and we came to an unspoken agreement where at least they attempted a little work each lesson, even if it was only ten minutes. So on the last day of term the class from hell disintegrated, falling apart like an overripe custard apple spilling its black, shiny seeds onto a cracked table. There were even token presents from the girls with a few stray tears, and a smile from the boys. When they left, the silence was stale but long overdue. With relief I placed their folders full of torn paper ready to be thrown into the recycle bin. Their school days were over.

Just a week and a half before Cuba, I was counting down the days to my departure but was ensconced in the daily delights of my Summer School and my four grandchildren who always came for that special week. I relished looking after four children again and delighted fiendishly in spoiling them, engineering dressing up games and pretend grown-up dinner parties with children's champagne. But no matter how hard I tried to make the event formal, it always deteriorated into a rabble of naughtiness with everyone collapsing in fits of giggles. On their last evening I took them to a restaurant not far from the cottage, walking along overgrown paths hazardously strewn with giant stinging nettles, while the roaring traffic inches away sped past. We had a fun meal together and I allowed myself one glass of red wine which was accidentally knocked over in one of their over-zealous moments, spilling down my new blue dress, deeply staining the front. They thought it was hilarious having to walk home with me trying to hide deep purple stains over my breasts and stomach. "She stood in the kitchen in her bra and washed her dress!" reported the youngest to her mum on the phone. Nothing ever was missed!

Just as we were about to play a game in the kitchen, a stranger phoned. It was a man. The children all wanted to listen, adding their comments, relating the saga of my wine-stained dress and me standing half naked in the kitchen. He seemed very nice, explaining that a mutual friend had given him my number. We arranged to meet that Saturday. Despite my misgivings about blind dates, I thought another embarrassing evening wouldn't matter as I was soon to be out of the country.

The departure of my little brood was sad as always but the date with Saul was on my mind. I was nervous. He stood waiting for me with a bunch of roses outside a nearby hotel. He kissed me and the sun shone triumphantly, springing out from behind the shrouded clouds in a golden haze. He bought me an old book of familiar quotations from poets and playwrights. He even quoted a passage from Shakespeare, which came alive under the spell of his deep Welsh tones. Two bottles of champagne later I asked to touch his calf muscle, explaining, "I couldn't possibly like someone with chicken legs!"

Years of rugby and training men in the police force had hewn muscles of rock out of his rugged body. He was just a little older than me and was fun to be with, sharing his unusual life as a James Bond-type hero as an undercover agent and assassin in Northern Ireland, which he had long forsaken to become a criminal lawyer. When I told him I was leaving for Cuba in four days, he tried to persuade me not to go, even offering to pay the full amount of my trip, but I couldn't explain my commitment to the journey and my inner purpose. I had to go despite the very tempting offer, and nothing was going to deter me from my quest.

We met on Saturday and on the following Wednesday, the day before I was due to leave for Cuba, he bought me a beautiful ring. "So that you come back to me," he explained in a serious, meaningful tone. We said goodbye in a romantic miasma and promised to speak every day. He handed me some envelopes containing a series of notes, one for each day, and he said he would try to learn to text so that we could communicate.

The next morning as gentle light sifted through the curtains, after all the months of longing and looking forward to my adventure, instead of racing to get up I lay there for a while, gently twisting my magnificent gold, diamond-encrusted amethyst ring.

CHAPTER 3

Cars Have Personalities Too!

*Each one of us carefully dances our name in
the sands of time but with one gentle hint of a
breeze, all our steps are lost in the dust.*

As I left my homely cottage with the sun rising through the glistening trees, I thought of Saul and our first meeting, and our hopes for a future together. Leaving this time was different from my last major expedition, which was clouded by a series of disasters including a threatened bomb attack on the airline on which I was travelling. This time I was calmly confident I would reach Havana safely and successfully meet my guide and the rest of the party as scheduled. After the last struggle to make the rendezvous deadline on time, I arranged to have two days and nights in a luxury hotel in Havana to prepare for the journey before transferring to a less auspicious side of town.

Waiting in the airport lounge, I tried to imagine Havana. I had preconceived ideas, one of a romantic notion of a pretty Cuban girl rolling a large cigar in her thighs, posing suggestively against a paradisiacal backdrop of sun, sea, and jungle plants. I had a cosy vision from an advert for a tropical drink of a close-knit community barricaded in a bar, partying all night, drinking exotic cocktails, whilst dancing salsa as a raging hurricane tears the street apart. Further, my expectations were formed from old films of tobacco plantations, slavery, huge *Gone with the Wind* plantation houses, colonialism, Ernest Hemingway in his hideaway bar drinking endless mojitos, plus Che Guevara, Fidel Castro, Cadillac cars, and finally, the Buena Vista Social Club.

The mundane flight droned on with the obligatory films and stopgap intermissions. I amused myself by organising my notes and itinerary, begrudgingly allocating time to photograph classic cars which I had been asked to do for an article. I wondered why I had agreed—I knew very little about cars, not even my own, and viewed them merely as a means of transport, so the idea of photographing boys' toys did not appeal in the slightest. I checked my notes and read: "Only Cuba has the conditions necessary for preserving and honouring the total history of the classic vintage car, transforming it into a national heritage." It was one national legacy that didn't inspire me and I intended to take only a few token photographs to comply with the editor's request.

I read further: "Havana is one of the oldest cities in the Western hemisphere, with a huge range of multi-cultural influences making it a strange and exotic hotchpotch of architectural images, with its mix of Baroque and Neoclassical monuments, arcades, balconies, wrought-iron gates, and secret courtyards." The description conjured up images of the old part of the city of Barcelona, where I had spent a great deal of time during my work in Spain. I imagined huge wooden, ornately carved doors leading to enchanting bijou courtyards hidden amidst ancient cobbled streets. I was cautioned about *jineteros* (translated as "men riding on the backs of the tourists")—men who were on the lookout for single women to take advantage of, and who were a special breed of Cuban who did not work but lived off immoral earnings especially from women *jineteras*, who offered sex.

So, armed with warnings and cautions, I nervously stepped off the plane on the outskirts of the city into the dying swelter of the late afternoon. The journey had been ordinary, uneventful, and even tedious, and as passport stamping and baggage reclaiming didn't take too long, I quickly followed everyone into the main exit that was awash with a flood of multi-coloured beach shirts, friendly ebony faces, and the smell of foreign spices and cologne turning acrid in the subsiding heat. As I stood in line to change currency, foreign voices bleated across the slippery mosaic tiles, ranging from Spanish, African, Caribbean, and Creole. Immersed in the throb and hubbub were lines of people waiting for incoming passengers. Some held name placards, some displayed company messages, while others excelled in the leisurely art of people watching. The queue for money seemed endless but I was relieved when I walked out into the gentle breeze to find a long line of taxis waiting for hire. I had been issued another warning before leaving and that was to make sure any taxi I hired displayed a licence, as many were illegal and might take you for more than just a ride!

The taxi driver knew my hotel and bounced into his seat with a self-important flurry. My fatigue lifted on our way to the great city as we picked up speed past the industrial estates and the wasteland billboards towering over a huddle of makeshift shacks stacked on the rich red earth. Evidence of the last hurricane lay strewn across scrubland with palms and tropical trees decapitated and ruptured in the brush. As we drove into the last blast of sunshine, swathing the sky in a pink terracotta wash, we turned off the freeway into a suburb thronging with a strong community pulse. Mums and dads herded their young ones across the busy road while the elderly gossiped in clutches outside the supermarket. Couples, husbands and wives, boyfriends and girlfriends, were shopping together holding hands, as youngsters on bicycles wove in and around laughing and shouting to one another. A holiday, Friday night, relaxed atmosphere set the scene for the weekend.

Just as we were slowing down to pull up at a set of traffic lights the unexpected happened. It was a magical moment born out of nothing, coming from nowhere, taking me completely by surprise, as waltzing down the hill with great ease and pizzazz was my first encounter with a classic, vintage car. Something peculiar happened to the non-car loving, non-mechanical, non-tyre-changing me, which altered my whole idea of the classic shebang. I fell in love with the green and gold Cadillac as it conjured images of a bygone era of film stars, Marilyn Monroe decadence, silk stockings, and diamond encrusted dresses with pink feather boas and champagne cocktails drunk from shiny black high-heel shoes. It was as though I was suddenly living a part of my childhood engrossed in a dream world of the famous film stars of the fifties. The glitterati of my infancy sprung to life.

The proud momma was brimming to the full with family members plastered against the windows, overloaded like a large lady in a tight dress. A young mother sat in the front eyeing me disdainfully as I stared at them, while her little daughter on her knee smiled a toothless grin, bobbing her African curls as her grandmother and other various members of the family sat respectfully in the back. Taking a closer look at the magnificent rolling saloon, I was dismayed to see brown rust everywhere eating into the shiny green and gold body work, with bits of metal hanging off at all angles. It was a miracle the car was working in its sad state of decay. Little did I know that the car was to exemplify the state of Havana, nor did I realise that this first sighting would turn into a crazy obsession to photograph every vintage car I spied.

Driving into the city I passed through periods of history in old colonial Havana with rich architectural flourishes of quaint balconies awash with ocean-blue paint, and Baroque, Rococo, Art Nouveau, Art Deco buildings all left untouched, nothing replaced by high rise office buildings. All was authentic Havana, no imitation suburbia. But I was shocked to catch glimpses of inward decay—like the deterioration of the green and gold Cadillac—as buildings on the outside retained vestiges of past glory but were internally crumbling. Facades of large houses were torn away revealing families struggling to exist. I had not expected to see such blatant decline underlying a deep internal struggle, yet there were no beggars on the streets.

The light began to fade and a sense of quiet settled over the city as men in white vests hung over their balconies smoking, discussing the day's events with their neighbours, while their wives busied themselves hanging out washing like bunting at the fair, wrapping the busy city in a comforting shawl of domesticity. I thought of Che. Would he be disappointed by the increasing corrosion of the city's infrastructure? We passed a crumbling wall with bright blue graffiti scrawled across it, hailing: "Fidel is a country." The idealism seemed soured at the core of the apple which had once been so tempting. We pulled up outside a luxury hotel in the main part of the city and I felt a flush of guilt at being treated like a queen, while across the road a row of bicycle taxi men watched, pacing out their lives in the unending heat, measured by their short bursts of toil night and day, for little reward.

Inside, the lavish interior made me forget the world outside and I became enchanted by the sumptuous elegance of the sweeping staircases, lit by a myriad of tiny lights leading up to a glass heaven shrouded by trees and palms. A quiet hush descended around the bar and lounge under the watchful presence of the security men dressed in black suits and sunglasses who were strategically perched by the stairways and lifts. The men in black took their job seriously, standing on guard in a paradise dream world kept secure only for the rich and tourists. I was shown to my room, which was more of a mini-apartment than a bedroom, and boasting every luxury I could desire. Appeasing my conscience, I told myself that I deserved an oasis for two days before immersing myself in the journey to come, knowing that before long I would be faced with my silly phobias of insects, creepy-crawlies, filthy lavatories, dirty accommodations, unclean beds and bathrooms. As I bent down to adjust my bedside lamp, a nosebleed gushed and I rushed to the bathroom to clean up, noting all the goodies on hand: shoe cleaning equipment, bath and hair wash, a plastic cap, a comb, and a sewing kit. Built-up pressure from the flight soon abated and when my ears popped I felt better. My phone bleeped. It was a text from Saul who had never before learnt the art of texting, but through sheer necessity had mastered the technique. He called himself a caveman, finding anything technical, alien. He implored me again to take the next plane home and although I was grateful for his concern, I was adamant that I had to complete the course and secretly follow my desire to learn about Che.

I turned down the air conditioning, preferring to feel closer to the city in its natural heat. I opened the windows and let the humid air burst in as the daily tropical downpour ceased. Children in the park opposite came out to play, hurling themselves along the slippery wet park slabs creating an amazingly long slide that glistened under the streetlights. Tourists stopped to watch them glide from one end of the square to the other on their bottoms, amidst whoops and yelps of dizzy laughter. After showering I dressed in one of the few pretty dresses I had brought and sauntered down to the main bar for a snack. I ordered my favourite fried oyster salad and a tropical fruit cocktail. Amidst the sophisticated clientele I felt slightly uncomfortable. A single woman is always an enigma, especially to the men in black who kept a furtive watch from a respectable distance. Travelling solo can be very lonely, especially when couples are sharing the day's events wrapped in each other's eyes, and embarrassing when you spy the Mariachi band serenading each table in turn. I dreaded them bursting into song around me. I hid behind a potted palm and hoped they wouldn't descend upon me. Thankfully they passed and entertained the next table with their rendering of "Guantanamera."

After my meal I felt smugly satisfied, cosseted in the lap of luxury, unlike my previous adventure where I had to spend a frightening, uncomfortable first night in the airport. Back in my room I watched the nightlife from my window. There was an invisible heaviness in the air that arose from words unspoken, formed through the pursed lips of the waitress and the sad posture of the street vendor across the square. From my window away to the right, I could make out dim electric lights of families living in the once-grand mansions now apportioned to flats with fragments of their accommodation open to the night sky. I wondered how they managed in the rain.

I closed the window but left a small crack in the thick, maroon velvet curtains, as I was afraid of the dark. Total blackout panicked me. When I was two years old, just after we had moved to a new house built on an ancient Druid burial site, I woke every night screaming, "There's a lady in my room—there's a lady!" My parents grew weary with lack of sleep and tried everything. Even a sleeping draught from the doctor had no effect, as I still screeched each night, terrified of the woman. One night both parents were woken by deathly shrieks and they shot out of bed to discover a thin sheet wrapped around my neck and tied to the cot bars. I could not possibly have done it myself! I couldn't breathe; I was choking and gasping for air. My parents were horrified to imagine someone or something had tried to strangle me and they later burnt everything that was associated with the room.

In the morning I rose to a bright new sun. I opened my curtains to a city already in motion and went down for a hearty breakfast. The dining room was fantastic, and featured a ceiling sculpture of the inner structure of a Viking long boat. I was presented with the greatest choice of breakfast feasts I had ever seen or tasted. The food was incredible and it was difficult not to be greedy. I sampled a vast variety of tropical fruits and pancakes with traditional cooked foods, cereals, jams, honeys, and bread of different varieties and I imbibed more cups of coffee than one person should normally drink at breakfast! I left the dining room fully sated, ready for my business meeting with a tour guide, but when I reached his desk he politely informed me that I was over an hour late. Smiling, he said that many people forget to alter their watches! Apologetically, I sat down and discussed a possible itinerary for my two free days, booking a few tours which would leave me enough time to explore the city by myself.

When the business was completed I decided to take a walk down to the harbour. I knew if I continued in a straight line after turning left from the hotel I would eventually reach the sea. After a terrible time on my last adventure when I got lost in Merida, I always take a map or make absolutely sure I know how to return. By ten-thirty the sun was already scorching, so I sought the cool shade of a narrow street lined with tall neoclassical buildings divided into flats with balconies bulging with washing, caged birds, tin cans, and potted plants. An old man knelt on the kerb tying up fruit ready for the market and I paused to watch him dispatching the small green fruit into bags. He looked up and held out a round, plum-like fruit with soft, sweet pink flesh. I tasted it and smiled. He laughed, giving me a handful, and I offered to pay him but he refused. Thanking him, I walked on with my gift.

The rest of the street was quiet but I was dismayed by the general decay and the inevitable destruction of the buildings eroded by weather and a lack of care and maintenance. Magnificent carved wooden doorways hinting at a glorious past were left to slide into insignificance hidden beneath layers of dirt, dust, and grime, receding from the pride of craftsmanship that once created works of art in a heyday of opulence. Similarly, beautiful wooden arches leading to intriguing courtyards were disintegrating, almost deliberately to allow tenants a non-ostentatious living space, as though they were embarrassed by grandeur. The continual struggle to survive was echoed in the crumbling bricks, peeling paintwork, and broken plumbing.

Farther along, I turned into a square where a band of teenagers, always curious about visitors and their lifestyles, sat on a wooden park seat and greeted me with warm, friendly smiles. I shared my fruit with them as I learnt about their struggle to pay for their education and their dual lives working whilst studying. Their poverty didn't affect their ambitions but beneath the cool acceptance of *Fidelismo* was an edge of resentment toward the prohibition of Cuba's interaction with world technology. Orlando, one of the boys, asked me where I was going and if he could accompany me. At first I was wary of his offer, but his manner wasn't forceful and as he explained he wanted to practice his English, I acquiesced. He showed me the way to the harbour and the little market by the magnificent medieval fortress but, naively, I had no idea that the market would be so sparse. I was shocked to find only a vegetable stall with a scant selection of plants and fruit spread across a wide table to make the goods appear plentiful. There was an African stall selling a few hand-carved statues and a stall owned by an Englishman with uninteresting tee shirts on display.

I thanked Orlando for his company and made my excuses to return to the hotel. He was very pleasant and offered to show me around the next day but I did not make any arrangements. I watched as he made his way down a narrow alley in the bright sunshine, his black head bobbing in and out of the morning crowd that had gathered to queue at the butcher's, where fly-ridden meat rations lay uncovered on an open slab, dumped on a bloody block ready to be collected. I turned back toward the compact square with its neat miniature park lovingly tended by an old African man in worn dungarees, struggling to bend to tweak out the stray weeds. Like a honeybee entering a garden for the first time, unaware of the vast variety of flowers close at hand, I suddenly realised that parked in every available space and corner were wonderful vintage cars of every colour and description, each exuding a character and history of ownership so individual and unique that I quickly became immersed in my new-found occupation of photographing them.

I was intrigued by how each car could be so different. In England a car was a car, a mode of transport offering varying degrees of speed and luxury, streamlined into characterless efficiency, whereas parked around the Havana square each automobile seemed like a member of a family, like pets waiting obediently for their owners. I marvelled at my own response—*I must be affected by the sun*, I thought, as I had never felt anything other than indifference to cars. It was strange that each model communicated its gender name as though each car related its own story and history in florid detail. I spied over in the corner Henry, whose battered, dull-green, dumpy saloon body with a cracked silver bonnet, newly sporting a white mudguard, was still his owner's pride and joy. Next to him was a superior male, Percival, who was a bright red, sparkling Chevrolet exuding a hoity-toity air of exclusivity. Perkily parked under the shade of the trees, so as not to get her bright pink skirts dirty from the crusty dust, was Myrtle, with her polished, disco-pink sexy body. Farther down by the bank aristocratic Charles, with his sleek back bonnet encased in shiny chrome accessories, waited with an arrogant air of quiet boredom and almost seemed to preen as I took shots of him from all angles. I captured them all for my collection and wondered at my children's response to my newfound hobby as I couldn't even remember my own car's registration number!

Feeling pleased with my collection, I meandered down the nearest side street back toward my hotel, passing a gathering of street artists and an opportunist preparing to entertain the tourists with his dog's antics. The scruffy mutt lay spread-eagle on the concrete path with his eyes closed, revealing his scabby underbelly, while the man placed a phone receiver over his ear to make it appear as if he was listening to someone on the phone. I quickly snapped the shot and moved on to where a few feet down the street I spied a delightful cheeky puppy peeping behind a green weathered doorway, his little grey and white face intent on making mischief. I took advantage of the shot and captured the little fellow with his impish grin. The heat by eleven o'clock was debilitating, sapping energy drop by drop like a slowly leaking tap, so I was relieved to sip a fresh, exotic fruit cup in the hotel lounge before continuing my exploration of the city. I was keen to find the National Opera House, the Grand Theatre de Cuba, and if possible book for a performance.

Back into the startlingly bright midday glare, I smiled, remembering the song lyric "Only mad dogs and Englishmen go out in the midday sun." I wasn't mad—I just didn't have time to languish in the hotel because I wanted to get out and experience the city. I knew the theatre wasn't far from the hotel but the heat made any slight distance seem wearisome. I hadn't walked far when a young man in front turned around and asked what I was looking for. When I told him he said he was going that way and would show me. He seemed friendly and keen to get where he was going. He pointed to a building nearby but walked me down a street bustling with morning business. Flat concrete houses, multi-coloured, were crumbling amidst rubble and buildings which were either going up or collapsing down. The road was littered with building debris, bricks, mortar, and lumps of concrete, yet amongst it all, cars of character sat back preening in the poverty-ridden backdrop of chaotic decay. A black and white spotted Dalmatian dog panted in the shade as a family breakfasted by the side of a suspicious green and white frumpy Cadillac, Mildred, who was probably used for mafia outings to obtain illegal goods for the black market. A shiny white and red Chevrolet, Dicki, waited calmly outside dingy quarters in the potholed road and I wondered where I was being led.

"The National Theatre?" I enquired.

"I pointed it out to you!" he stated. I hesitated. "Would you like to see where Hemingway drank mojitos?"

The situation was not what I intended. I had so easily been duped after all the warnings. Stupidly, I was foiled. Yet I was not in any danger and I argued with myself that I was seeing a part of the city that was not scheduled and I might as well go along with the arrangement. The bar was small but electrically charged with *Cubanismo* rhythm bounding from a small group in the corner but I instinctively knew it was not the original bar. However, customers were caught in the spell of the beat; syncopated lyrics pulsed across the counter where a woman handed me a drink.

"What is this?"

"Is alcoholic drink," my guide said nonchalantly.

"I don't want it—you drink it!" I said suspiciously, afraid it might be spiked or drugged.

"I don't drink," he replied quietly.

"I am going!" I stated blatantly, but I had no idea where I was and was relieved when he followed. "Take me back please?"

"Okay, okay, I take you back. First would you like to see cigars?"

I didn't say anything but I followed him down a side street where he knocked at a door and I thought we were taking a shortcut. A man opened the door and the smell of fresh tobacco wafted into the open air.

"Good, hey, I give you good price!"

The heat, the deceit, the potentially dangerous situation—it was was too much for me and I screamed at the top of my voice,

"I hate smoking, I hate cigars. I don't want to buy any! Now get me out of here!"

The two men were shocked by my sudden outburst. They obviously didn't want any bother and quickly ushered me out into the main street in the bright sunshine.

"Now take me back," I ordered.

He nodded, leading me to where we had begun our ignominious meeting. "Please, lady, you give me money for my help?"

I looked at him and felt obliged to give him something; otherwise, I might find myself troubled in other ways. I gave him a small amount which he challenged but I didn't relent. He walked away with casual disdain and I sighed with relief to be back in the main square. I had been such a fool—after all my years of travelling alone I had to step into such an easy snare?

I needed a drink to recover, and vowed to keep my stupidity a secret, especially from Saul who would use it as a weapon to persuade me to return back home on the next plane. I chose a lovely restaurant near the National Opera House and took my time to sip a cool mojito, a genuine one. I admired the delicate piped-icing carvings on the magnificent building with its intricate white Baroque columns beautifully defined like wedding cake tiers, minutely sculpted, hailing the opulence of a bygone era of wealth and the imported culture of classical concerts. I stood excitedly at the entrance where the sheltered, church-like portals gave sanctuary from the broiling heat. Like the Grand Opera House in Paris, the long sweeping staircase suggested glittering images of bright chandeliers twinkling on the ladies parading their diamonds and designer clothes and preening alongside their generous husbands with their munificent bank accounts. But unlike the Paris Opera House, its grand days were merely hinted at in the fading facades of yesterday, where the powerful emotion of bygone performances was devoured and lay wounded, maimed by neglect, afflicted by the same decaying disease that affected the whole of Havana. Melancholy lingered on the dull stairway. Death hung in the shadows. Ghostly visages wavered in and out of long ago yesterday and I watched as they took shape then disintegrated.

I was unaware for a few moments of a guard peering at me from below and I softly asked him where I could make a booking for a performance. He pointed at a board with a handwritten poster announcing "The Theatre de Cuba, the People's Concert." I paid for my ticket excited at the prospect of the show and walked back to my hotel having succeeded in one of my goals for the day, and wishing desperately to forget my brush with a *jinetero*!

I decided to shake off the anger at my stupidity by taking the ornate lift to the roof garden where there was a beautiful swimming pool set out like an oasis in the sizzling desert. The view from the top was awesome. Havana lay sprawled like a tired, well-used prostitute, relying on the custom of old clients to survive the new times. I wondered what Che felt when he triumphantly drove into the city with the old regime folding into the cracked bricks of the pre-war opulence. I marvelled at his almost saintly adherence to the guerrilla war code, when he made one of his fellow soldiers return a car that he had stolen in order to drive victoriously into Havana, making him walk the rest of the way, scolding, "We are soldiers, not thieves!" Did Che on his exultant welcome slip quietly away from the crowds to be alone with his wife and family, surreptitiously avoiding the mass hysteria? I wanted to get inside his head and learn answers to the myriad of questions bubbling in my mind.

From one of the highest points in the city I surveyed an endless horizon of decaying buildings but I noticed a tiny fluttering of movement near my hand. I was amazed to see a minute hummingbird with its long, spike-like beak sucking the nectar from a single flower growing haphazardly through the iron railing. Its miniscule wings beat the air furiously in the heat, keeping it aloft above the droning traffic far below while it satiated its need. I was transfixed by the beautiful little bird's resilience and its plucky courage to fly so high when there was not another single bird around or stray flower growing precariously on the rooftop. I wondered if the little creature was real and not one of my visions, so I ventured closer to the edge of the rail where I could see the vivid blue markings on its feathers. It sensed my presence and I watched its teeny dark eye acknowledge me momentarily as it hovered in space, pausing before disappearing into the afternoon heat.

I caught the wonder of the moment and wrapped it safely in the soft tissue of my memory as I swam in the lagoon under the great scudding clouds, swirling and gathering, threatening the usual afternoon tropical downpour. When the warm rain fell I stayed in the pool, playing with childlike exuberance, disobeying the general mode of sensible behaviour. In Yorkshire it was rarely warm enough to swim outside and never hot enough to swim in the cold rain. At that moment in total freedom I was one with the sky, the water, and the air, close to the elements of my being, cleansed in the gift of life's flow, washing through time-less space. It was raining in the quiet of nothing and the moment for crying was past. There was a new love in my life. A new era was stamping out the old as I clambered out of the pool, tiptoeing past the attendant into the gold elevator, cloistered from the dampness of the tropical downpour.

It was early afternoon and the sun again burnt the streets, baking the shrubs in the park to a crisp brown. With a short time before my planned tour around the city, I decided to take a bicycle taxi to photograph more classic cars. I hailed one and explained my mission. The boy nodded, mounted his worn cycle seat, and attacked the pedals in the searing heat in his task to take me to capture rare species. I watched his muscled calves speed into action, steering his steed impressively through obstacles, ducking and diving in between the yellow taxicabs as sweat cascaded down his neck and back, seeping through his skimpy white vest. I wished I had worn a hat to protect my head as the roasting heat blistered my pale scalp. A few minutes later my driver slid off the saddle and stood with cloudy droplets pouring down his face, stinging his eyes, and streaming from his nose. Guilt-ridden at making him work so hard in the sweltering heat, I handed him one of my bottles of water and he graciously accepted it, smiling through a wet film on his upper lip.

I was thrilled at the treasures the boy found hiding down a side road, secretly stabled from the tourist track. Sydney first caught my attention, as perched on the top of his buff blue bonnet was a silver bird in flight with shiny wings spread ready for takeoff. Above the polished chrome front guard was a white plastic sign written in red stating, "Dodge 1949, Coronet." Jutting out above the front windows was a silver canopy like the peak of a baseball cap, giving him the comical, jaunty air of an elderly uncle. Next to him was William, with a shiny, red-berry body with two chrome stripes down the front of his bonnet, like silver elasticised braces, the kind that a middle-aged dapper dandy might wear to impress the ladies. The wiper blades positioned with one up and the other down added a sly, sneaky expression like a con man eyeing his next victim. Farther down the road was Esmiralda, sporting an ultraviolet lilac body with a bright white hood and white gothic patterns painted on the front of her bonnet, sides, and rear. "Pontiac" blazed across her chest in gleaming silver and with open wings in flight between her chrome bosoms was a red aeroplane, which altered the tone of her glamorous appearance into a sleazy, cabaret prostitute. By herself, shaded in a clump of trees growing out of the broken pavement, was Grandma. She had careworn mother of pearl paintwork, with dull chrome accessories and a high stub bonnet, like a buck-toothed rabbit. Her narrow front windows framed her faint eyes and a yellow taxi sign displayed over her right eye told everyone she was not too old to work!

There were so many interesting specimens and not enough time to photograph them; besides, the temperature was rising and the slightest movement made me leak under arms and down my back. I nodded to my bicycle boy to take me back and he shot into action heedless of the heat. When we arrived back at the hotel I gave him a surprise fee, probably the equivalent of a month's wages. His face beamed and his eyes sparkled with thanks. Dressed and refreshed, I hurried to wait for the tourist bus to take me on a tour around the old part of the city. Havana was very different from the unrealistic picture in my mind. I had not expected to see decaying buildings like broken eggshells, cracked and shattered, with tenants living inside, unprotected, open to the elements. Yet there were no hungry people on the streets or children begging. The shops were mostly empty with ghostlike manikins vacantly staring back at the public with nothing to offer. I had hoped to buy some tourist trinkets but there was nothing vaguely resembling a Havana keepsake, apart from cigars, not even a cheesy key ring or a plastic Che on a stick.

Our first stop was the rum factory. The smell of old Havana rum-soaked casks leaked through the main doors into the lobby. People peered from behind their monotonous tasks of rinsing, washing, corking, capping, and labelling the bottles that rattled along on an electric line, with each worker in turn adding his labour to the finished product. A couple of off-shift workers trundled up the stairs with their empty bottles to collect their quota of free liquor. As we followed them up the heavy oak steps, I detected an echo of history submerged behind the painted smile of the black worker on the varnished mural. It hinted at slavery and the pitiful lot of the African. Something distasteful lurked in the crevices between the barrels piled high to the ceiling, something unspoken, concealed behind closed doors and blanked by cordiality. The visitors poured into the various rooms where the techniques of making rum were demonstrated and samples were tasted. The rum was warming, trickling stealthily down the back of my throat, lubricating the dryness of the afternoon heat. I didn't buy a bottle but many of our party did and we ambled back to the bus on our way to the tobacco factory where the smell was tempting but the idea disgusting, like the smell of rich coffee with its tantalizing aroma but with a bitter aftertaste of tar. I didn't linger long inside as I had no interest in cigars and didn't want to be reminded of my embarrassing experience that morning.

The factory was buzzing with activity and was filled with an atmosphere of cool camaraderie. The guide explained that each morning there was an assembly for the workers where the management said prayers and read out messages. Then a reader came in and read the news to everyone while they meticulously rolled the papyrus cigar leaves into the famous Havana shape. The workers were allowed to smoke as they worked while in the afternoon they were read a story.

I loved the idea of the collective listening and wondered how effective the method would be if introduced into English factories.

I waited by the bus, watching two little girls cavorting around their front door enjoying the moment of being photographed. The rain began and we moved on to Hemingway's bar jumping over blocks of dried cement left haphazardly on the crumbling wet pavements, ducking through doorways, avoiding skips bursting with rubbish and broken furniture plus building rubble and spiked metal rods poking out dangerously at all angles. Electrical stores were mostly empty as the government did not encourage capitalism in any way, shape, or form and it was impossible to buy a toaster or a hair dryer from the shops—such articles were obtained from black market sources.

Our little group from the bus followed our guide to Hemingway's bar where he led us up winding steps to a small bar upstairs where a band played strains of forgotten Louisiana cotton-picking tunes. I shook off my jacket, placing it on the back of my seat as I rejoiced in the recollection of a sunny New Orleans afternoon. Alone with my memory, I was embraced in the warmth of the welcome. Someone from the bus tour sitting at my table bought me a mojito, and I was touched by his generosity and the camaraderie of the moment; for on a wet afternoon in Havana, in Hemingway's bar, far from my dance school and dull classroom of North Yorkshire, I was riding high on a wave of music, singing in a bar full of strangers brought together by the rain and cocooned in the lingering smell of damp raincoats, crushed fresh mint, honey, and rum-soaked lemon.

CHAPTER 4

The People's Concert

Don't dance before the drums begin,
otherwise you might be asleep when they do!
(from an old African folk saying)

W e spent a happy hour at Hemingway's bar before driving
up winding streets and alleyways delivering passengers
back to their various hotels. Mine was the last and as I stepped
off the bus into the sweltering humidity of the city square, I
began to look forward to the People's Concert. I booked an early
supper and changed into a dress that I had brought for the final
evening at the famous Tropicana nightclub. As usual the food
was excellent, with a myriad of choices, but I was too excited to
eat. As I rushed out of the hotel I was aware of eyes watching
from afar. The men in black viewed me with suspicion and envy
as I flitted around freely, coming and going alone in their exotic
city, aloof in a cloud of mystery. Eyes stared from the park
square as I declined saloon taxis and bicycle taxis, preferring to
find my way on foot in the dimming grey light as evening curled
around the skyline.

Ten minutes to six and I expected to see crowds gathering
outside the theatre for the six o'clock performance but there
was no one in sight except the bored lady in the ticket office.

The handwritten billboard specified a six o'clock start but the main doors to the auditorium were not even open. I asked the blank-faced lady selling tickets what was happening. She stared at me unenthusiastically and pointed to the board and shrugged her shoulders. I felt like a guest invited to a party that was deliberately being held somewhere else. Eagerly I climbed the black stone stairs and followed the sound of a piano in the distance. A small, rotund man stood at the top of the grand, sweeping steps carrying a bunch of keys and wearing a caretaker's concerned expression. He was dressed in shabby trousers and work-a-day tee shirt, with pale-rimmed glasses, and straggling grey hair plastered across the top of his head hiding his baldness.

"Could you help me, please—I'm looking for the concert?"

He looked at me quizzically and smiled, nodding. "It's happening there," he stated, pointing to a door along a vast corridor.

"Oh, I thought it would be in the main theatre?" I enquired disappointedly.

"No money; not open for a long time. The government they promise money, but lady there is none…you have very green eyes!" I was taken aback by his last comment and shyly smiled. "Your dress is Marilyn Monroe!" he grinned.

"Thank you, er…when is the concert due to begin?"

"Six o'clock, seven o'clock, when they are ready."

I was shocked to find such a lackadaisical attitude. In the theatre there is no such thing as "convenient time." After spending a lifetime locked to a professional time schedule, I found it hard to accept anything less. To conceal my annoyance, I politely observed, "This must have been an amazing place in its time."

"Indeed, lady. I have been here for forty years and all we have now is promises."

"Would it be possible to see the auditorium?"

"I am afraid not but I can show you some of the rehearsal rooms. Sometimes we have Saturday dance classes for children."

I smiled. How well I knew Saturday dance classes both as a child and a teacher. He opened a massive carved mahogany door and I slipped into a lost world of dreams. A vision appeared like a misty memory from the forgotten realm of the Russian Tsar's palace, where immense yet delicate ornate mirrors adorned enormous walls up to the beautifully carved ceiling bedecked with a rose centre display of crystal teardrops dangling, gently turning like a dancer's pirouette. A ghostly figure of a young man sat on the edge of a small, raised stage, wearing a white Edwardian shirt and maroon cravat, his ginger head bowed over a black walking cane with a silver handle. A large girl watched the street from an open window, her mind on other things. Others were totally caught in their own steps practising at the bar or diagonally gliding across the polished wooden floor in their long, old-fashioned pink net practice skirts and their thick flesh-tinted tights fighting muscle underneath their pale pink leotards, while their cerise silk ballet shoes prodded the wooden floor. I could smell the zest of concentration and energy pouring into the practice accompanied at the piano by a thin woman in a black, high-necked dress attacking the ivory keys with her bony fingers, swaying in time to her own rhythm, swishing the pages of music across the board without taking her beady, smouldering eyes from the dancers.

The sound of clinking keys brought me back to the present where the reality was grim. The beautiful mirrors had misted with age like an old lady's parched skin, dotted with black spots eating into the once-silky surface. The lumpy floor was no longer sleek and shiny but smothered in a heavy, dirty protective industrial covering infused with the rot of time and stinking of builder's sweat. Two upright pianos were dumped near the windows, their ivory keys yellowed like old men's cigar fingers. The backs were hacked away, revealing skeletal damage with broken and missing hammers. The wicked decay folded heavily into the greying night, reminiscent of a rotting elephant's carcase I had seen laying abandoned in the Indian jungle. That sorrowful graveyard was splintered with haunting traits of the magnificent creature's vibrant life, while vultures feasted on the once-majestic head. In the practice room some fractured floorboards stuck out from underneath the sheet. I couldn't imagine dance classes being allowed in the demolition zone, but then I did not know the real Cuba. The once magnificent room was lonely, bereft of joyful voices and shimmering bodies, with its imposing dance master buried long ago, together with his dreams of the perfect ballet.

As Philippe the curator locked the door, I could still feel the pulse of the dancers beating the lonely air, for even through the veil of death, a dancer recognises another. Our footsteps echoed through the dark, cloistered passage where stifled passion hung in the humid evening. Philippe accompanied me to another large, dark mahogany door down the end of the hallway where a few people entered and I mistakenly followed where faces stared at me from behind a large grand piano with the rehearsal still in progress.

"What time does it begin?" I enquired feebly.

"Eight o'clock," a large man replied.

I made my exit quickly and stood by a stone carved crevice, reminiscent of the kind which medieval castles employed to shoot arrows at their marauding enemies. I peered through the thin fissure to spy on the evening's activities. I was disappointed to find that the People's Concert was not going to be the professional show that I had anticipated and to discover them still rehearsing was shocking. I deliberated whether to stay. I had arrived just before six and it was nearly seven. With another hour to wait, I pondered whether it was going to be worth it. I decided that as I had bought the ticket I must stay, arguing with myself that a live performance always held some gem.

So I continued to wait, and watched the traffic swimming around the square. Classic cars of all colours and proportions swam in and out of the trees like exotic fish. Bright pinks with white fins, deep purples with lilac fronds, and electric yellows swished in the light evening drizzle interspersed with the ordinary, common taxis. I stared across at the tall, imposing buildings opposite. Cloistered in the abbey-like portals of the enclosed corridor of the theatre, whiling away the minutes, idly watching for signs of life from behind the closed door, Barcelona wrapped herself around me, recapturing happy times dancing and teaching choreography. I remembered the time when I had a few days' break and had invited my youngest daughter for a short holiday to show her the city. She was fifteen years old and was enthralled by the street performers in Las Ramblas. Our hotel was just around the corner from the famous avenue of daily live theatre. We were given a room in an annexe in the oldest part of the hotel where the floorboards creaked, dipping and rising underfoot as we tramped through endless glass safety doors.

Our room was long and narrow, with two single beds, a television, and bathroom. There was a large window shrouded in grey net curtains hiding a bleak office building just inches away, where the humdrum world of bodies in dark suits acted out the day mindlessly shuffling paper on desks. Drawing our heavy drapes, we turned on the lights to close out the grim scene and cast off our annexed capsule into unknown seas, drifting in a ghostly limbo where footsteps lingered from long-forgotten wars of Moors and Spanish kings, persecuted Jews, and Indian princes. We were eager to explore the city so we didn't bother to unpack because we wanted to watch an open-air concert in the square near the "goose cathedral," La Seu. We sat under the stars in the warmth of the evening as the music swirled around us before bouncing into the cosmos, vibrating through the ancient walls out towards the open sea.

When we walked back through Las Ramblas a cacophony of strains charged the air, screeching from mini portable sound systems, vying for the crowd's attention, as each variety act claimed their territory on the congested pavement. In the middle of the throng, a woman dressed as a snake coiled up and down a long piece of red silk dangling from a tree, while three dragons beneath her danced a macabre pavane. Meandering through the maze of magic, we slowly wound our way back to the hotel where my daughter, exhausted, went straight to bed. Just as I was settling into an odd Spanish wedding reality programme on the television, my daughter shot up, screaming, "Mum, Mum, someone touched my arm! There was someone next to my bed! I felt it, it was here!" she cried in a panic. "Please, please, Mum sit by me until I go to sleep?"

I calmly stroked her head, coaxing her to lie back down.

"Honestly, Mum, I felt it—it touched me here!" she wailed, pointing to the lower part of her arm.

I sat on the edge of her bed, reassuring her with soothing tones. It was not like her to be so disturbed. I stroked her head until she fell asleep, and watched her troubled face slowly relax and drift into slumber. In the quiet as she slept an oppressive nothingness hung, waiting to pounce, as a haunting melody hardly audible—like a solitary harp plucked in an empty hall—vibrated through the walls. The piercing silence struck like a quick, sharp, intake of breath on a frosty morning. The temperature grew icy in the dissolving moment, freezing backwards towards a second in time when terror struck the innocent, burning bodies, imprisoning them in perpetual shock, preventing them from realizing they were not in the realm of the living but were instead lingering spirits waiting to be released. They waited. They watched, slowly gliding towards me. They were encased in the ticking of the clock; imprisoned in the hum of the air-conditioning; they peered at me in the heavy stillness, pausing abruptly like the moment before a storm striking a calm sea. I resisted their presence and quickly clambered into bed without fully undressing. I refused to be sucked into the vortex of their existence and hurriedly jumped into bed, leaving a small light casting shadows over my daughter's face.

I was used to dealing with lost spirits and helping them to cross the line into their waiting world beyond, but as I placed my head on the pillow my body froze. All the hairs on my left arm shot up like the bristles on a harsh toothbrush. I wrestled internally with the phenomenon but my body was responding to something beyond my mind's control. My head was locked to my right and I could not move. A man was standing close to the bed on my left, near my arm, as others crept stealthily towards me. I was unable to move a muscle while inside my brain I struggled to coax my body back to normality. I refused to acknowledge the invisible entities until I was ready to receive them. In my extreme battle to push them away, my mind blanked and I woke in the morning to the awed memory of the haunting.

The night's unwanted visitors unsettled us both; my daughter was adamant that someone had touched her and, not wishing to alarm her, I tried to make light of the incident. We enjoyed a wonderful day meeting my son, who was studying at Barcelona University. My daughter was eager to share her experience with her brother and described what she had felt as we sat and watched the boats in the dock. My son explained that there was great upheaval centuries ago among the Moors, the Jews, and the Spanish and that many Jews had been burnt as they attempted to flee the city. It was not improbable that there were lost spirits in the ancient part of the city that had been burnt to death and locked in a limbo waiting for release.

Upon returning to our room later that night we switched on all the lights and my daughter insisted that I sit by her side until she fell asleep. While she slept the room's temperature cooled. The lights dimmed and I knew they were approaching. The pulse of time stopped, leaving a gap where the past stole in, breathing sorrow in an icy mist. This time I lay back with my head staring up at the ceiling. As they approached, my body involuntarily went into shock, as the hairs on my arms and the back of my neck stood on end like iron filings on a magnet. I closed my eyes. A hand touched me. I allowed a picture to form of an old man wearing biblical robes. He had a long beard and a dark face. A young boy stood next to him wearing a cream and blue tunic in thick weft cloth tied round the waist with a rope belt. As I allowed them to take form in my brain, others came forward to be acknowledged. I learnt that they were a religious sect on the run from persecutors and had taken refuge in an anteroom in a church. They firmly believed they would be liberated but they were burnt to death still clinging to their immovable faith, believing beyond death that they were not dead. They diligently waited for someone with the energy to open a doorway through their dark tunnel to lead them back to their spiritual home.

The next night I knew I would try to help the lost souls. After my daughter fell into a deep sleep, I crept into bed knowing they were in the shadows waiting. The lights lowered. The air grew still and cold. I closed my eyes to begin my deep breathing, taking myself under the normal level of pulse rate and heartbeat, slowing everything down. I encased myself in a protective film so that I would not be severed from my body and sucked out into limbo with the spirits. I entered a grey bubble of energy swirling in white translucence, hurling me into a timeless tube, until I stood in the sacred silence of the dead. The ancient smell of religious ceremony was thick in the musty air. In obedient silence they waited. Pale faces stared and the veiled heads of the women turned upwards to greet me, unsmiling, uncertain, accepting their fate with absolute trust.

In the action, I was not afraid. I simply gave myself to the mission. From afar I could see my body breathing. Purple energy hovered above and around me. A gap manifested through my solar plexus opening a portal to beyond as a bright runway shone through the aperture, past my daughter and out through the window. It was a stairway of light gleaming to illumine their way home. First the old man approached gently, calmly, graciously, with gratitude glowing from within. He passed through me. Suddenly, the exodus happened quickly. Energy struck like lightning bolts across the room, cracking the ceiling with whiplash pulses, beating through me as they passed like a rush hour crush to cram inside a tube train. Momentarily aware of two aspects of myself, one inside my frame and the other outside, I watched my daughter being thrown around her bed, convulsing as spirits passed from me through her and out through the window. Flashes sparked over our heads, ricocheting off the walls, exploding joyously, lighting the room with a myriad of tiny fluorescent stars exploding in the air seconds before vanishing. I don't remember sleeping. I don't recall gliding back into my body. I woke the next morning to see my daughter's peaceful face, smiling in her sleep. The room was tranquil. The air was light and warm. Golden rays trickled through the creases in the curtain and I knew that time had regained its normal pace. The sun beamed a bright welcome back to the world of the living while the spirits had departed to their sanctuary at last to find their true home.

A flurry of voices burbled up the staircase, breaking the spell of memory, pulling me back to the living moment. It was eight o'clock and the People's Theatre Company was finally ready. I followed the trickle of visitors into the council chambers meeting room with its white marble floor and an ornate coat of arms of Galicia prominently set above a large window draped with pale blue velvet curtains. Philippe had organised a meagre lighting system with a couple of lights barely making any difference to the brightly-lit electric ceiling lights. Highbacked hard chairs were set in rows with a grand piano positioned stage right. I took a seat at the end of a row down the centre aisle and watched as people began to quietly filter into the space. I counted twenty-nine in the audience, not realising that three-quarters of the people were performers. After some secret signal, Philippe took his auspicious seat behind the paltry lighting equipment and from a side door an African man and woman entered, singing a song and throwing boiled sweets into the audience from small baskets. I suddenly realised with inner dread that I was stuck in an amateur concert, caught in a web of enthusiasm dripping with star struck operatic singers. After spending a lifetime choreographing amateur musicals just to pay the rent, I had no desire to sit through school concert material performed by people whose heritage held much richer treasures than pseudo-English Edwardian choral works.

Sitting in front of me was a middle-aged European man, Gary. His thin, bottle-blonde hair was stiffly coiffed and his face was finely made-up with lovely bright red lips like a pantomime Dame. When he got up from his chair he smiled coyly. He sang a song overflowing with rude innuendos and double entendres and when he alluded to his sizzling-hot penis, miming to the old black ladies sitting in the front row, I prickled with embarrassment. After an uncomfortable few minutes of Gary's music hall charade, people applauded politely and he bowed low, making way for the *Carmen* ensemble. A group of women tottered into the arena, all shapes and sizes, mostly Spanish/African, dressed in homemade red skirts adapted to fit each unique figure. Their heights varied from small to very tall. The small rotund ladies produced high wailing voices, and the tall slender ones growled in deep basso profundo tones. A middle-sized, middle-aged lady in glasses at the end of the line attempted to conduct the ensemble with unusual hand gestures and occasional flicks of her hips in a vain attempt to conjure the saucy moves of the sexy gypsy Carmen. The group made explicit efforts to recreate the passion and smouldering glances of the chorus as they swished their homemade skirts like small children displaying superficial temper tantrums, whilst blinking their eyes wildly like puppet dolls in the hands of unaccomplished puppeteers. I was relieved when they exhaled their final note into oblivion, abandoning the stage in a flurry of animated pride, waving like children at their first Nativity concert.

An African quartet took their place. Two very large, tall men and two very small, round men stood nervously before us. Comically the small men poured forth deep, bear-like notes, while the tall men sang in sweet falsetto tones in an alarmingly convincing manner. I vaguely recognised the tune, squeezing my brain to pulp out the melody that was obscured by their strange rendition of groups of notes I knew so well. Suddenly, when they sang "Michelle, ma belle" I realised they were crooning the Beatles' famous ballad, "Michelle." Having fathomed the actual song and placed it in my mind where I could mentally sing along, their medieval, disharmonious interpretation lost me and left me pondering how they could have interpreted a simple melody in such an unusual way. However, their four-part version of "Three Little Maids from School" from *The Mikado* was acceptable, especially with closed eyes, and the words sung in English with a Spanish accent added an exotic flair to the pseudo-oriental operetta.

During the short interval I realised my presence amongst the congregation caused curiosity as I sat alone, knew no one, and was not a performer or a supporter or a friend or a relative of anyone. I appeared like a cuckoo in a nest of blackbirds, so obviously not one of them, no matter how loudly I applauded the acts. When Gary came out of a side door wearing a pair of red, worn boots made into tap shoes, which clinked and clacked mechanically on the marble floor as he sauntered back to his seat, my spirits lifted—I love tap and had taught my own genre of the art form for many years. The women in red skirts fluttered in and out of their friends and families clucking with pride, puffing out their generous chests as they nestled back into their places ready for the second half. Philippe flickered the lights to alert everyone that the second act was about to begin and an African man set the scene by singing "Old Man River" in pure Paul Robson tones, which was wonderful. The vibration and profound resonance of his voice transported me to the Deep South river banks in Louisiana, in the cotton fields and the tobacco plantations with the smell of gumbo wafting through open windows. He was my gem for the night, set in a cluster of fake sparkle.

Next to perform was Gary. He had a sound cabaret voice, but as the song "New York" flowed into each verse without one single tip-tap, I began to suspect the worst. When he finally gave a little flurry, I was embarrassed beyond measure. He patted the marble tiles with odd single clacks, which even my baby class could have produced. I bit my lip, trying to disguise my feeling of humiliation for him. How could he present such feeble footwork in front of an audience whose heritage was steeped in the most amazing and intricate steps? Again the audience politely clapped as Gary wiped his beaded brow and sat down preening like a full-plumed peacock. The rest of the concert drifted by with excerpts from Gilbert and Sullivan and other well-worn melodies until the last coda rallied in four-part harmony to a rolling crescendo with everyone holding onto the last note until all breath was squeezed out, wheezed out, tapering into the void beyond the pale velvet curtains. I rose to leave but sat down again as a line of performers queued to accept a box of sweets which they received like Oscar trophies. Eventually I escaped, running down the empty sweeping steps and avoiding the call of Philippe behind who wanted to show me the nightlife of Havana.

After the rising expectation and build-up of excitement during the day, all I wanted was to free myself from the People's Concert. Outside I breathed a deep sigh in the warm evening air and ambled back to my hotel. The concert had been an experience, disappointing but unforgettable. I wished I could have shared it with Saul and we would have laughed together. I looked up at the night sky where the moon was smiling. I wondered if he was sleeping; it was too late to phone or text. I had such wonderful dreams for our future together. We could share so much. I would have to slowly and carefully unravel my psychic side, because to a lay person the matters of the paranormal could be too difficult to accept. I did not want him to think I was crazy and scare him away. It was quite normal for anyone who got close to me to see, feel, and experience strange things and I wondered if he was ready for that. Would he accept me, and my true nature? How could I explain leaving my body sometimes at night to help rescue lost spirits?

I remembered a very sweet experience when my children were young and we lived near a beautiful pond. There was a little girl who lived at the top of the street and whose mummy I befriended. She accepted my psychic slant on the world and discussed many aspects of extra-sensory perception as she was a medical nurse and had a different perspective from a scientific viewpoint. One night, her little daughter Sita was worried and upset because her father was working away and she feared that something dreadful might happen to him. In my out of body wandering, I found her walking in her nightdress by the top of the road. It was chilly and there was no one around. Her little body was cold and I took her hand and told her that her father would be fine and that she must go back to bed. So I led her back to her bedroom and snuggled her down under the covers and stayed until she fell asleep. For me, that was a normal event and I did not think about it until a couple of days later when I met Jane, Sita's mother. She smiled and gave me a quizzical look.

"Thank you!" she said.

"For what?"

"Taking care of Sita."

"Oh!" I replied, a little reserved.

"She told me you took her back to bed when she was outside looking for her father and you stayed until she went to sleep!"

"Yes, that's true."

"I'm not going to ask how you did it. I only know what Sita told me was the truth and just to say that I am so glad you did, what you did, thank you."

It gave me a warm feeling to know that the child accepted the happening quite naturally and related the event with a casual attitude, as though it was an everyday occurrence. When I was out of my body, I appeared to her like my normal self and so it was not a frightening phenomenon. Children cannot be fooled. They are still close to the essence of being and see what others cannot. The curtain between worlds is flimsy and it is not until they learn to pull down the curtain tightly and close off the sphere beyond that their second sight is blinded.

As I lay my head on the pillow and night closed in, my mind drifted back to the comical Carmen ensemble and I fell asleep with the strange strains and visions of the People's Concert vibrating in my head.

CHAPTER 5

Visions

You must be able to dance backwards
with the same confidence as forwards.
Never look back, just do it!

I woke early, realizing my new adventure was about to begin. I slipped out of bed and stood watching Havana embrace the dawn. Parades of morning shades streaked pink across the midnight blue, casting away the darkest hue of brooding, black clouds. The miracle of morning unfolded as the sun rose spectacularly over the city and with one glimmer, lambkin clouds shimmered over the ancient bricks and I wondered at what precise moment did the day begin? The curtain up on the first scene cued clattering vendors into the square, setting up their stalls as the bicycle taxis began their wait for custom while the shoeshine boys yawned and watched for their regular customers. I sighed, not wanting to leave the comforting hotel luxuries, and decided that before taking a taxi downtown to my rendezvous with my travel companions, I would hire a bicycle taxi to photograph more classical cars.

Back at the hotel after my brief photography outing I gathered my things, knowing that in readiness for a new adventure I had to temporarily sacrifice all the luxuries and comfort that were part of another lifestyle. I had to embrace the unknown and be prepared to forgo my privacy and share a bedroom and bathroom with strangers. The taxi driver looked puzzled when I asked to be taken downtown to an inferior hotel and as he lifted my bags out of the cab I understood his concern. The hotel was squeezed in between a small pizzeria and a fast food café. There was a garage and a parking lot opposite. The road was potholed, uneven and worn, speckled with litter and unwanted packaging from nearby shops. A large empty wooden crate lay smashed by the kerb with sharp splinters jutting out onto the pavement. I was dismayed as I dragged my bags into the small, dismal lobby after the gracious splendour of the Palm Court International Hotel. I checked in and was told that I would be sharing with another woman who hadn't yet arrived. I took the tiny lift up to my room, which was compact, clean, and adequate. There was a sense of one night stands, business men watching porn on the television, weary student travellers, and lonely tourists hovering in the dimness. I chose a bed, placed my bags on the end, and left to investigate the rest of the hotel. A sign to the swimming pool intrigued me, so I took the lift to the top floor and alighted into a large café area, similar to a school canteen. The sign directed me to a small space enclosed by a plastic canopy where I was shocked to find that the swimming pool was a large tin tub pulped with people. I turned away suppressing the thought of "people stew" as the pool was a large pot where body germs could thrive and fester, simmering in the heat of unclean bodies. The idea of having a cup of coffee from the café was quickly abandoned so I walked out into the glare of the afternoon and meandered around the back streets.

This part of Havana was certainly different from the city centre. I wandered into a bakery that was part café, where a few elderly people spooned out time and whiled away the hours staring at empty teacups and half-eaten cakes. I ordered a take-away coffee and a sandwich. Back in the searing heat I traced the pavement where tufts of grass broke haphazardly through the cracked tarmac. I marvelled at a single white flower flourishing in a desert of concrete, its delicate face smeared with grime. An image of a black daisy appeared fleetingly in my mind, struggling to exist in alien confines, and I was reminded of a strange vision that appeared to me from a train window as I travelled towards Dover to catch a ferry to France. I was journeying to Italy over land to choreograph some new work in Lake Garda. As the train slowed when it neared a station, but did not stop, I caught a glimpse of an empty platform. The scene was grey. The day was dismal. The grimy, neglected buildings were left to rot, besmirched in every corner with faded, luminous graffiti. Standing on the edge near a silver wire fence was a naked, black teenage boy, his eyes pleading, boring into mine. Suddenly from nowhere his body was splattered with white paint and he stood humiliated, screaming in silent pain, beseeching me to do something. I recoiled from the window in shock, gasping at the sight. I looked around—no one else in the carriage had seen the apparition. The horror of the vision remains; the look in his eyes especially will always haunt me.

When I found my way back to the hotel, I sat in the cool of the dim lobby watching the comings and goings of the clientele. I managed two hours of patient waiting before the pangs of hunger moved me to try the pizzeria next door. I indulged in a glass of wine and a seafood pizza. Another hour dwindled. I sauntered next door to the lobby and sat until I spied an English woman registering at the counter. I heard her Birmingham accent clearly above the Spanish chatter. Her strong voice came from an emaciated body. I ambled up beside her and overheard that she was sharing the room with me. Hilary's skeletal arm and bony hand held out a welcome. She explained that she had just arrived from another trip and was dying to go upstairs and wash her clothes. I said I would meet her along with the others at six o'clock in the lobby. She was the head of English in a school in Birmingham and seemed a lovely person. She had beautiful, long, wavy brown hair, but her delicate frame worried me. I thought she had wanted to punish herself for some reason and had become anorexic. Perhaps the trip might help to cure her in some way and encourage her to eat.

I lost another hour by walking to an intriguing building just around the corner from the hotel. It spiralled up like a giant helter-skelter with pockets of interesting art and craft stalls hidden in various corners of the levels. I walked past a few people gathered around a table at the entrance and made my way up to the first level but a man followed me. I was afraid, so I quickened my pace, clutching my handbag, and began to race up the steep slope, sweating in the great heat of late afternoon. As I turned around I saw that he was fast on my heels. I began to run, my heart pounding. I could feel the heat of his body closing in on me. A hand grabbed my shoulder. My heart pumped and my legs jellied as I stopped and saw a man smiling at me.

"Please, missy, you didn't pay to come in?"

I was shocked. It hadn't occurred to me that I had to pay to get in the place. I gasped then laughed and so did he. I gave him the token entrance fee and continued on my way, trying to blend into the material stall to shake off my embarrassment. The helter-skelter art emporium was full of local crafts and I wished I could have bought some of the pottery and paintings, but there was no room in my rucksack for such luxuries. After wandering through the amazing maze with its tantalizing smells of little booths offering different worldwide cuisines, I realised it was time to get back to the hotel and begin my adventure with a group of strangers, wondering what trials lay ahead.

Back at the dingy hotel, a cluster of people had gathered in the lobby including Hilary, who smiled as I sat down. A young Australian woman with white blonde hair and a voluptuous figure sat facing everyone in a short skirt that revealed her athletic legs. She held a clipboard and ticked off names as people arrived. Carol was our leader. She resembled an upbeat, Australian Marilyn Monroe. Hilary sat next to a beautiful young woman, Simonise, who was also from Australia. She had a tall, slender, model-like figure with long, blonde, straight hair and a sweet smile. A middle-aged overweight Irish couple ambled out of the small lift and beamed as they introduced themselves, Paddy and Mira. A young boy of about nineteen years of age waved enthusiastically from the bar and joined us carrying a fruity cocktail, greeting us in a flurry of English public school bravado, calling, "Hello, I'm Edgar. Pleased to meet you all."

Two more Australians joined us, introducing themselves, "Hi, I'm Eric, and I've never travelled before in my life!" His young wife echoed his sentiments. "Hi, I'm Charlie, and I've travelled lots, but I decided before we had a family that Eric ought to see something of the world, so be kind to him, folks!"

We all laughed and Eric blushed, shyly smiling into his chest. Across the room sitting primly together were two young Swiss women, one with black hair, Jane, and the other with mouse brown hair, Marie. They sat with straight backs, attentively listening to the conversation like two old maiden aunts eager to join in the party games but never quite plucking up the courage to revel in the fun. After everyone made their introductions, Carol gave us our instructions for the morning flight to Santiago de Cuba and then asked if we would like to have dinner in the Spanish quarter to sample wonderful authentic food and watch the flamenco dancing. We all thought it was a great idea, except the Prunesquallors (a nickname for the two Swiss women which I concocted from Mervyn Peake's *Gormenghast*). At least they were not like a couple from my previous trip, nicknamed "the complainers" as nothing was to their satisfaction and they continually grumbled and bickered.

As we trundled through the streets to an old part of the city, conversation bubbled. It was always a relief to get past the initial meeting of one's companions, placing everyone into convenient boxes, labelling them according to compatibility. I was glad that there was no one in the group with whom I might become romantically attached, as I had promised Saul to be faithful even though we had only known each other fleetingly. His beautiful ring kept me company in lonely moments.

Twilight shades of purple and pink streaked the sky with firefly flashes as we strolled through the ancient streets. Fallen ashes of grey bleached away the day, making way for night to flood the scene in a cosy screen of deepest blue. Excitement stirred as the overture began, the floodlights blazed as we entered centre stage to take our places in the unfolding saga of the new adventure, and what better place to set the scene than a sweltering cavern with a roasting spit that crackled and spat, hissing a welcome as we were shown to rough wooden tables in front of a bare-boards stage. Spanish musicians sat on old upright chairs, plucking frantically at chords, striking the air with heated passion as the Flamenco dancer blasted quick lightning rallies like gunfire shot from her shoes, across the stage, drumming through our table, vibrating through our hands, churning our glasses of red wine as she flashed her skirt revealing black knickers. A flurry of waiters attended to our needs, bringing the spicy flavours of Spain to our table while the music and dancing throbbed and robbed the atmosphere of air, making us gasp and gulp more wine from rustic brown pots.

Satiated with wonderful food and our fill of red wine, reeling with the dancer's twirls and stampede of castanets with plucked melodies of lost loves and forlorn young men, we drifted out of the cavern into the humid night. Hilary and some of the others decided to carry on to a nightclub but Paddy, Mira, and I needed to retire in preparation for our early flight. When I switched on the light in the bathroom, I discovered that Hilary had decked it with washing bunting. The tiny cubicle resembled a Chinese laundry, with underwear hanging from every available space. I was shocked at all the thongs on display, so tiny that they were like eye patches or stringy slingshots. How could she wear such scanty articles? I settled down, relieved that the sheets were clean, and drifted into sleep, knowing that when Hilary came in I would soon be disturbed—such was the price of expedition travel!

The next morning we were up bright and early, greeting each other in the restaurant like old friends. The Prunesquallors were meticulously turned out in demur cotton blouses and sensible trousers. They looked up from their toast and jam and waved politely. I sat next to Hilary and coaxed her to eat something for the journey; she made a fair attempt at eating her fruit and yogurt before returning to our room to finish her packing. Carol was busy in the lobby organising our taxis to transport us to the miniature postal airport, where all the internal mail was sorted and flown across Cuba. Ten of us piled into three taxis and sped out through the centre of Havana past the open land on the outskirts of the city to a compact airport constructed in the middle of shrub land. We watched as our bags were flung into the micro hold of the tiny plane along with mailbags and strangely shaped parcels. I enjoy flying on small aircraft as the sensation of being high in the air is more acute than in a large plane, like riding a roller coaster with the dips and loops gripping in the pit of your stomach. I love the takeoff and landing, with the bone-shaking, rattling and rolling sensation as the noise of the throbbing engine gyrates and makes your teeth chatter. Others in the party did not share my enthusiasm, as didn't Hilary who sat next to me with sweating palms. The flight was only short and it seemed no time at all before we were alighting in another microscopic airport, collecting our luggage, and boarding our little rickety coach nicknamed the WaWa bus, which was to be our home for the duration of the rest of the journey. It was just big enough to take our luggage and house the whole party.

In high spirits, we claimed our seats and drove into the rising heat of the morning. Santiago de Cuba was hotter than Havana and the bus was not air-conditioned. Carol played us a CD of the previous group's musical efforts, reminding us that we were in for a treat: taking percussion lessons with some well-known artists. We were also scheduled to cut a CD of our own as a highlight to the finale of our trip. All that seemed far away, almost incomprehensible at that moment when our little WaWa bus was bouncing in and out of the potholed roads, beating a track through rough-shod highways, pounding our way to our homestead houses. We arrived in the hot, dusty city, cradle of the revolution and father of traditional *son* rhythms, in the late morning when the city was alive with its internal throb. Santiago and the Oriente area have a large population of Afro-Cubans due to slave labour from Africa brought in to work on the sugar cane and tobacco plantations and to increase the labour force in the mines and ranches. The faces in the streets reflect this heritage, unlike the people in Havana where the Afro influence is slightly more diluted.

We were taken first to Carol's homestead family where we were assigned our various adopted families. The houses were extremely deceptive. On the outside they appeared dilapidated, crammed together in linear rows with crumbling paintwork and decaying masonry, but inside they were miniature palaces. The front room of all the homesteads was a showcase of accumulated wealth, overflowing with middle class trappings of pottery, ceramics, knick-knacks, bric-a-brac, religious statues and family photographs in expensive silver frames. Farther down the street from Carol's house was mine. The door was opened by a large, overbearing man with metallic grey hair and thick-rimmed glasses. I was ushered in and was amazed by the décor of the room, which was designed in a lavish Mexican/Spanish style. My host's mousey housewife peeped out from behind her husband's tall body. She peered over her silver specs like a sweet Mrs. Tiggywinkle, wringing her hands over her clean apron. The master of the house laid down the law like a strict parent and told me I was not to have a key but I must ring the bell when I wanted to get in. I sheepishly asked if I was out late did the same rule apply and he nodded, stating pompously, "Someone will always be awake!" There was no trifling with him and I thought he must have been a formidable father.

He showed me to my room upstairs. The staircase was unusual, like the white-pebbled seaside steps winding down to a Cornish beach, with no handrail to steady or guide oneself. At the top of the stairs stood Maria, the house owner's sister, who was a small attractive lady smiling a warm welcome. My room was clean and adequate with an ancient air conditioner in one corner which, when turned on, vibrated like a worn-out cattle lorry juddering its way along a rutted highway. Mr. Gazeereth explained how it worked and that whenever I left the room I had to turn it off. He was most insistent about this, and like a shy child I nodded affirmatively. The bathroom next door was clean, but my phobia of spiders and insects always made me nervous about things lurking in corners and I checked behind the shower curtain to make sure it was clear of crawlies. On the veranda was a small birdcage whose occupant chirped from time to time. His restrained warbles upset me and I longed to open the little trap door and watch him fly away. Over the rail was a view to the open courtyard with foliage sprouting upwards and outwards. It always intrigued me why the houses had a jungle growing in the middle and how they were open to the sky and subject to all manner of weather changes.

Farther along was a small kitchen where I was to eat alone. Maria did the cooking for guests. She told me that she had a daughter and showed me her photograph hanging on the wall. Upstairs was Maria's domain and as she clattered in the kitchen she chatted. She had adapted the cooking space into a tiny restaurant for one, using her own creative ideas as to what a visitor might find attractive. A chequered green plastic cloth covered a tiny table. In the centre was an ancient, ornate cruet set, plus a small black vase with faded silk flowers. There was an ancient sink with a worn wooden drain board with shelves underneath harbouring a collection of old steel saucepans like the ones I used to play with as a child to make mud pies. There was a tiny fridge, an elderly gas cooker, and through a glassless window sounds of a hen scratching secretly were just audible. Discoloured artificial sunflowers smiled apologetically from the top of a cupboard and a string of waxen, dusty fruit dangled over a battered bread bin. Foliage from outside poked a friendly greeting inside, while sham flowers and plants inside made the cubby-hole claustrophobic and uncomfortable. As I sat down to eat a strange luncheon, a collection of African masks and small statues peered at me from a shelf opposite.

I was not hungry but I forced down some of the chicken stew. I didn't touch the doughy white bread accompanied by butter sachets, but I did eat the fresh fruit and drink the carton of juice. I felt guilty at eating so little, not because I realised how difficult it was to live off rations, but because I didn't want to offend Maria. I hoped the beautiful soap I had brought for presents for the homestead families lessened the offence. I had been told that beauty soap was expensive in Cuba, so I had brought a good supply to give to my hosts. I made my apologies, stating our group had a meeting at Casa de la Tova, and greeted Edgar outside my house. He was a charming boy—reminding me of my son—with impeccable manners, who insisted on helping me to find my way to the famous café. Casa de la Tova is famous because the Buena Vista Social Club used to play there. In the afternoon it becomes an old-fashioned tea dance emporium downstairs, set out with white tables and chairs under a greenhouse canopy of indoor flowers and jungle shrubs. As we entered, the gentle scritch-scratch of maracas echoed around the room and elderly guitar players in their seventies strummed contentedly, nimbly fingering florid, embellished arpeggios with swollen, arthritic fingers. The eighty-three-year-old female lead singer was marvellous at crooning old Cuban folk songs. I bought one of her CDs and she gave me a kiss. A flash vision of her as a young woman reached in my head and tumbled back out again and I sighed for the loss of her youth and wondered why anyone has to grow old.

We sat at an extended table in the centre of the café and ordered various drinks. Everyone was coaxed into a peaceful stupor as the music lulled us contentedly in gentle melodies until the band changed tempo and played hypnotically, syncopating the beat, luring us with sensual drums accompanied by *palitos* (sticks) into a seductive mood. The rhythm was a rumba (from the word *rumbear*, which means to have a good party time), but it was slower than the normal rumba which indicated that it was a *yambu*, which is an older person's rumba played slowly and which is highly sexually charged. It simulates the story of a man's pursuit of a woman and the sexual domination of her. As I sipped my mojito, one of the café's professional dancers tapped me on the shoulder and asked me to dance. The group all cheered and I couldn't refuse. We had the floor to ourselves and slinked in a mock-seductive style over the tiles, adding touches of suggestive steps wherever and whenever the music dictated. I felt safe in his leadership as he was there to entertain the people, not for a romantic liaison. We stayed for a couple of hours relaxing in the restrained atmosphere of the 1920s tea hall, while the exotic, sexy beat pulsed beneath the polite, genteel facade. Then Carol organised three taxis to drive us to the castle on the hill near the bay to watch the special cannon ceremony that is performed each evening at dusk to celebrate the revolution's liberation of the people.

The light was dulling, blending into the steely, calm sea as we stepped out of the taxis feeling the breeze across the ocean cooling the humid twilight. We had time to explore the ramparts and inner dungeons and Edgar made me laugh as he pulled mock faces of victims from inside the prison bars. The air was quiet and strangely expectant. I wandered to a tiny turret and gazed out to sea. Simonise was hanging over the ancient bricks taking photos and I thought how brave she was to take a year's world tour by herself, needing time after a collapsed love affair. I thought of Saul and wondered what the Welsh caveman was doing. Couples holding hands leading each other over to the cannon fortifications signalled a closeness of a special moment. I wondered if Saul and I would do such things together in the future and if we would love one another into old age. The first time I put my head on his chest and heard a mechanical thumping, I was alarmed. He told me he had a heart valve and that he could promise me fifteen years at most, and as he held me in his arms he whispered, "All I want to do is die wrapped in your arms with my head on your breast!"

A strong, chilly breeze caught me sinking in the moment and I shivered. A vision of a man waiting to die, lying on the floor with his back to the dingy wall, waiting in the dark in an old schoolhouse, wavered above the glassy grey sea. Pain wracked his body, forcing his soul to fly…the vision faded. Che…

I turned to witness the curious cannon ceremony as seven young Cuban teenagers marched across the ramparts in perfect unison. The cold white ancient bricks, pitted with the years, watched the sinister scene set against the vast sea on one side and a scrub wilderness on the other. The parade was lead by a dedicated young girl who stomped toward the squat cannons that were aimed and ready for action. The seven youngsters were dressed in starched white uniforms. The girl in front wore a calf-length white skirt and a white blouse with a frilled yolk and high neck collar trimmed in red. The others wore white trousers, black Nazi-style knee-length boots, beautifully polished, and black belts anchoring swords on their left side with buckled black belts worn diagonally across their chests in pirate fashion.

Solemnly harmonious, each with their beige straw hats turned up in front revealing the Cuban flag, they carried an air of the past, reminiscent of their ancestors' fight for freedom from slavery. Like old dry lavender, retaining a hint of the smell of fresh buds yet preserving the essence in closed pods, the youngsters re-enacted their history with stern sincerity, safe-keeping the core of their forebears' pride. In a quietly alarming manner, their movements performed with such dogmatic determination reminded me of the Hitler Youth in their energetic innocence. There were no adults overseeing the proceedings. The teenagers were totally in control of the operation. The leader governed the ritual, waiting to give the orders while the other three stood guard. Two boys saluted and moved forward to ram the cannon ammunition into place with long steel poles. A boy played a bugled salute that plaintively floated out to sea. The cannon fired with sombre funereal dignity and boomed across the vast horizon into the depths of forever as the failing light and grey smoke fused into the dulling sea. Just as dramatically as the procession appeared, it disappeared, bringing the curtain down on the daily evening service.

We turned our backs on the blackening ocean and boarded our taxis back to our homesteads where we prepared for a different kind of ritual: the night scene, the dance dream of lurid passion enticed by heated bodies entangled in the fandango of the steamy night, thrilled and tantalised by the throbbing live music in the dance hall of Casa de la Tova. Upstairs in the long wooden hall our party sat enthralled at the dancers performing their stylised versions of salsa movements. It was the locals' turn first to show off their skill and prowess before the floor was opened to the general public. Suddenly, when the performance ended men crept from under floorboards and out of walls, pouncing on unsuspecting people and not heeding refusals as everyone danced with anybody and everybody. Language was not necessary, only communication of moves, and when the dance was over you passed onto someone else to experience their style.

The clammy humid air did not affect the dancers as they bounced from one dance to the next, basking in the sticky glow of their efforts. Poor Paddy was plagued by the toothache and consoled himself with Irish whiskey, while Mira was thoroughly enjoying herself in the fling of the moment, being spun and manipulated into strange positions, girlishly giggling and shouting above the blare of the music, "I didn't know salsa was like this! We didn't learn this back home in Ireland!" as her arms became stylistically entangled with a stranger. Carol waved as she dragged on a cigarette, ensconced in the embrace of a past boyfriend. Hilary was on the balcony enjoying the attentions of a well-dressed teacher from the university. The Prunesquallors with their usual demure postures sat politely sipping orange juice, while the dancers multiplied around them, conquering all space, closing in like locusts on a ripe corncob. Edgar was slowly dwindling into a comfortably drunken stupor with his fresh face puffed and reddened by the sun as he sat imbibing copious amount of vodka, being in no fit state to dance. Simonise was jubilantly throwing herself into the rumba. The Australian couple were downing pints of beer, happy to be spectators at the masquerade. As the music momentarily paused, a general hush spread throughout the hall as the last remaining member of the Buena Vista Social Club ambled across the floor to speak to fellow musicians. He was greeted with a round of applause and waved to everyone as he took a seat to listen to the music.

Soon afterwards, the heat, the travelling, and the day's events made me too tired to stay longer. Back at the homestead, true to his word, Mr Gazeereth got up to let me in. My room was roasting but the air conditioning was so noisy. I was thrilled to see a message from Saul and to know he missed me as I missed him. I had not felt loved for a long time and the feeling gave me comfort and strength. Resigned to the dreadful noise of the air conditioning, I slept fitfully, especially after seeing a flying cockroach jump near my bed. Drifting in and out of reality, wafting on a sea of past visions, memories hazed like mirages in a steamy desert. Knossos hovered through hidden corridors, pushing forward to enter my consciousness, fighting to be reborn in my mind but as the light of the present began to dribble through the thin curtains, I was relieved to find myself in the bedroom in

Cuba. I could hear gentle clattering from the kitchen and knew Maria must be making my breakfast. I wrapped a towel around my hair and returned to my room. I had my first dance lesson to look forward to and I was hungry. Maria had made me a formal breakfast with eggs, bacon, and toast. She was pleased with my clean plate and I excused myself to prepare for the day. My lesson was at eleven o'clock in the morning and I planned to first take a walk around the city and photograph more classic cars.

As I walked out into the heavy heat of the morning, locals stared from their front doorsteps. Walking up the hill to the main thoroughfare was tedious and a film of dusty grime polluted the air, leaving a taste of soot on my lips. I needed to find a shop where I could buy water. At the top of the street was a supermarket but it was not well stocked. It was set out like a closing-down sale with goods piled in different corners, haphazardly stacked for people to pick up randomly. It was only after I had walked past a few shops which had either ceased trading or were open and had nothing to sell, that I realized how bad things were for the people. Window after window echoed the same dull emptiness. Dreary, drab, half-whitewashed shop windows lined the busy street. I stopped by one which forlornly bore traces of someone's thoughtful departure. The empty shop was a pitiful plea from an invisible presence against the washed-out economy with a single white bow left on a mat of artificial grass and a bouquet of faded flowers arranged on a stand. A garish manikin with gaudy makeup and a coquettish long blonde curly wig balanced on its head stood dressed in a dingy long grey tee shirt mocking the opulence not offered to Cubans. I took a photo of the bleak scene.

Farther on I found a warehouse full of second-hand clothes, shoes, and uniforms which people could buy very cheaply with or without ration coupons. I picked out a grey and orange long-sleeved shirt for dancing and bought it for about a pound. The house where I was to have my lesson was around the corner down the next street and when I knocked I was shown into a hallway where my teacher was just finishing a lesson with Eric and Charlie, who beamed through a haze of air freshener and sweat. It was an odd place to have a lesson. It was a small rectangular white hall with a green and white tiled floor. There was a compact table in one corner with a small tape recorder perched on the top next to a fridge. A black plastic armchair was angled at the side and a bicycle was parked against a wall. A large fan whirred in another corner. My teacher had a familiar face, wearing clothes almost identical to one of the dancers from Alvin Ailey's company that I had seen years ago. He wore a bright red peaked beret the same colour as his tee shirt, and white cotton slacks. His dark hair and eyebrows were greying but his body was trim and muscled. He was a gifted dancer and as soon as he took me in his arms we fell into the steps. His style was old-fashioned which suited me and contained a mixture of steps from the mambo, rumba, and conga, making it more of a Mozambique with *bata* drum music. We had to keep stopping to dry our hands in the relentless heat. The hour passed too quickly and he asked me if I wanted to teach dance at the Universidad de Santiago and begin that December. Although it was a fantastic offer, I could not accept—there was too much back home anchoring me to Yorkshire.

I could not contemplate leaving the children in my school. We have one purpose: dancing out our lives in a safe haven while the world outside rages. I watch as my students dance out their fears, their growing pains, and their joy. Like a family we close ranks against intruders and the world outside. We dance on. We face ourselves through the steps and dance for others. Sometimes I see their invisible dreams twirling beside them like obedient shadows. From the inner temple of life I guide them, urge them with my energy to fold and stretch, curl and glide. Over the years many, many children have passed through the dance school, and each time they are ready to fly the nest I resolve my heart will not be broken. When they walk out of the door for the last time I know they are unravelling the umbilical cord and I am determined not to love so hard again, but then the round repeats itself and a new batch hatches through the door, and I think these are my last chicks. I think I couldn't love them as much as my last babies but they take hold of my heart. Walking in through the door shyly holding onto their mothers' hands, the new batch in their miniscule uniforms stand before me looking up with their trust in my hands and hope in their toes. I study their toes. How beautifully they point them. I watch their legs. What control for ones so young. I am amazed at their timing and upper body flexibility. I pull myself back from admiring their natural talent. I do not want to love them. But inch by inch, little step by step, I can't help myself. I have beautiful babies again and the surge, the great maternal urge, floods out. I am hooked, telling myself that perhaps when I have seen this batch through to the end it will be the final curtain.

"Let's do the sun and moon dance!" I suggest enthusiastically.

They all laugh and a little one shouts, "We don't have a sun—it's the stars and moon dance!"

"Oh, yes, silly me! George, you're the moon and all you little ones are the stars. Let's get into our places. George, are you ready? Now let's make sure we all have our feet together like this!" I demonstrate feet in first parallel. "What's this position called?"

Hands shoot up and a tiny face in front of me smiles and shouts, "Ooh, ooh, I know!"

"Yes, what is it?"

"Feet in first paradise!" she coos.

Feet in first paradise—how I wish we could always have our feet in paradise. I smile as I drive home through the glare of the evening sun along a straight stretch of motorway thinking of "feet in first paradise," when a light reaches out from my solar plexus and extends in a never-ending golden pathway towards the sun, trailing children's dancing arms and legs in a perpetual arc towards forever. I know my purpose.

CHAPTER 6

The Music of Knowing...

*Dance when you're young, dance when
you're old, dance even if you're shy,
or confident and bold; dance in the morning
when the sun shines bright; dance in the
evening and in the dead of night; but never
dance if you don't like the music!*

The next day after another wonderful lesson I had arranged to
meet the gang in a different café where they had assembled
to discuss the day's activities. Seven of us elected to go to the
famous Moncada Barracks where Fidel organised his first
revolutionary attack to dislodge the government. Carol organised what she called a "coconut taxi," which was a massive red
Cadillac car with a friendly driver. Somehow we all piled in and
Carol, Eric, Charlie, Hilary, Edgar, Simonise, and I spontaneously burst into laughter as we pulled away into the sweltering
streets. It was like a *Guinness World Records* stunt to see how
many people we could fit into a small space. The raucousness
continued all the way to the barracks, making the driver smile
and sometimes join in our laughter. As we tumbled out, the heat
assaulted us, suffocating our high spirits, and we crammed into
a doorway to escape the searing rays. Carol went inside to buy

our entrance tickets but came out saying we didn't have to pay because they had forgotten to renew their license and we could get in free.

I glared across the empty parade grounds. The walls were pitted with gunshot holes like smallpox dents on a smooth skin. I felt a tingle, a small connection with Che, and I shivered thinking of his execution. Inside there were glass cases of guns, ammunition, blood-stained clothes, and photographs of soldiers killed in the skirmish, but what affected me most was the dungeon and the waiting room where people waited their turn to be tortured.

The prison bars were heavy, black wrought-iron railings that confined a small space. Momentarily I had a vision of the faces of men held captive inside. I gulped back the picture, not wanting to see the torment and the heavy oppressive energy hanging over each man. The before-torture waiting room was terrifying. It was a small space with wooden benches. The visitors and members of our group happily walked in and around the tiny space like tourists at Buckingham Palace. But I couldn't go in; I just hovered in the doorway. I couldn't bear the thought of waiting before knowing I was going to be subjected to immense pain. The vision persisted of the slumped bodies on the benches, the bleak terror reflected in their eyes. I had to turn away.

Our visit lasted for about an hour and our friendly Cadillac man was on hand with our coconut taxi to take us back into the town. On the outskirts of the main thoroughfare we meandered through craft stalls and I bought a trio of hand-carved dancers in three tones of wood, dark brown, cream, and fawn, with the romantic dream of building a new home with Saul and creating a special heaven for us both to peacefully retire.

As we walked on, outside a rundown bright blue house a band strummed strains of Cuba past. An elderly African man with a white cap and white shirt shook a pair of electric blue maracas, like the little boy standing next to him emulating his every move, with his shirtless young body shimmying in the glaring heat and beaming a wide grin. A large man playing a huge double bass stood lost in the rhythm, while another pluck-

Lesley Ann Eden

ing a Spanish guitar swayed on a broken bench. An elderly man wearing a dark blue beret and sunglasses sat on the pavement picking at another guitar. Next to him was a tiny bed of earth lovingly tended and planted with baby shrubs amidst the broken slabs and crumbling debris of the decaying street. Here was the throb of the city, the music of the past blending with the folk of the present.

Hilary and I stopped to enjoy the freedom of the music, soaking up the beat, allowing our feet to gyrate and syncopate, lost in the rhythm pounding in the heat, taken, with vibration, without hesitation, or heed for discreet polite appreciation, we ingested the seed, the creed, of yo mama, imbibing the rhythm, feeding the people with light of their sowing,
forever in creating the music of knowing,
the gift from the gods,
fodder through strife,
zest of the moment,
the life-saving life,
the urge beyond
being,
music
freeing…

The air was electrically charged with what we had come to experience and we were not disappointed. From then on there was no second-hand acceptance of synthetic salsa. The pulse was in the street, all around, everywhere. We understood how the people danced and sang through their struggles, surviving the worst times. The night soaked us in salsa vibrations at Casa de la Tova. For me it was a delicious feast I could savour and ingest, ready to store to take back to my own school. Our sun-red faces beamed in the dim light, all set to throw ourselves into the throb of the crowd as the nightly ritual had become part of the journey. We were drugged by the pulse, addicted to the steamy scene of the music and the dance as we partied through the night.

The next day we were invited to watch the Ikarache dance group in their studio, which was the church and home of the

Voodoo religion for that area. The building resembled the stylised architecture of a Baptist church with open archway entrances on two sides. I was shocked to see the condition of the place. Through one portal I gazed up into the broken open rafters, afraid to stand underneath in case the roof caved in. Rotting floorboards and decayed brick were decomposing in the humidity. Thick wooden beams were left open to the sky, prey to all weather conditions. Shockingly, two small black faces peered down through the gaping hole in the ceiling as they knelt watching the proceedings in their open breeze-block room where their family squatted. The state of the hall was deplorable, with open electric cables trailing down dirty crumbling walls that were covered in unfinished pencil sketches. An imperial crown surrounded with doves hiding in leaves next to a squat naked man dominated the drawings. There was a framed photograph of a youthful Fidel on another wall, but a larger photograph of Che watched over the Black Voodoo Mama shrine where chickens were sacrificed. Two bunches of plastic flowers arranged in the midst of broken branches and a tiny palm tree adorned the altar. Laying underneath was a Voodoo Mama doll and pink and orange raffia cheerleader's pompoms strewn haphazardly on the floor.

The church buzzed with preparation for the performance. In one corner a woman sat having her hair plaited in tiny knots, while groups of young children drifted in and sat watching the white visitors with great curiosity. As we took our places on concrete benches we watched the dancers limbering up with their shiny athletic bodies gleaming in the heat. The black Voodoo Mama, the witch-queen, stood overseeing the whole spectrum of events waiting for her money. She exuded a masterful, powerful presence dressed in her ceremonial robes of white and red with matching large turban. Her large frame moved slowly, like a cargo barge on a narrow canal stealthily negotiating turns and twists of the river, as she moved around her table of wisdom displaying her dried herbs, spell book, strings of beads, and an empty plastic cup (which I guessed might be for drinking sacrificial blood). When Carol handed her our money she beamed a wide grin, shaking her gigantic, white circular earrings in a jovial thanksgiving.

The drummer and percussionists began to take their places warming up with resounding thumps from the deep bass *djembe* drums, pounding resounding earth-shattering vibrations that cut through the dense heat with rolling rhythms that hit the pit of your stomach with shrill expectancy as the beat coiled and bounced off the walls. Primitively the call reached out to the people who began to pour into the small hall. I looked up to the gaping hole in the ceiling where a thick crowd of black faces stared. The dancers blazed onto the floor in a flurry of colour, performing the history of the dance of the rumba, in which an old man first discovers the steps as he walks shakily with the aid of his stick. Soon the rhythm rocks his body and he throws away the stick, enticing the village to dance seductively with him. The dance was brilliantly executed with fiery energy in the cloying heat, oiling the male dancers in a layer of glistening sweat.

The next dance was equally energetic, performed in couples with the men wearing long white cotton trousers and bright red shirts with orange and white frills on the shoulders. The women wore a traditional costume of white calf-length full skirts with a light blue trim, white bodices, and dark blue scarves anchored over their shoulders with small white kerchiefs tied around their heads. They were beautifully in time and lived each step. I had been trained in African dance and when we were invited to join the dancers I disregarded my injured leg and delighted in the joy of the moment, dancing with a lithe, athletic partner who was surprised I knew the routine. The children in the audience enjoyed our display and cheered. The air was thin and pungent with incense and perspiration. The Black Mama nodded approval to her dancers, puffing on her cigar as she perched on a high stool. Our group loved the show and Hilary hoped to witness one of the sacrificial rituals, but the next day we were scheduled to travel in our little WaWa bus to Camaguey and after another night of dancing and partying I was ready to cash in on some sleep.

That night, sleeping intermittently disturbed by the rattling air conditioner, I was woken at four o'clock by a dog barking and a cock crowing. I lay awake in the seething heat, having decided finally to turn off the air conditioner. The memory of Knossos kept floating, drifting in and out of my mind like the gentle flapping of a single sail on a calm sea. The opera experience back home had opened up a fissure in a sealed cave of memory and I was being lulled back to an incredible event that I had tried many times to record, but at every junction something always prevented me. Floating in a hazy mist, I allowed myself to return to the astonishing encounter with the past at the palace of Knossos…

Back, back… I submitted to the call and drifted to the time when it all began on a hot morning, walking a dusty road with my family in a tiny Greek village on our way to catch the early bus to Knossos. My youngest daughter Greta was nearly five years old and had a shock of straw-white hair that fuzzed in tangles. Her large, deep brown eyes shone with mischief. She was a sweet cluster bomb always ready to explode from one extreme of emotion to another. My son Branden, serious and deeply embarrassed by his sister's persistent naughtiness, had fair hair and ocean blue eyes and was mature for his eight years, hiding his hurt emotions under a canopy of sensibility, but fearing the imminent break-up of his parents' marriage. The reason for the holiday was to try to mend our broken relationship, but it was too late—the dancer and the rock climber had fallen too far into the abyss of distrust. We were civil to each other, avoided close contact, and walked purposefully apart in the rising heat, watching the children. We had promised them a trip to see an historical palace and Greta was excited at the prospect of perhaps meeting a real princess.

As we neared the village, stray dogs grunted in the shade. Even at eight o'clock in the morning the heat was unbearable. A few other passengers straggled along the sandy road to wait with us in the shelter of the closed shops. When the bus eventually arrived we accepted the old, dilapidated boneshaker with its uncomfortable seats and we were patient when it scraped up hills and lurched insecurely around country village roads, but we were not prepared for it to break down in the middle of a rural village. An angry German man shouted at the driver; a young Italian man stamped his feet and gesticulated; we sat on the back seat enduring the baking pressure penetrating the old tin bus. The driver got out and disappeared into a small throng of villagers peering at us from the pavement.

Greta began to howl because she was thirsty and Branden sat silently moping, with his tired red face in his hands. Gavin got off the bus to look for somewhere to buy drinks. It seemed the elements were conspiring against our visit. Ten minutes later, after Greta had worked herself into a fevered frenzy, Gavin returned with bottles of water and lollipops. The bus driver, wiping his red face, asked everyone to get off the bus as a replacement was on its way. Half an hour later, we trudged onto a slightly better bus and spent the next hour wending our way through dusty tracks and village roads until we reached the outskirts of Knossos. The air was oppressive, hiding an invisible darkness. The road to the palace was disrespectfully lined with street vendors and market traders, inciting an outraged anger deep within me. I had no idea why my response was so intense. Perhaps I was just ill-tempered after the awful journey and the rising heat. When we finally alighted from the bus I was dismayed at the piles of rubble and shocked at the huge crowds flocking around guides holding up umbrellas. I shared the children's disgust and disappointment at finding only wreckage, and a voice inside my head screamed: *"This isn't it, this isn't it at all! This is not what it's like. This is not what I remember!"*

I pushed the voice away. How could I remember? What could I remember? I had never seen the palace before. The children were hot and cranky and not even another ice cream could placate them. "I want to go home, I want to go home!" wailed Greta. "This isn't a real palace with a real princess. I want to go home," she cried, hopping from one foot to the other, never still. Branden sat on a pile of bricks, also complaining in his quiet way. It was too hot and there were too many people and it wasn't a palace at all; it was only broken walls and pots. Looking at their tired hot faces, we parents both agreed we had to take them back. From a distance I heard a guide's clear voice above the din, "…and this section is the queen's chamber." In the broiling moment, a deep chill quivered through my body. The present shifted from one time span to another and back again, like a volcanic rumbling under the earth shaking the fabric of a house. I felt dizzy and held onto a crumbling wall.

"The queen…the queen…Chry…." I almost remembered her name. It nearly rolled off my tongue in disgust.

"Come on Mummy!" urged Greta. "We don't like this place, do we, Branden? It smells!"

I became confused as I tried to locate certain landmarks, as though seeing the place through someone else's eyes. I felt lost, like a child separated from its parent in a crowd. Through the throng I heard a sharp voice, *"And this is the queen's bathroom…"*

Bathed in a shockwave of terror I ran toward a mound of broken bricks with little Greta in tow. I stood shaking, glaring at the familiar dolphins.

"Look Mummy, they're smiling…"

"I know, I remember…," I whispered, feeling the memory invade my thought, striking with a deep ode of despair. Suddenly the air was too thin. I clasped little Greta to my chest and ran with her to the alley of trees farther down. I needed oxygen and the cool of the shade.

On regaining my balance and breath, we walked back to the bus station as Branden and Gavin eyed me curiously. Back on the bus the children slept while I inwardly battled with mixed emotions. I was angry at something. I was afraid of something hidden in the back of my mind. I was annoyed with myself for being angry, and upset not being able to share my emotions with my estranged husband. The whole day had been a disaster. Images from hidden caverns in a lost memory fought to regain credence, but as soon as one bubble expanded into focus, it burst back into oblivion. The memory was always just out of reach.

I was relieved when we arrived back at our little rented house tucked in a valley under grey and purple mountains, with the deep azure sea only minutes away. Life returned to some semblance of normality. Branden went with his father to paddle in the sea and Greta stayed with me while I prepared the sup-per. I watched her from the kitchen teasing a tabby kitten in the bushes while I chopped the carrots. Rapt in the mundane chore I allowed my mind to drift back to the dilapidated palace where a voice beyond recognition was struggling to be heard, but my reverie was interrupted by a high pitched squeal and the screech of brakes swerving on hard tarmac, followed by the clang of something metal striking against our brick wall. I shot out of the door to be met by Greta holding a young man's hand, leading him down the garden path like a little lost lamb. "Come with me, my mummy will make it better for you."

I smiled. She had utter faith in my healing gift. The poor young man in his late teens was Italian and didn't speak any English but he trusted the little blonde girl who had watched him fall off his scooter and had helped him to get up. He sat in the kitchen while I bathed and bandaged his badly cut knee. He stood the pain quietly as I lifted out pieces of grit with a pair of tweezers while Greta held his hand, telling him a story about her pets and he silently nodded, not understanding a single word. After I had tended his wounds, Greta and I watched him shakily pick up his damaged scooter and wheel it reluctantly down the road. I looked up at the brooding mountains and heard a voice in my head, *"...the queen's chambers...her bathroom..."*

An icy finger of fear warned caution, which I brushed away warily, returning to the kitchen to finish preparing supper. The evening was pleasant and we ate on the veranda under the powerful, watchful presence of the grave mountains. When the sky turned inky black with silver threads, I put the children to bed and avoided conversation with the man I had deeply loved. I stayed watching the stars and embroidering under the dim lamplight.

The night was still and my time alone precious. I was afraid to think of the future but knew that our marriage was beyond repair. I gazed at the stars. Each one appeared so close, so tangible that I could reach out and touch them. In the safety of silence I crept back into the house. My babies were peacefully asleep. Branden, with his little sunburnt nose peeping out from under the sheet, looked angelic, while Greta, naughty as ever, had put on her swimming suit over her pyjamas and lay sleeping with her bottom in the air and her chest on the pillow, her face turned to the side wearing her swimming goggles! I gently eased off the goggles and placed her carefully back under the sheet. As I entered the bedroom I was relieved to hear Gavin snoring in the single bed by the window, so I quickly undressed and sank under the sheet and closed my eyes. A noise in the corner disturbed me. I thought it was Gavin getting up to go to the lavatory. I feigned sleep and lay still but the noise, strangely unfamiliar, made me peep.

Standing in the corner I could make out a figure of a man's bronzed chest with the lower half of his body wrapped in a white towel. I thought it was Gavin. Another unfamiliar shuffling noise made me take another peek and my heart stopped. It wasn't Gavin—he was fast asleep—but another man. I broke out in a clammy sweat. What should I do? Scream? I couldn't even breathe! There was no air in my lungs to gulp. I tried to make a noise but my voice was blocked, frozen in terror. I tried to move but I was petrified, locked in a freeze frame horror film. It was not a nightmare, it was real. I could see only a portion of a stranger, only his chest, not his head. His upper body was golden, bathed in gleaming oil, which glistened in the light from a strange-smelling lamp. I could not see beyond his knees, only the pale, thickly woven cloth, which was tied under his stomach and folded in pleats over his thighs. He wore bronze wristbands on each arm. In his left hand he held a long spear. I could see his chest gently rising and falling as the torchlight cast dancing shadows around the room.

Without warning, I was whirling, swirling down a tunnel, and came to rest inside the body of a nine-year-old girl. She was lying on a basic wooden four-poster bed with thin white gauze curtains hanging down from over the top in a small white stone outbuilding. Inside her body, through her eyes, the view of the man was restricted because of the position of the bed and the height of the gauzes. I wasn't sure whether I was she or she me or where we mingled. Her words became mine as we fused into one. It seemed as though she had been waiting for me, hanging onto a thin thread of life.

I knew her name, my name: Izatah. I, me, she, was tethered in torment. In the being of that moment, I became her and felt my feet tied at the ankles with my left foot over my right. It hurt. It was sore. I couldn't move and I couldn't sleep. Bile trickled down my throat mingling with a rancid sour taste from my nose. I shook in a fever hovering between bouts of boiling inside to bitter cold outside, as droplets formed on my skin, aching, icy to touch. I squirmed and repositioned myself so that I could see the man. He smiled, hiding his concern. His face was large, smooth, and round. His head was bald and shiny under a pewter helmet which came to a point at his forehead, and which was engraved with a snake's head, denoting he was a servant of the queen. Inside Izatah, I acquired information about her life. The exchange of thought was like a memory stick storing knowledge from a computer. I knew every moment of her life as each second was transferred to my brain and became mine. Or was it mine in the first place? I cannot say. I could not distinguish her thought from my own. I can only relate the event as though I were she.

The guard in the corner was a eunuch. He watched with sad eyes, helpless to prevent my torture. I remembered his name with affection: Xabin. In better times he had played games with me and brought me pieces of bread when I was hungry. I watched his body stiffen and his gaze drop as an overpowering scent of musk flooded the tiny antechamber, mingling sourly with the goat's grease lamp that sputtered and gasped in the draught. The queen's low whispers hissed across the lonely silence. Evil pervaded her being like a diseased liver, overshadowing life with a malicious canker. She craved depravity and was addicted to the delicious taste of agony suffered by her victims. She glided forward to the bedside, revelling in my battle. Xabin shuffled. I dared to stare into her dark spiteful eyes where flames spat, reflected from the torch. She licked her lips, anticipating triumph, sealing the final touch as she bent low and forced me to sip from a tiny phial, but I pursed my mouth. She cut my lip as drops dribbled through my teeth. Xabin coughed nervously as she made her swift exit. The liquid burnt my mouth. Black bits of burnt flesh dribbled down my chin. Xabin rushed from his post to wipe it away and ran back, afraid to be caught. Brown welts began to rise above my skin, her skin, our skin. My breath was closing down...her breath...Izatah...

CHAPTER 7

Time Shift

*You must always endeavour to move
in time with the music, even when
you are out of time with the world.*

Visions of the horrendous scene trembled in and out of focus as I was brought back to the present and realized that I had to get up to make an early start to travel to Camaguey. The horror of the revisited moment was too much to bear and I needed to adjust my mind to the needs of the day. In haste I prepared my bags and felt little appetite for breakfast. We set out at six o'clock the next morning after packing our little WaWa bus in the deserted, dusty street. For a while we had enjoyed the luxury of staying in one place but it was time to roll on to the next phase of our journey. The atmosphere in the bus was that of a happy and contented group who had settled into each other's ways. We had our own seats and dozed sleepily, hardly speaking as we chased away the night's revelry. Paddy still had the toothache but bore his pain quietly. The Prunesquallors were not sleepy, having left the party early in order to prepare for the day's rigours; they chirped quietly to each other like two contented canaries. Edgar was on time even though he had spent a heavy night drinking. Carol, who was a good leader, was always on hand to give help and sat singing along quietly to her walk-man. Hilary's health concerned me, as I feared she didn't eat much, though she partied well.

I relaxed back in my seat and watched the world go by. Set-tling into our travelling mode of dozing and sleeping, I fought for a while to keep my eyes open but gradually succumbed to the rocking of the bus lulling me into a faraway feeling where my breath, her breath, Izatah's breath, was curdling, suffocating in a sea of rising phlegm. I was returning to the scene of her deathbed, her murder. I didn't have any thoughts of my own life as I knew it, only that of the little girl and her suffering. I was lying in her body in a tiny antechamber in Knossos Palace. She wanted me to share her life's story that became my life in the hours through the night as it unravelled before me. She showed me everything—I lived her brief laughter, her sorrow, and her fears, feeling each unjust blow of fate as my own. She told me that sadness is sadness no matter what era or time zone you are caught in. You feel it: pain is pain, for the human condition never alters even though our surroundings are in continual flux. Being drawn back to tell her story, I became her reality using her words, describing the details of her short life…

I am four years old. I am laughing. I am riding on a plump cushion along the vast black and white chequered hall set out like a huge chessboard, pushed along between my grandfather and my father. We are happy. My mother is expecting a baby and we are waiting for news. The oil lamps flicker and dance as the light evening breeze flows through the open corridors. The terracotta walls are painted with scenes of dancers, jugglers, and acrobat performers parading around a big black bull that is fiercely stamping the ground to make the dust rise like the time of the great bull festival, where dancers gyrate and cavort with a bull's head covering their lithe bodies, performing the Minotaur ritual. There is no such animal. My father explained it all when I was very small. He said the half-bull, half-man creature was only a symbol of the rites of nature which were danced out each spring. The blood sacrifice of the bull was necessary to yield good crops to give thanksgiving to the nature gods.

In the quivering lamplight the figures painted on the walls spring to life, jumping and turning in the air, while the ladies in waiting with their charcoal eyes stare at us. My grandfather is not as tall as my father and he has white hair. He is wearing a dark, wine-coloured tunic with a heavy leather belt knotted at the waist. He has a gold chain around his neck embossed with a bull's head. My father is taller, darker, and has kind eyes. He is dressed in soft, long robes of gentle blue and is wearing a huge gold ring also embossed with the same bull's head with wide horns sweeping upwards and outwards. The ring glints in the torchlight. The bull is our symbol for life, for he is strong and virile and brings us luck.

"More, more, again!" I cry, wanting the fun to continue. My nurse, Evtie, moves forward to relieve them of their duty. The guards stand miraculously still, gazing past the scene. Expectant silence hangs in the air as we wait. The sound of bare feet padding along the tiles alerts us. A coy, breathless servant girl hands my father a purple ribbon that he lifts to his lips and kisses.

"Izatah, you have a baby brother!"

Grandfather lifts me high above his head and laughs. We are all happy. Later I am taken to my mother's chamber. From the dim flickering torch above her head, her dark eyes appear sunken. She is pale, and lying propped up by many pillows. She opens her eyes when I kiss her hand and she smiles weakly. Her face is wet. She nods to the cot beside her and I spy a wriggling bundle of dark hair wrapped in a blanket. I cannot see. The nurse lifts me up to view a red, wrinkled face with an open gaping, toothless mouth, like a baby bird waiting for worms. What a lot of fuss for such an ugly baby! He cries with his arms flailing the air and the sound echoes through the palace. It is a lonely sound. He is taken away and my mother sighs deeply as though she is in another world. I leave her to sleep. I am hungry. Evtie takes me to see her friends. It is not allowed, but no one is looking and everyone is feasting. She does not take me back to my room but lets me sleep on a cushion near the window as she and the other servants drink wine, laughing and singing into the night.

As the early morning light chinks through the white gauze drapes I sit up. All around they sleep, making rough noises. I shake Evtie and she wakes. Nervously she hurries me back along the cool corridors to my room before the rest of the palace wakes. She tells me not to speak about our little secret adventure. I nod in accordance. Soon she is washing me and braiding my hair with gold beads that clink as I shake my head. I am dressed in a new shift made of soft cotton embroidered with flowers like the blossoms in the spring meadow which grow on the far side of the palace, where there is a shrine to the god of nature that we garland with petals. Evtie sometimes takes me there to escape the hot afternoon, the time when the palace doors are opened, for they are designed each in line to allow the air to breeze straight through from one end to the other. Evtie calls it "changing the air time." I drink warm milk and honey and watch from my window as the palace wakes. Servant girls with hibiscus flowers in their hair creep softly across the courtyard in their scant sandals. They carry water in large pots. A girl runs in wide-eyed. She whispers to Evtie then leaves. Evtie looks worried.

"Can I see Amah now?" I question.

Evtie turns away and brushes my neat bed. "Later," she sighs.

"But I want to go now—now!"

"It is not possible," she affirms.

"No, no! I want to see Amah now!"

She sidles out of the room leaving me alone by the window. Strange sounds whip the morning. Someone is wailing. The servants are running. Shouting rises to the boil above the parapet and more wailing echoes around the courtyard. I feel lonely. Today is not a good day. The sun is shining and is in the usual place but all around it is dark. I have a new dress and a new baby brother but where is everyone? I wait. I wait. The sun now is high and still no one comes. Where is Evtie? I am thirsty. It is a feeling I have never known. I do not know where to go to find drink. Evtie always brings it. I push my door open. I am alone. This has never happened before. Where shall I go? I have never been alone. It is a harsh feeling. A guard eunuch moves forward and smiles, placing a hand on my shoulder to guide me back to my room.

"Where is Evtie?" He does not reply. I do not understand that he is not allowed to speak to me and I am angry. The long gauzes waft gently as a new servant woman appears with a tray. "Where is Evtie?" I demand.

The woman smiles, bows low, then disappears leaving the tray. I sit on the cool floor and I am alarmed but awed with a strange sense of adventure as I eat alone. Broth spills down my clean dress and breadcrumbs tumble around me. If I had a pet monkey it could eat up the bits and I would not mind. A short while later Evtie sidles into the room; her eyes are red and swollen. She does not smile and only clicks her teeth when she sees my dress, which she quickly changes without speaking. I do not speak. I want to punish her for leaving me but she doesn't notice. There is an unusual unfriendly silence between us. She takes my hand and leads me through a hushed walkway that is normally buzzing with crowds. My father's throne is empty. I am taken to a small room that I do not know. It is another throne room for the high priest, with a large bowl in the centre rippling gently with water and shining like a glass mirror. My father stands with his back to me. His hoarse voice comes from afar as he orders Evtie to leave. He turns his face to me. He is changed. His cheeks are sunken under his eyes and his brow is furrowed like the fields at the turn of autumn. His eyes are watery. His black hair is streaked with silver strands. He is both fall and winter. Spring and summer have fled his soul.

"Amah has gone to heaven!" he whispers.

I remember the words. I remember the scene. I remember the emptiness.

Amah was dead. Part of my life died with her. Words drifted in and out of my head.

I rarely saw my father smile or laugh after that day. He never spent time with Vangelis, my brother, never held him or watched him play. When I was allowed to see him he would smile up at me with his toothless gums and coo. When he cried I could always soothe him. His little hands learnt to reach for my hair and pull it hard. I missed my mother's arms and the comforting smell of her body. Evtie did her best but as my father's daughter, I was expected to come to terms with my grief alone. No one spoke of my mother again. My life was empty, huge, and vast like the dark gigantic jars in the store hall when drained of the last drops of eucalyptus honey; no matter how hard you strain to retrieve the last trickle of sweetness, it evaporates, leaving a crusty rim, mingling with a sharp medicinal aftertaste.

When Vangelis was two years old he could walk and trot after me calling, "Ztah. Ztah." Sometimes we were taken near the sweeping steps down towards the meadows where the servants allowed us to play. It was a joyous time of freedom. Vangelis did not know our grandparents because my mother's parents had died in a fire and I had not seen my paternal grandparents since Amah's death, but one day they appeared as Vangelis and I were rolling in the sweet-scented grass. The servants hurried to flick bits of dried weeds and seeds from our hair. Our grandparents smiled distantly and talked with a strained affection. They led the way back to the palace where my father waited. He smiled. He looked better. Standing next to him, much too close, was a younger woman dressed in fine white silk robes with blue and turquoise edging that glinted in the sunlight like minute jewels sparkling in the early morning dew, rippling on her undulating breasts.

My father held out his arms to me and I ran full pelt at him, feeling the ground fall away beneath as he swung me around like in the old days. When he put me down he took a long look at Vangelis who had my father's face and my mother's sweet eyes, but he did not hug him. The woman edged me away from my father and stood between us. I did not like her eyes. They lied. Underneath her painted smile was bile. I could taste it, smell it under her breath. She coiled away from me like a sly snake ready to strike. She knew I knew her true nature. Our battle began before we were even introduced.

"Izatah, this is Chryanaida. She is to be your new mother, and my blessed queen," announced my father with crystal clarity. There was no room in his tone for arguing. She could never be his blessed queen. My mother was and always would be his only queen!

"She will come around," whispered my father too close to her ear, too close to her body, too close to her breasts. He leaned into her and drank in her smooth deceit.

"And this must be little majesty Vangelis!" she crooned, but although he was small he was not duped by her cheating mouth. He wailed loudly in her ear and she recoiled, momentarily letting her mask crack as she hissed, "Please take him away—poor thing must be hungry!"

The servant girls sneaked a sideways glance as Vangelis was hurled away speedily, while I was allowed to sit next to my grandparents and be served rich delicacies. Golden liquid was poured into small shiny goblets encrusted with opaque pearls and I was allowed a sip. It tasted like honey but felt like fire spreading into my chest. I didn't speak but listened to the talk of ceremony, banquets, and the reeling of long names and faraway places. My grandmother pecked my cheek and asked me to give Chryanaida a token goodbye kiss but I ignored her as I flung my arms around my father and ran out of the chamber. Her stare shot after me, stabbing into my back like a poisoned dart and I knew she would seek revenge.

Amah's death drastically altered my life but I was certainly not prepared for the next stage of change that swept through the palace like a tormented swarm of bees, mercilessly stinging everyone in its path. A few weeks after I met Chryanaida I overheard Evtie whispering to one of her friends that the "painted bitch on heat" had moved into Amah's apartments and was demanding attention every minute, night and day, running all the servants into a ragged panic. Nothing was right for her, nothing agreed or suited her, everything had to be manipulated according to her demands and repeated until each minor detail passed her scrutiny. Altering my routine was part of her scheme. Usually I was allowed to discreetly wander the palace with Evtie. I could walk through the great hall where two thrones stood side by side where my father held court, administering justice to farmers, beggars, and nobles. We could walk down the great stone steps to the massive store hall where the farmers stored their grain, wheat, flour, wine, vinegar, honey, goat's wax for torches, and salted fish and other smoked foods. Sometimes I accompanied Evtie when she had to collect a portion of nuts and grain together with a flagon of honey.

The great hall was a wondrous emporium of smells emanating from the great vats and clay pots, taller than me, oozing delicious, tantalizing aromas from exotic concoctions. It was dark and womb-like, lit with goat's grease torches which sometimes crackled and spat when caught by a sudden breeze, like when the huge wooden doors swung open, or the small side door was left ajar, but mostly they gave off a golden dying glow like the sun setting over the mountains, with an unmistakable smell of cooking fat mingled with rich hot sauce. In the secret pantry of feasts, I would watch Evtie unscrew a clay stopper from one of the vats and I coveted the golden treacle-honey as it slithered into her pot. Sometimes she would let me catch a sticky clot in the palm of my hand and lick it clean. When she replaced the stopper a small amount escaped and I would be ready to catch it in my open mouth. It used to make Evtie laugh and say, "You honey pot, with your heather-honey eyes!"

The palace was a whole world—so big it was a city, so vast that you could never know it all. I was not allowed to explore beyond our small kingdom but my little world shrunk when she took control. Evtie always woke me with my breakfast and prepared me for the day. Similarly at night she stayed with me and slept at the foot of my bed. Chryanaida set up a new regime. I was not allowed in the main palace at all, not at any time. It became a forbidden area. I was only to be fed at the set meal times with no food or drinks in between. No treats allowed. I was not to see my father unless he initiated the visit. I was not to see other children as I was deemed a bad influence. I was to be up and out of my room before the palace rose, in order to receive tuition from a tutor, which would take up most of the day, and by evening I was to be back in my room where I would take my evening meal alone. Evtie did not like the new system. I had to sleep in my chamber alone with a guard outside my door. Evtie said my baby time was over.

The tutor was better than I expected and in his own way was a kind man. I did not realize how hungry I was for knowledge and instead of hating the lessons I looked forward to them. Xabin, my eunuch guard, also secretly enjoyed the lessons because sometimes I would catch him mouthing the answers to himself. I soaked up all the information set in front of me like fresh rain in a dry well. I liked the sense of purpose the knowledge gave me and at bedtime my head would be stirring with all kinds of ideas inspired by the day's input of history, language, science, and poetry. One day in the small wooden room, I heard voices. I knew it was Chryanaida's entourage. I could smell the musk of her perfume long before she appeared. I spilt water and vermillion mix over my reed slate and Manos, my tutor, shot up from his slumber and feigned anger as a maidservant scurried to clean it up. At that point of confusion and rebellion Chryanaida entered. It was a perfect ploy to make her think I hated my lessons. She left as abruptly as she had entered and Manos lifted his eyebrows in cunning understanding, never uttering a word, except to ask how I knew she was coming. I told him I heard her and smelt her perfume. He looked puzzled and asked me if I often heard things or saw things or smelt things which other people could not. I did not reply but he gave me a knowing glance. Xabin shuffled uncomfortably but smiled.

So my new days passed better than expected. Evtie always found a way to sneak me extra food and sometimes I would find sweet treats under my pillow. I was nearly seven and I looked forward to a special celebration for my birthday, but on that day none came. Evtie said my father had not forgotten but he was away and would surely see me on his return. He did not. Evtie brought me a special secret feast and Xabin looked away so as to pretend he had not seen the indulgence. He also took me on a secret walk around the palace. Evtie dressed me up as a servant child and covered my head with cloth. I was shocked to see how things had changed. All the main inner court servants had new robes with Chryanaida's snake emblem embroidered on the shoulder. The throne room had new paintings of my father with a new queen by his side. I asked to go to the great store hall and at first Xabin was afraid but he checked with some other guards to see if it was clear. When we entered, the old familiar flavour, smell, and womb-like protective atmosphere flooded me with memories of my babyhood. I stood in the middle of the honey jars and wept. Xabin allowed me a few moments, then he patted my shoulder and, although he was not allowed to speak to me, he whispered, "Remember now—you are seven!"

He was right. Seven was important in the Minoan calendar. Seven was magical. Seven was strong. Something special happened every seven years in a person's life and I was going to be strong like the number. Before we left I persuaded Xabin to turn away while I unplugged a honey jar stopper and drew a gleaming slither of sweetness into the palm of my hand and gluttonously licked it clean. What joy! I felt seven times better. On our way back, Xabin had to duck into a crevice behind another guard. Chryanaida was parading with her entourage along one of the main corridors and I stood with a crowd of servants as the hem of her robe scratched passed my cheek. A rush of excitement flushed as I wallowed in my anonymity. Her odour's dark signature of snake venom, datura, black dried blood, and a feminine smell concealed by musk trailed after her, leaving in her wake her unmistakable warning of evil.

After my seventh birthday, which was totally forgotten by my father, a flurry of months passed in preparation for the great wedding. Evtie had to make sure that I knew the drill. We practiced together where to walk, how to bow, when to bow, never to speak, where to stand, when to sit, when to kneel, never to hold a gaze to my father or her, the one the servants called in secret "painted bitch on heat." Sometimes I would whisper those words to myself, repeating them with great vengeance. I even taught Vangelis the word "bitch" which he would repeat like a coded mantra. When the wedding day dawned the sun was circled in a red cape. It was not a good sign. The birds were hushed by a whining wind blowing from the west and took shelter, hooded by the trees. I walked onto my terrace and held my hands out to the sky feeling a warm tingling surge through my palms. Invoking energy from the sky was natural and I asked the great ones to help me through the day. Somewhere in the great universe my mother was watching and I felt I was betraying her love. I asked her to forgive me.

Evtie breezed in and asked me to stop my nonsense and hurry up! The preparations were lengthy. My long hair had to be plaited, intertwined with gold thread and little sparkly gems. It took hours! A golden half-moon coronet was inserted on my head and looped through strands of hair. It felt awkward to wear. I was helped into a heavy gem-encrusted gown with a long train by two servant girls who were assisting Evtie. They played with the rings and jewels and were admonished by Evtie for trying them on. I didn't care. They could take the lot! However, when I was shown the final ensemble I liked it. I seemed to shimmer from head to toe in gold, even my face was brushed with a light gold powder which glinted when it caught the light. I paraded up and down for Xabin and he bowed, stifling a giggle. Evtie nervously ushered me into my place in the never-ending line of dignitaries as a fanfare of horns echoed and resounded through the great hall. I was obedient and did exactly as I had been taught. Vangelis marched behind my train and inadvertently stood on it a couple of times, almost tripping me up, but his nurse striding beside him managed to sweep him back just in time to keep the procession moving.

From a distance I saw my father waiting near his throne, wearing his ceremonial crown and robes. A whole array of priests, government officials, and vestal virgins threw flowers and rose petals into the air. It was hot under so many clothes. The air was thick with incense and sickly citrus perfume. I had not eaten much and my stomach bubbled. I was thirsty and my mouth was dry with acrid heat from the myriads of candles blazing on the altar. My face itched with the powder and tiny streams of wet began to trickle down from my scalp onto my nose, dripping into my mouth. I tried to wipe it away but the powder smeared my sleeves. Suddenly I was near my father who smiled, although I don't think he really saw me. The procession halted and I took my place. There was a pause then she appeared. I stared. I blinked. I glared. Under her heavy gold crown and glittering finery were enormous diaphanous eyes of an insect set in a black spider face. Her mouth leered, revealing a row of white fangs. Her arms uncoiled and curled out towards the crowd. I stifled a scream. I was watching the hideous creature as she mooched forward, spider-like, luring her innocent fly into her sticky web to feast on his pure heart. She was a black spider…an obnoxious, flesh-devouring beast.

"The painted bitch on heat is a spider!" I howled, bringing the whole ceremony to a hushed standstill. Screaming and screeching, I threw myself at my father's feet wailing, "No! No! Can't you see she is a spider, the bitch is a spider?"

Vangelis thought it was funny and repeated "bitch" like it was a game, his little comical voice ringing through the roaring stillness. A guard plunged forward and whisked me up high as I kicked, flailing the air. Above the crowd I caught a man's eyes leering with the same watery quality as the female spider. He knew I saw them both as they really were and in the knowing, in the seeing, he realised my secret, my psychic secret.

CHAPTER 8

Return

It is not the song but the singer...
it is not the dance but the dancer...
it is not life it is the living...

Chugging along in our little WaWa bus, I was hurled back into the present as we stopped and pulled into a sandy lay-by to pick up two men in dark uniforms. I was stinging with the horror of the grotesque spider and tried to clear away the memory while attempting to listen to Carol explain that our new passengers were an extra driver and an engineer. I wondered why we had such luxury but farther along the tiny roads I understood the need. The wrecked highways were a mass of potholes and as we jarred in and out of the broken rubble, the cracked windows of our bus juddered and shook to the point of shattering. The noise of the engine and the rickety joints of the seats combined with the creaking undercarriage and whinging gears forming a Stockhausen symphony and drowning out the Beach Boys single of "I Get Around" on the hissing PA system. The reality of the uncomfortable ride helped me to acclimate to the seriousness of the present, as our bus wrestled with the rocky, muddy terrain.

We passed a truck stuck in a nearby flooded brown river and caught a glimpse of people being rescued in tiny boats. By the side of the road a broken old bus waited for a replacement as people poured out to find shelter from the sizzling heat under forests of palm trees. Farther along, a cattle truck bursting with cramped people battled with the craters, its wheels slipping and sliding desperately to maintain momentum as the poor passengers inside were flung from side to side. On and on we bounced our way to the famous church El Cobre Basilica, where the patron saint of Cuba, the Virgin of Charity, is revered. As we swerved in and out of gaping holes, I spied two beautiful yellow butterflies flittering among the brush scrubland and I said to myself, *Today is a day of butterflies.* I glimpsed more bright yellow species gathered in a cluster over some bushes, like dancers poised gracefully, floating effortlessly in the bright light. I have a special affection for butterflies and remembered a strange occurrence in school in the drama studio.

It was a dark, bleak, winter morning and I was watching a class noisily immersed in their improvisation. In the womb-like darkness of the studio with its cold, sepulchral, high drab ceiling and cheap black curtains, the students acted out visions of their lives. I sat at my desk, remembering a wonderful student who had been killed outright by a large truck that hit her head-on while she was riding her bicycle. I recalled her unique energy that lit up dreary routine with her open smile. Suddenly the class spontaneously hushed and stood still, gazing upward. I followed their eyes, straining to see what had caught their attention. In awed silence an amazing red butterfly danced gracefully toward me. The whole class was mesmerized, hypnotised by its sense of purpose. It knew exactly where it was going as it shimmered toward my desk where at first it hovered, then came to rest on the paper I was marking, almost touching my hand. Peace encapsulated the moment as the class suppressed a gasp when it fluttered a little, then took its place again near my hand. It paused for a few seconds and I held my breath, afraid to disturb it with a whisper of air. But then it twirled backward and began its ascent like a rising star vanishing into the darkness. The ruby-red butterfly appearing in the dead of winter was unique, like a precious jewel in the dark, just like her, my star student, when she was alive.

Back on the bus the group slept until we revved our way up a steep incline and came to a halt at the top of a rise next to the famous Basilica. There was a slight breeze ruffling Hilary's hair and I spied a glimmer of fear flash across her eyes. As we stood looking out across the valley she confessed her concerns about her health. I tried to comfort her, reminding her that we had seen so many beautiful yellow butterflies, which were a good emblem of hope; we could invoke their bright vibration to heal her. Yellow, the colour of high thought, could be used to help her. She seemed happy at that idea. When we entered the church heavy with incense, burning candles, and floating prayers, I wanted to laugh because even in the confines of the hallowed sanctum vestiges of Cuban music were bursting from every possible shelf and table.

Displayed on the powder blue wall was an old saxophone hanging next to the gold filigree ornate altar where Jesus hung on the cross under a red dome, while below a fiery sea of candles rippled. Relics from all walks of life were offered—even Fidel's mother had laid a gold guerrilla fighter at the feet of the Virgin. I offered my thoughts for Hilary's wellbeing and drifted out into the bright sunshine to take photographs of a battered vintage car perched near the edge of the precipice. Once the group had taken in the holy vibes from the shrine, it was time to make our way to Camaguey back on the WaWa bus with our new driver taking over and the engineer at the ready with his toolbox. The heat intensified, making the metal sides of the bus too hot to touch, so I had to be careful not to allow my bare shoulders to rest against the windows.

My eyes closed and I had no energy to fight the pictures of Knossos quivering under my eyelashes. I fought the vision for a while but succumbed to the lullaby rocking of the bus as I was being drawn back to Izatah, back to sharing the repulsive memory of the creature and the disgusting sight of Chryanaida's true nature. Through Izatah I could see the bulging, opaque eyes boring into the fibre of my being. The eyes of her spider mate with his vulture neck registered with mine, warning me not to interfere as I was hauled up in front of everyone and bundled away to a small room at the far end of the palace. The door was locked. I threw myself onto the wooden bed and cried until all was lost in a bleak void.

When I woke, a tray had been placed by the door with water and dry bread. I had sealed my fate. For the first time I undressed myself, leaving the royal robes and jewellery scattered on the floor. I scraped the crown from my head but left the beads and gold thread as it was too difficult to unravel. My white shift was cool and not cumbersome like the robes. Gold smears ran in stripes down my face and I washed them away in the water pot and sat watching the moon glide and slide across a slippery velvet sky. No one came to put me to bed. Across the courtyards I heard the throb of music and singing. No one came. Through the buzz of the night insects, dancers shouted. No one came. Waves of dread rose and fell in half dreams as I sat curled up by the door. The heaviness of nothing and the emptiness of everything was suffocating, like being trapped under a great stone. I was helpless, unable to undo the damage. No one kissed me goodnight. No one came. I don't remember when the night faded and when the dawn rose but the next morning Evtie picked me up from off the floor and hugged me like a baby for a few moments before the eunuch guard came.

The days passed in prison-like simplicity. Months dwindled and whittled away. I was not allowed to be tutored by Manos. I could only walk on my terrace, sleep, and eat. I was not allowed to see Vangelis. Evtie saw to my basic needs and was never allowed to stay long, but she did tell me that my father had been informed by the queen that I had been sent to live with a religious order in the mountains and that the money sent for my keep was used to pamper the queen's personal, selfish whims. She also whispered that the queen was about to give birth. The news shocked me and I wished with all my heart that she would die in childbirth. I wallowed in her screams when her time came. When the palace shook with her wailing, I rejoiced. But she didn't die. She and her son thrived.

One day in spring after my eighth birthday—which was not celebrated or recognised by anyone—only Evtie dared to serve me extra bread. It was just after the quiet time when the palace was aired each day and the main doors aligned with each other were opened wide to the world; that time had a new meaning for me because I overheard two servant girls bearing water jars walking past my veranda, and I heard them say it was "the time of fluttering bed curtains when the queen played games." I couldn't imagine what toys she had or what might amuse her. It certainly wasn't the time for games! It was a time when on waking everyone busied themselves, and so I knew it would be safe to sneak over the terrace toward the steps which led to the meadows. Halfway down was a small courtyard leading from the joint chambers of the royal couple and from there I heard voices. I hid behind a bush and spied children playing, watched over by their nurses. I immediately recognised Vangelis. He was four years old. He had grown so much. He had our father's bearing and regal manner and a look of mother in his eyes. He was standing by himself, not joining in with the others. He stood gazing out toward where I was hiding. I wanted to run and throw my arms around him, curl him in my love, and tell him everything would be fine. I hurt inside and bit back the tears.

A figure came out into the bright sunlight. There was something about the stranger I recognised but it was a faint glimmer of a past memory. One of the servants bowed, and with an immediate jolt like a lightning bolt, I saw my father in the old man's body. I was shocked that he could have deteriorated so rapidly. He was bent in pain and could hardly walk. Then she appeared in all her deceitful glory. As ever, she was beautifully decked in jewels and finery and strutting with authority. Next to her was the man with watery, glassy eyes I had seen at the wedding. He brushed past my father with disdain. I stood by the bush, unkempt and dishevelled; he would never recognise me. Father's dead grey eyes were expressionless. I knew she was slowly poisoning him, sucking out all his will to live. He was a shadow of the person I once knew and loved. There was nothing left, only a vague impression. She had stolen his soul.

She turned toward the bush, and I dropped down to the earth quickly, knowing her gaze was straining, sniffing the air like a hungry wolf, realizing prey was hiding. She scooped everyone inside, almost knocking my father over in her swift dismissal. The vulture followed. I had to turn away from the scene and scurry back to my cell, shaking and seething with anger. I was just in time to see Xabin ambling through the door with my usual tray of bread and broth. I had the notion that he had to go to the kitchen and scout for whatever was left; my meal was never prepared or thought out. It was just scraps. I dropped down behind the small wall which enclosed my cell and sat holding my knees to my chest, burying sobs. Xabin knew to find me there and stood shielding the sun with his friendly, large frame. He was not supposed to speak to me, but that was in the old days before I became a nobody.

"Come now, little one, what is the matter?" he whispered.

I looked up into his leathery face, unable to speak as the tears bubbled.

"Come, come…," he motioned as I slipped into his strong, gentle arms. He held me like a baby and pretended to throw me over the wall. Soon he had me laughing and he put me down, frowning with concern. "Now tell me—what is wrong?"

"Do you see my father?"

"Sometimes."

"Is he sick?"

"I do not know!"

"I saw him today."

"Mmm…I see…"

"I must see him! I have to speak to him! I have to…I have to…," I sobbed.

"It is not possible, but who knows? If you wish by the light of the guiding moon, it may be so!"

Xabin was always on guard from late afternoon all the way through the night—not to be there if I needed anything, but to make sure that I remained a prisoner. Sometimes we played games. Sometimes I told him stories that were buried in my head of faraway places with strange people and peculiar flying machines. In his simple way he cared for me and delighted in the tales of beyond our land. In this way we passed the night until I fell asleep wherever I dropped and he would pick me up and place me on the bed. He allowed me to watch for the moon to make my wish. He stood by as I implored the great silver spirit to help me and he added his own prayers. A few days later, Evtie rushed secretly into my room. She looked different, older. She said she was going away to be married. She hugged me and left a stray tear on my cheek, saying, "Tomorrow at 'hush' time go to the great hall of books. Go in secret and hide like before."

"Why?"

She did not reply but gave me a last kiss and left. Xabin came later that afternoon and gave me a quizzical look. But I did not share my secret. I pondered the message and weighed the time, counting the moments until I made my escape. No one was around to keep watch. The palace rested in a quiet hush breathing the fresh air on a sunny breeze which wafted through the great doors. I covered my head like a servant; my clothes were too dirty and torn to worry about being noticed. It was easy to scamper through the great hall, past the throne room, down the main aisle, to a side corridor on the left where the great room of learning waited. The handle was heavy and for a moment I was afraid I could not move it, but I pulled down on it using my body's weight and it eased open.

The room was covered from wall to wall with books with a large table in the centre with carved wooden chairs and soft cushions. A noise outside made me drop down behind a large cupboard. I heard someone shuffle to the large table. A chair scraped. A hefty book was taken down and slumped on the table. Pages were quickly turned until there was quiet. I peeped from behind my hiding place. An old man with quivering hands was reading the script, tracing each word with a shaky finger. His long, thin grey hair straggled onto his shoulders. His head was bent in the book and his wiry, white beard strayed onto the page. His knees quivered as he read and his poor sandaled feet were ingrained with deep red sores. I thought he was an old priest. I wandered near to his seat and stared up into his face. Involuntarily I let out a sharp cry: "Father?"

He stared. I stared. His gaze held mine until a small glimmer of recognition lit his dying eyes.

"Child, oh child, what have they done to you?" he whispered in a frail voice…

The trance was broken as the bus swerved and juddered, screeching a high-pitched whining as the brakes refused to respond but the driver hauled us sideways and the brakes obeyed under his skilful manoeuvring. I brushed away stray tears that had welled up in the recall and quickly coughed myself back to the present. I didn't want anyone to see me crying—how could I explain that I was reliving another life in another time span in Knossos Palace? Retracing another zone is always disconcerting and it's sometimes hard to adjust back to the reality of the moment. So as we approached Camaguey I sat up, taking deep breaths to soak up the new scene, focusing on the road and how it evened out to a modern thoroughfare where a train track ran parallel to the street. A horse cantered cheerfully past our bus as we waited at the crossroad. We had travelled along the Carretera Central to the third largest city in Cuba and I leaped forward into the present to adjust my mind to the delights of the city. I enjoyed its colonial heritage so evident in its buildings, plazas, and *tinajones* (large clay pots used to collect rainwater). I did not know very much about Camaguey except that it was the home of the Ballet de Camaguey, the second most important dance company in Cuba.

As we approached our new destination, Carol explained that the city had been the first in Cuba to transmit radio and television programmes and had also been the first to build an airport with commercial flights. Amusingly, she added that the city had been designed with a deliberately confusing street pattern in order to disorientate any intruders. I did not find that comforting as I tended to lose my way easily and had a fear of getting lost, like on my last trip in Mexico. As we rounded a corner in the centre the streets seemed very narrow and an unusual tower jutted out of a flat building painted in bright pink with maroon edging, like an eccentric birthday cake. Past another corner a similar building with a round bell tower painted in bright blue with white icing edges like a wedding cake stood near a block of grey buildings, and next to it—less ornate and flashy—was the bank where high on the roof a picture of Che looked down on the high street. He was everywhere. His face beamed from shops, cafes, and restaurants. Passing through parts of the city the bus turned around and pulled up on the outskirts next to a large hotel. It was to be our only luxury stay in a tourist place.

Hilary and I shared a room overlooking a vast expanse of open scrub jungle. We threw our cases on the beds, as we didn't have time to unpack because the group was scheduled to explore the city. The best way to travel around was a bicycle taxi. Hilary and I shared one and the rest divided up, riding out in a flotilla of wheels, following each other like a fairground ride. We weaved in and out of the small streets until we came to a wider road where Che's face was emblazoned on a café front: "Che Commandante, Amigo." His presence was etched into the bricks and mortar. He was the people's hero. He was the fabric of the city, never to be forgotten, eternally deified.

The heat stifled the air, forcing our drivers to fight for breath as their muscular legs attacked the pedals like gladiators charging into battle in their chariots. We stopped briefly by a small vendor's cart for the riders to rest and take a drink before resuming our wheeled tour. While our athletic gladiators rested for a few moments, the group decided to investigate a baker's shop across the way. From the outside it resembled an old French patisserie but inside it was disappointing, as there were only a few cardboard-like small cakes in the display case together with a couple of bread buns. There were crisps, fast food snacks, and Coca-Cola drinks in a machine—totally out of character with the setting. Hilary bought an uninteresting cake but didn't eat it. Most of the group bought cold drinks and I bought a Sprite. Back on our bicycle taxis we felt like royalty surveying the locals. We drew up in a fascinating square where the inhabitants had been immortalised, created in brass for posterity. When we arrived, the characters came out of their houses and took up their positions next to their sculpted doubles so we could take photographs of them for a small fee. There was a middle-aged man reading a newspaper; lovers sharing a flagon of wine; old women whispering and gossiping, drinking cups of tea; and other family groups. It was weird seeing both the statues and the real-life models posing side by side. Hilary took my photograph next to an old lady appearing to whisper in my ear. Then a group of little girls gathered and wanted their pictures taken with me by the group of old women. It was a fun interlude before we pedalled on to our next place of interest.

We stopped by beautiful, bright blue filigree iron railings where houses of the same hue with ornate shutters, reminiscent of Barbados beach houses, were set out in a square at the bottom of a steep incline. At the top was an old church overlooking the Caribbean-style area, keeping a dour, watchful eye over the congregation. A long-haired, thick-coated dog lay sprawled in the dying heat near a bush; its fur was matted and flea-ridden. She had beautiful pleading eyes and I resisted the pull of petting her and took a photograph instead. A group of boys played nearby, laughing, displaying rows of healthy white teeth and I thought of the children back home who probably by their age had at least one filling. These children, although they were not wealthy, looked strong, well fed, and happy as did all of the children we encountered playing in the street. Che would be proud to witness this and to know that part of his idealism was being fulfilled.

Farther along we came to a strange cul-de-sac. A hush descended as the dying heat calmed. The square in the cool of the evening was a meeting space where all four quarters were occupied. In the far left corner by some steps, a unit of the police force were holding their evening's briefing. A senior officer standing in front of the corps shouted orders as the men and one woman stood to attention. They were dressed in light blue shirts with dark blue edging around the collar with navy epaulettes on their shoulders. The officer's voice boomed across the flowers, slicing the calm with a serious edge, threatening business. Their presence was peculiarly at odds with a clutch of shy nuns diagonally opposite who were taking their routine stroll, dressed in missionary white habits with starched white veils. Their elderly faces hidden behind uniform grey glasses appeared at ease with the world, unlike the taut, strained expressions of the police. In the far right, a team of elderly men played a leisurely game with short sticks and large flat counters in the dry, dusty earth.

Diagonally across from them was a very different quarter, where a large house on the corner lured the curious into its portals feigning a museum, art gallery, and objets d'art collection extraordinaire. It was a magical emporium of secrets stored, bought and sold, lost and found, painted and created. Inside I recognised the work of an artist whose paintings are world famous. Her style is unmistakable: bold, brilliant, stripy, one-dimensional flat cats preening, with wide-open eyes in fluorescent colours. There were even small models of them lurking in hidden corners. In the same brazen design, black Caribbean characters smiled with pouting red lips as they lazed under palm trees or waved from bicycles. The artist smiled as I admired her work. I wished I could have bought at least a small token of her art but I did not have the money. Inside the cool, dark haven, the high walls were covered from ceiling to floor with paintings in a myriad of styles and subjects. In one corner a huge canvas stared menacingly with a bleak, black background with the outline of a white water buffalo painted in bold lines, dripping driblets of paint trailing off the bottom of the picture. Hanging next to it was a massive interpretation of a masterpiece, a scene of an old gramophone and the archetypal dog with his ears cocked to one side listening to music, painted on a red and orange mottled background. Cupboards, chests, and dressers were piled together and festooned with antiques and reproduction knick-knacks. It was a warehouse of lost furniture. In the centre of the first room a dazzling eastern lantern twinkled above the congeries of old chairs, and a bright blue shutter opened onto the busy square outside. Mobiles hung from the ceiling, dangling precariously over our heads. We didn't stay long and soon made our token thanks to the artist who graciously acknowledged our visit.

Back in the square life had drifted away. It had changed to a vacant sanctuary of darkening pressure, with a leer of watchful waiting as the blackening sky threatened thunder. Through the emptiness our feet echoed across the park as we scurried back to our waiting chariots. Our taxi drivers did not wait for each other to progress through the streets in a formal parade but instead raced their bicycles in a rush to reach the outskirts of the city before the storm broke. The previous bustle was squeezed into closed corners and sucked behind locked shutters, draining all colours from the street in a grey haze of foreboding. Our driver momentarily stopped to pull a plastic tarpaulin over our buggy to protect Hilary and I from the impending squall. Suddenly the built-up pressure in the air cracked, tearing the sky with pink electric streaks of lightning that perforated the charcoal clouds with shards of orange and yellow gashes. The rain pelted our driver, lashing his back with welts of fury. Raindrops as large as hailstones struck the tarmac, beating a drum roll as we raced along the main highway.

Inside our cocoon the torrent was all-invasive and through the din I had a strange impression of being inside a buggy pulled by a black horse. Instead of travelling forward I was reeling backward, riding back through time watching small children appear on ancient wooden verandas lighting fires for their evening meal, watching the steam rise from blackened cooking pots, viewing old men in strange robes peering from behind filigree shutters. I struggled to breathe the present. The air hung heavily mantled in a hushed guise from an era without extraneous noise from radios, televisions, or mobile phones.

I looked at Hilary, wondering if she was affected, but her eyes merely reflected my guilt at watching the poor man strain in the rain. We were uncomfortable with the human imbalance of the moment, with the obnoxious thought of slavery just licking its wounds around the edges of the last century. On and on the poor man pedalled as the road turned to a stream under his feet and his body morphed into the slithery skin of a slippery eel, his lithe muscles rippling under his soaked tee shirt. The sensation of moving backwards instead of forwards peaked towards the end of the main street and dissolved as we neared the modern hotel complex. Hilary dashed in and bought the man a couple of cans of beer and I gratefully handed him a generous tip. He beamed thanks, dripping crystal droplets from his nose and face.

Inside the hotel the warm, damp evening was locked out and replaced by icy blasts from the air-conditioning. I shivered in the unnecessary temperature drop and changed into some warmer clothes and wandered around to find the others. Some were cosily coiled around small tables in a tiny bar, but I didn't feel like burying myself in booze so early in the evening. I found some of the others drinking coffee in the lounge but I was restless and couldn't sit chitchatting. I realised I was hungry and made my way to the restaurant where some of the others were tucking into a three-course buffet. I decided to do the same and paid my money but realised too late that the food was not very appetising. The boiled stew with lank carrots had a layer of congealed grease simmering on the top. The vegetables were over-cooked and teetered on the grey side of fresh. The salad was passable and the fruit cocktail edible. I had an overbearing feeling of not belonging and feeling lost. I didn't want to sit with anyone. I didn't want to talk. I just wanted to hide within myself. I toyed with the food as the clank and clatter of sleek, shiny cutlery beat a reassuring cacophony in the background.

After a less than satisfying dinner, I ambled out of the restaurant and sat in a soft-cushioned sofa, sinking deep into the recess and, being small, with my little legs dangling in the air I felt like I was being eaten by the upholstery rather than relaxing in it. I was hauling my bottom out of the rear of the sofa in an unladylike manner when a man sat down beside me. I was occupied attempting to liberate my backside from the nether regions of the settee when he spoke in Spanish and asked me if I was staying at the hotel. I can't quite recall what I replied but it made him laugh. Awkwardly we continued the conversation but I was not in the mood for making small talk. He even asked for my room number, which I blatantly refused to provide and so he backed away in search of another conquest.

The dark crept in, bringing nippy chills lurking around corners in the cold, air-conditioned corridors. It felt like winter and all I wanted to do was curl up snug and warm in bed. A sharp pang of homesickness caught me off balance as I shuddered in the lonely moment, wondering what the Welsh caveman was doing. I tried to phone him but I lost the connection and decided to meander down to the bar to see what the others were doing. Small groups of our party were scattered around the lobby drinking coffee and a few were in the bar but I didn't want to attach myself to any. Instead I resigned myself to an early night, shivering in the icy bedroom but not wishing to turn off the air-conditioning as I knew Hilary preferred it on. I curled under the covers and locked out the day but as I stared at the blank white wall in the dimness, I was hauled back into Izatah's body; back into the turmoil of her being; back inside her head; back to the great hall of books where the dusty musk of ancient knowledge pervaded the ominous silence that brooded over a festering grievance.

CHAPTER 9

Seeing Is Believing

When you take the moves into your being,
into your heart and through your body,
you will not only learn to dance, but fly!

Back in the moment at Knossos, where time ceased to count, when it was too late for regrets and too soon for action, my father in the library wept, flooding his old grey eyes with fresh vision. I threw my arms around his shrunken body and for a moment we were locked inside old memories of rosebud kisses and golden laughter, but a sharp sound outside the door alerted us. He pushed me away and I hid as a guard appeared. He was led away and when all was quiet I crept out and looked at the book he was studying. It was filled with pictures of herbs and plants and symbols of magic. A scraping sound near the door made me retreat to my hiding place from where I spied a servant nimbly taking the book. When no one was around, I scampered back to my cell and waited and waited. No food came. No Xabin appeared. The afternoon became night and still I was forgotten. I was afraid my meeting with my father had damned him and we were both at the mercy of her will.

When night imprisoned day in a bleak, black mantle, I fell asleep near the door but I was woken by brutal hands. I rolled around on the coarse, splintered wood that pierced through the sack in which I was bound and cut into my cheeks. A dark, rough man tied a band tightly around my mouth. My feet were bound with a leather strap and my wrists were held fast with a rope. I was scooped up in a sack and carried over a shoulder then hurled into a creaking cart and trundled away. I heard voices and horse's hooves cantering over rough ground. I rolled around as the cart bounced across its uneven track. Then the air closed in around me and sounds were muffled. Snapping and cracking of twigs thrown up by the cart's wheels resounded in a hollow. The cart stopped. My heart thumped through my ribs, shooting up to my mouth as I hit the ground with a thud. I tasted blood and then felt nothing. Voices drifted in and out of the distance until all was quiet

Wood smoke—cooking smoke—choked my throat. Water, cool water refreshed my mouth, my face. Smarting cuts were cleansed with kind hands. Smoke, smoke, warm smoke, curling above, reeling below. Hot broth, sweet soup, gurgling through my lips, down my chest. Rest, rest, sleep. Open eyes, clear skies, no longer smoke, only light, wondrous day. An old woman's face peers over mine. She is wearing thick brown serge cloth. Her hands are gnarled like the bark of an oak. She smiles a toothless grin. I sit up. I hurt and ache. She laughs. I try to stand. She slaps her thighs and bleats like a lamb. I am alright…

The next morning, back in my bed in Camaguey as I came to, my throat was sore and my head throbbed. I had caught a chill from the air conditioning. It was hard to swallow and my glands were swollen. Hilary also had a sore throat, as did a few others in our party as I discovered at breakfast. Paddy still had the toothache and was assured we would find a dentist at our next destination, Trinidad de Cuba. Outside we packed the WaWa bus for our six-hour-long journey across Cuba to the exotic town of Trinidad. It was warm but not too hot, and I revelled in the comfort of the sun after the cold night in the hotel. Back on the bus I sucked throat sweets and felt better with the prospect of seeing new places. Saul had texted me and intimated marriage. I liked the idea and felt secure in his newfound love for me.

Boarding the bus everyone was pleasantly looking forward to our new venture with the chance to have drumming and percussion lessons. By this stage of the journey everyone appeared like old friends, relaxed in each other's company. The bus chugged its way along the main roads until we came to a small village with a thriving market in the centre. We were advised by Carol to stock up on food as we had a long and tedious journey ahead and although we were scheduled to make comfort stops, food was not always guaranteed to be found.

The market was an amazing hotchpotch of stalls set out on a piece of wasteland. I imagined a medieval market to have been similar, with the same kinds of smells and flavours wafting in the air; with meat on open slabs infested with flies, and stray dogs wandering nearby ready to be fed scraps; while all manner of rice and wheat pulses were decoratively laid out on dirty, flat tables with fruit stalls displaying melons and papayas cut open with myriads of black flies juicily feeding off the pulp. Fish stalls stinking of fish guts and soft roe mingled with hardware booths reeking of black grease and petrol, combining to taint the air with pungency unique to the market. Evidence of ration books and scarcity of produce was apparent as lists of goods which could only be sold with tickets were on display everywhere.

As we walked around the people smiled and were friendly. One local showed his amazing tattoos. On his right arm smiled Che, and on the left was Fidel. He loved Che and so did everyone; he was the people's hero. I could imagine Che receiving a magnanimous welcome amongst the crowd. No one had ever touched the hearts of the people like he did. Again Che was everywhere, ingrained in the dust, maintained in the stores, hailed from the rooftops, and harmonised in folk songs. Carol recommended a local sweet speciality made of nuts, a little like nut toffee brittle which some of us bought to munch on the bus. Many bought fruit and biscuits, but none of us bought anything meaty or spicy. Wandering around near the edge of the stalls I spied an old donkey tethered to the bushes. He wore a hat with his ears poking out in a comic fashion. Next to him, half hidden under the bushes, was an amazing red Cadillac. I loved its bold lines and show-biz glamour. It must have once been wonderful, blazing with colour, but it had been left to fade and rot, hiding its former glory under weeds.

We didn't spend too long in the market and were soon bouncing our way through miles of open brush land. The sun was beginning to sizzle and heat up our little tin bus like a barbeque griddle. Without air conditioning, all the open windows rattled and whirred making conversation difficult, so we all retracted into our own little worlds, lazily watching the countryside chug by. In the quiet of my mind, as the bus droned on to Trinidad de Cuba, I remembered my horror at waking up the next day after the incredible journey to the past. My first reaction was disbelief. It was not possible to be taken back to live another life. The very thought of it unnerved me and flooded me with all kinds of doubts and fears, but no matter how much I tried to escape the memory, I knew deep within that it had actually occurred.

My experience of being hauled back in time had definitely happened, and my memory of it was still razor sharp, for as I remembered the morning after my journey back in time, as the early morning sun streaked through the slatted wooden shutters, I stared hard at the corner where the eunuch had stood the previous night and noted it was completely empty. The silence jeered a mocking warning that all seemed normal and I got up to examine the spot. It seemed a silly worthless thing to do, but nevertheless, for my own peace of mind it was necessary. There was nothing there, no trap door, no false panel, nothing other than an ordinary bedroom wall!

I hurried to see the children. They were just waking. I hugged them both, relieved to find them safely in their beds. I couldn't shake off the life I had entered. I couldn't remove the sights, sounds, and events which had been played like a film in the back of my subconscious. As I busied myself making the breakfast, I remembered that the previous day at the palace we had bought a map and guidebook in which I could check out all the places little Izatah had shown me. The first place which was so vivid was the chequered hall. I doubted whether in those times they had such strong geometric designs. My hand shook as I opened the glossy book. There it was! The chequered hall with the tiles set out in black and white like a chess board, just like the one I had seen in Izatah's memory. I was shocked and had to sit down.

"What's the matter mummy?" questioned Greta, wrapping her bed-warm little arms around my neck.

"Er…nothing. Drink your orange juice."

She slipped away to the table where her brother was eating his toast. "I can swim under water without breathing and you can't!" she blurted out, teasing him and sticking out her cheeky pink tongue.

"No, you can't!"

"Yes, I can!"

"No, you can't. You're fibbing again."

"Yes, I can, I can!" she screamed. "The man last night taught me!"

An alarm bell clanged a warning. "Man? What man?"

"Last night he came and took me outside where there was a swimming pool in the middle of the garden."

"There isn't one, so she's lying…"

I knew she wasn't. I could tell by her face and her eyes—what she was saying was the absolute truth. She was naughty and mischievous, but she never lied; in fact, she told the truth to an embarrassingly detailed degree.

"Who was this man?" I enquired softly.

"Just a man and he was dressed in a funny costume and he was nice."

"What happened?"

"He just took me to the swimming pool."

"Which isn't there!" taunted Branden.

"Well, it was last night!"

"Alright, you two! Just be quiet, Branden, and let her tell us. So what was this swimming pool like?"

"Just a swimming pool and the man showed me how to swim under water without breathing. It was easy!"

Thoughts raced. He, whoever, he was, had been sent to entertain Greta while I was deep in another sphere. Obviously someone didn't want me to be disturbed. My legs jellified. My heart raced. I had tried to sweep the experience away but it was becoming dauntingly clear that the evidence from all sides was too overpowering not to believe.

"Did the man say anything?"

"He said we shouldn't disturb you!"

"Oh?" I nearly choked on my coffee.

"The swimming pool was really nice! It was lit by torches!"

"Ahhh…!" I screamed inside my head. The whole palace had been lit by torches and my own daughter had an experience at the same time in a place "lit by torches." I was stupefied. It was one thing to have an encounter on my own terms, but for my baby to be involved was another matter.

"It was a dream!" guffawed Branden.

"No, it wasn't. It was real!" screeched Greta. Gavin had gone for an early morning run and would have scotched the argument but Greta was adamant that it really happened, and continued howling.

"Alright, alright. I believe you, darling. I know it's true."

"I stayed for a long time, so I know it's true!"

I believed every word. "Did he take you back and put you in bed?"

"Yes!"

"Well, that was alright then?"

"I'm not saying any more!" To this day my daughter can recall the encounter and maintains the man was her guardian angel.

"Okay, sweetheart, it doesn't matter," I sighed as I bit my lip, trying to hide my rising terror at the thought of her innocent trust placed in a total stranger, albeit one from thousands of years in the past!

After breakfast the children ran out to play in the bright sunlight and I was left in the kitchen to ponder the information. I checked and rechecked the chequered hall and its position. It was exactly where Izatah had shown me. I looked at the great storehouse of pots where the supplies were kept and, likewise, it was as I had seen. Everything was just the way it appeared in her memory. Down at the beach, under the shade of a huge umbrella, I allowed the tears to well and fall. All around me the scene was normal, with families basking in the sun and children frolicking in the crashing waves, and yet in my head a little girl waited to die. A whole night had been spent in sharing her life and I feared another would ensue. I knew she would show me the rest of her story and I was afraid. I was a coward.

It was not what happened that scared me, but the thought of how I was taken. It didn't hurt. There was hardly any sensation in the actual transportation. It was just the thought of it that terrified me. As I looked around, I saw "ordinariness." Everyone living an ordinary existence. How could I ever expect anyone to understand my journey back to the past that was so extraordinary—even I have difficulty in believing it happened, but it did and I knew that a second episode was inevitable.

The bus trundled on, endlessly pounding our way to Trinidad de Cuba, and I couldn't help my thoughts returning to Crete. Back in the scene, in our little apartment in Crete, by early evening after the first night of my episode with Izatah I was restless, trying to avoid thinking of bedtime. I was afraid of returning back into the past, yet nervous in case it didn't happen. Suddenly a knock at the door startled the children and I hurried to see who it was. Greta ran to the door and beamed a welcome to the young Italian who had fallen off his scooter the previous night. He stood smiling, holding a bunch of flowers in one hand and his girlfriend's hand in the other.

"I er...wanta to, er...say thank you madam for your gooda 'elp. I am now betta."

"I told you my mummy would make it better for you!" gushed Greta.

We accompanied them back to the gate, not able to communicate through words, only hugs, and watched them walk arm in arm down the road. Back in the kitchen I put the beautiful roses in water and watched one petal from the bunch fall silently, its perfect cup turned delicately up towards the brooding mountains. I placed it next to my mouth bruising the soft tissue, releasing the fresh oil which lingered momentarily on my lips.

The roses were a lovely gift, anchoring me to the moment, but loitering in the background, lurking behind the chores, waiting in the wings was the fear. Fear of the night, fear of death, fear of the unknown.

The evening took its usual course and after putting the children to bed, I sat nervously watching the mountains. I didn't want the man to come again and take care of Greta. Whatever happened, I knew she would be safe but the thought of her being with a stranger was terrifying, especially an unknown entity from the past! Her experience made my own believable but more horrific in the thought that the whole event was manipulated by some thing or someone who needed me to know the truth. I was afraid to go to bed. I postponed sleeping for as long as I could, drinking too much wine in the hope of escaping the pull back. I watched and waited until the stars studded the black sky in a cascade of silver. When my eyes began to close, I knew I must face the inescapable fall through time. As I crawled into bed, the room was quiet, but I felt a heavy watching from someone far away. Once under the covers, everything went into overdrive. I hardly had time to register the eunuch back in the room, standing in the same spot in the corner of the bedroom, before I was back inside Izatah's mind. It was as though I had never left and we resumed her story quickly. It was easy, not at all frightening…

She was standing—I was standing—in a ramshackle hut in the middle of the valley forest. A sage old woman had found me in a sack with my arms and legs tethered. My captors had left me for the night wolves to devour, because their religion would not allow them to kill a daughter of the king. They had not counted on the ancient, wise witch of the forest to save me. The old woman was a healer; her humble shack made out of broken branches and dried goatskins sheltered her from the harsh winds. Her little fire smoked in the bright breeze drying her freshly gathered herbs and flowers from the forest hedgerows. A cooking pot dangled in the middle over the fire and the smell of rabbit stew with wild garlic was enticing. She motioned me to sit down, gurgling a strange language and, hovering over me, she dusted a powdery substance over my head and body and danced a little jig. Then she handed me some hot broth and sat at the shack's door smoking a clay pipe and squinting her eyes at the cool, cloudy sky.

I felt fine. I was strong enough to walk. After I ate I knew I would leave and she knew it too. Her words were not mine but we both understood. I hugged her and she didn't move; she just kept on glaring at the sky. I walked through the forest on and on. Sometimes I ran a little, scattering the birds with the crack and snapping of broken twigs beneath my feet. The palace was high on a hill and I was down in the valley, so I knew that once out of the forest I would be able to spy it dominating the skyline. I had no doubts about my purpose of returning safely, I just knew I would. Safely back, I had to dissolve into the working tissue of the main body of the palace. I could easily hide and be lost in the sinews of the strong arms of the workers, all pumping, pulsing to keep the main arteries feeding the greedy heart of the repulsive spider.

I had to reach Vangelis. I had to save him. We could run away together and be free and live by the sea and catch fish and go swimming whenever we wanted, with no one to tell us what to do. We could have pet monkeys and feed them on dried fruit and honey. All these thoughts kept me going, kept me plodding, one foot in front of the other, up mounds and down hills, through streams and round bends. When I heard voices or saw a settlement I hid, and ran when it was safe. I trudged all day from early morning until the sun was sinking. The lights of the palace twinkled for miles and miles. In the dark it was not so difficult. The moon kept peeping from behind her shroud and lit my way. It was not so far…not far…not too far…

I am hungry and thirsty but I know where to go. The great hall will provide all. Keep on, keep on, the moon urges and when I catch up with her, she hides and moves farther, pulling me onward, like a magnet with her invisible silver thread. I am nearly there, through the trees, across the meadow. I know where to enter without being seen. It is late evening and the servants are gathered around their fires, eating and talking after their hard day. I slide on my stomach through scented grass and slip into a side door near the great kitchens. Only a few tired voices echo across the clang and clatter of dirty dishes scrubbed in the huge vat. Leftover food is piled near the door and hastily I scrabble at what I can fold in my torn shift.

The shiny pots around me gleam like mirrors. Someone stands before me. I do not recognise her. She is thin and tall with a mass of dark hair matted and chinked in places with tiny gold beads which have become embedded in her thick curls. Her face is brown and stained. Her green eyes recognise and register herself, long-forgotten, newly honed in the shape of a survivor, a fighter, a warrior against the web of deceit, spun so charmingly, blinding everyone in a lacy veil of lies. I leave the child behind and accept a new world…I know what I have to do.

I know how to creep down the corridors toward the great store hall. I know how to slide into the underground tunnels where the water rushes down pipe gullies. I know how to slide down the back chutes into storage rooms. I know where to hide. Armed with my spoils, I squeeze through the rough wooden portal inside the great womb of the palace where there is peace and calm and I surrender my being. In hazy warmth of content-ment, wrapped in the familiar smells of goat's grease, honey, dried fruits, and vats of vinegar, I eat and eat and drink red wine. Curled up behind the grain bags I close my eyes, falling into a world long lost, of Evtie and my mother's kiss. In the early hours of the morning the keepers of the hall enter to measure out grain for the farmers, provisions for the palace, stored nuts and fruit for the workers, and a hefty helping of treats for themselves which they hide under their shawls. I watch them from the safety of my hideout.

At first I am cautious not to stray too far away from the hall but then after a while when I am certain of my nonentity status, I am able to wander farther with my head covered in a dirty cloth. The gold beads tangled in my hair are the final remnants of who I was; I need to steal a sharp knife and cut off my curls. I scurry to the kitchen in the dead of night. It is easy. Only a few guards are on duty and the kitchen has many sharp utensils. I snatch a small curved dagger and run back to the great hall where I sit munching nuts whilst attacking my hair, carving it off in handfuls, which I pile up neatly beside me. A few stray mice and the occasional rat come to watch. My head feels so light and free. Slash, slash, the knife cuts through the strands. I run my fingers through the tufts, shaking my head free of the stray strands and skip around the hall to show off my new look. I decide to keep the knife and use it to pry open a jar of juicy black olives, being careful to select just a few and replacing the lid, hiding the broken seal. In the glinting lamplight I catch a glimpse of my reflection in a large wine jar. I look like Vangelis. I look like a boy. I challenge the reflection with my knife and look ferocious, growling quietly like a wild dog. I know what I must do! I must dress as a boy. Become a boy. In the morning I resolve to venture down to the servants' quarters and take a shift shirt and loon trousers from the bushes where the women wash their clothes. I will have greater freedom as boy. I will bide my time and learn how to get close to Vangelis…Sleep, sleep—I wade through the murky waters into oblivion.

Days, weeks passed. I was never hungry or thirsty again. The great hall was my provider, my protector, my home. I even gained some weight and felt healthy. As a boy I mingled with the crowds, the servants, and the farmers. I spoke to no one and kept my own company, watching, waiting, and listening to gossip. I learnt that my father had died. Chryanaida ruled with her venomous friend as her advisor. But with her as ruler there was a distinct quality in the air of something sour; something not quite as it should be; something curdling the milk; something stealing the laughter and making it rain on the inside when the sun was shining outside. Close to the ground, I heard macabre whispers of deadly deeds performed by Chryanaida and her high priest deep in the bowels of the palace where screams cut the night's edge with ungodly executions. I heard them say that the dead were not laid to rest. I heard them whisper things that were never meant for the living to hear.

One day I saw Xabin and he stopped abruptly, opening his mouth to say something, but he changed his mind and hurried on. I continued to walk down the heaving corridor, packed with traders who had come to barter goods. I always kept my eyes down and never exchanged glances with anyone. That way I became anonymous, invisible to the world, making it possible for me to sneak undetected into areas I remembered. Sometime around my ninth birthday—I wasn't too sure of the day, but I knew it was at hand because the little lilac flower smock blooms, which grew abundantly in the meadow had come into flower— I managed to catch a glimpse of Vangelis wandering alone in the enclosed courtyard. He was five years old and, like me, tall for his age. He looked sad. He aimlessly threw pebbles into the air, mindless of where they landed. I wanted to run to him but I held back in case of danger. Instead I whistled in the air and he caught the signal. He stood still and listened. I made a sound that I knew only he and I could recall: the sound he used to make for my name, Ztah. I blew it to him on the breeze. A flash of recognition flew across his eyes. He repeated the sound looking in my direction but a servant came running out and shooed him back indoors. His little pained face told all as he tried to look back. He remembered—I knew he remembered me!

I bit back the tears and fled to the safety of the great store hall. I had to be near him, I had to speak with him, had to hug him and kiss his fraught little face. The next day I dared my chances to seek him out at the same time and place. He was there. I made the sounds. He smiled and returned them on the wind. I stood up and waved. He looked confused. I made the noise so that he could see my lips move. He ventured near, repeating the sounds, until we both stood nose to nose staring into each other's eyes. We hugged and cried and laughed, dropping down behind the hibiscus bushes. He ran his hand through my clipped hair and touched my face, unable to take in my disguise as a boy. I tweaked his nose. There wasn't time to exchange news but we agreed to meet every day, if it was safe for us both. A call sent him scampering back to the servant but I was happy.

During our brief time together, we made plans to escape and talked of all the things we wanted to do and how we would grow up and avenge our father and make life good for everyone in the palace. Vangelis told me of rising fears of plagues, floods, drought, and famine wrecking the land, as he had overheard the servant's gossiping. They spoke of black blood found in the chicken's eggs; dead fish rotting in the sea; unripe harvests; poisoned grain; sour wine; and worst of all, the prophecies from the wise men who read the signs and foretold of a thunderbolt which would wreck the palace with a great fire, destroying all within, killing everyone, and burning all the land for miles around. Evil above and below would make the people bleed until their blood turned to water and the water turned to bile and nothing would be left except the dry bones in the infertile soil, leaving only dust and ashes. The prophecies made us fearful for our future and we plotted to escape: we would make our move on the eve of the great bull feast when the crowds would be too thick for us to be noticed.

On the eve of the great festival, dancers and acrobats were training in the ceremonial arena and teams of servants were rushing everywhere. I waited as usual, watching from the bushes, but Vangelis did not run through the curtains to greet me. Instead, he walked with his head downcast. I was about to whistle when I saw that she followed. She had grown fat, with puffed cheeks like a stuffed boar's head crammed with fruit at the harvest feast. Her eyes bulged encased in a spider's glare and her pudgy arms toyed with Vangelis' shoulders in a mock-motherly fashion. Suddenly her fists clenched and unclenched, and she pushed Vangelis down the long flight of steps to the courtyard below. In slow motion I watched him bounce, turning in the air, splitting his head open as the crown of his skull smashed against the rocks. I saw the back of his head was a red mash. He spiralled and his body rebounded like a floppy rag doll falling from step to step until he reached the bottom. She paused and waited for him to land in a crumpled heap before crying after him, shouting for help.

From afar I heard myself yell. From outside myself I saw her look up at me with the same hatred she had tried to hide so many years before. When I returned to the moment, amidst shouting, wailing, and howling I ran, brought to my senses by her glare.

But it was too late. I knew she knew and like before she would wreak her revenge.

I ran back to the great hall. She knew my disguise. Outside the hall and along the tiny corridor guards were on patrol. I asked a keeper what was amiss and he told me that for some time thieves had been helping themselves to the stores and that a new system of security had to be adopted. I thought I had been so clever only taking small amounts from each sack, but they had not been fooled. I didn't know where to go. The soldiers would be searching for me and from her description they would know what I looked like. I needed to be invisible again. Suddenly the smell of incense wafted heavily in the late afternoon, drifting over from the temple. They were mourning Vangelis. The idea of hiding down in the vaults seemed the best, so I hurried down the winding stairs, down and down into the dark below. But I was not prepared for the horror that waited.

The flickering lamps drizzled dollops of fat onto the stone floor, congealing in white piles and as I raced I slipped and crashed down a few steps, cutting my shin. I clung to the wall as I saw Chryanaida with the vulture, her partner, standing over the body of Vangelis, cutting out his heart. I froze in terror. She put the bleeding organ to her mouth and bit into the flesh. Her mouth was wet with his blood—my baby brother's blood—smeared over her face. I crumbled to the floor. There was nothing, only blackness.

Izatah's memory blurs and judders in and out of focus. She recalls fainting, falling, being strapped and carried until she is lying where I first found her, tied to the rough bed with Xabin in the corner watching over her. This time there is no escape. The poison has nearly completed its round and she accepts there is little time left. The queen will have her way but she will not have victory. I lie quietly within her conscious mind, unable to bite back the disgust. I pause, waiting for her body to close down. I am with her. I will never forget her. She knows that one day I will tell her story. Our membranes grow weak. I am unfolding from her and she allows me to move outside of her being and walk toward the door where Xabin stands. He knows there is a ghostly spectre in the room comforting Izatah.

Suddenly, she calls, "The dancer has come for me—the dancer with stars in her eyes is here!"

Xabin watches.

"Look—she is here. She has come to dance with me. She has come to take me away...we will dance together..." She softly closes her eyes, and is gone, past her pain and the terror of her existence.

CHAPTER 10

Red Alert

When all is harmonious in the dance,
all is well with the world!

On and on the bus droned and I kept Izatah's memory close. I remembered how I felt the next morning, waking up after the second and final fall back through time. As I woke, a part of me drifted, like a lost sailboat slipping its mooring in the dead of night. Like a tiny speck of dust, a particle of nothingness wandered into the cosmos. Under the covers, private in my grief, I sobbed. I had never lost someone closer to me than myself and the pain, like a dried coconut husk rolling on a deserted beach, echoed a constant hollow emptiness. The early morning sun streaked in through the shutters of our vacation apartment. There was no Xabin waiting and watching. I was drowned in the injustice and her innocence, drained dry in the cages of white bones left ragged in the rock of worn-out emotion. Her anguish gagged in my throat. Her bitter bile lingered on my tongue. I made a pact with myself, resolving that whatever it took I would speak out and write her story, no matter how incredible it appeared or the outcome of people's reactions. I naively had no idea what lay in wait, or just how difficult it was going to be and how, at every junction, something would conspire to deter me from my goal.

Travelling on and on in our little WaWa bus the hours dwindled, bringing us nearer to our destination. In the glare of the blazing heat we turned into Trinidad de Cuba. The town was aglow in a myriad of flat-roofed, multicoloured houses basking in the bright sunshine. We bounced up and down, in and out, of the potholed roads through a maze of linear streets built originally in 1514. The town breathed a warm welcome under the impressive lushness of the Sierra del Escambray mountains protectively watching in the distance, and encompassed by exotic white sandy beaches and the tropical blue sea. Trinidad would be where we would face new challenges of our music and dance course and make our CD. Our homesteads were to be shared with different partners, apart from the two married couples. Simonise and I had been assigned a house together. I found the arrangement of living in a stranger's house uncomfortable, especially knowing that we were neither relatives nor friends. We were there for the sole purpose of earning the household extra money. Communication was unnatural and awkward at times, but we gained a glimpse into the true picture of people's lives.

Ours was a small house in a long row of what appeared on the outside to be dilapidated buildings with paint peeling from multicoloured house fronts, with white iron-framed gates that slid across the house at night. From the potholed road, we walked straight into the small front room with a television and sofa, where the owner's daughter sat watching her favourite programme; she hardly looked up as we entered. Next, through an open archway, was a small dining area with a modest table and four chairs near a compact kitchen. Up the stairs were two bedrooms. Ours was the back bedroom which had an en suite shower and toilet but the other bedroom was just an open space with a bed, cordoned off by a flimsy curtain. The husband of the household was a friendly and handsome man who, being a waiter at a nearby large hotel, possessed enough savvy for dealing with tourists. The wife, Margarita, was a large, strong, domineering woman who eyed us suspiciously and kept watch over her shoulder at her husband. We were always encouraged to eat our first meal in the new homestead with the family, as it gave them extra revenue and was supposed to be cheaper than eating out. They took our order for our evening meal that would be served to us around seven o'clock.

In the heat of the afternoon we explored the area and were taken to a nearby central arena up a steep incline where musicians gathered at night and the community partied until the early hours. We sat in the shade under a tree near the bar, which resembled a dull, flat, concrete, dank green, council outhouse, and we drank beautiful mint-scented mojitos. As the late afternoon rolled into the early evening, casting long shadows over the concrete arena, Simonise and I ambled back for our evening meal. The family were gathered in the front room around the television and we felt like interlopers sneaking into a hallowed space. The children were ushered off to friends for the night and we were able to eat in relative peace.

The first course was a wholesome and nutritious homemade soup which Alfonse, the husband, had made. It was served with cheap white doughy rolls and plastic butter in sachets. We were asked if we would like wine and were shown a bottle—which I suspected was purloined from the hotel—and were overcharged for the privilege. We had both ordered a seafood dish for our main course which was quite tasty but sitting in that false situation with both husband and wife hovering and us not able to speak freely was like a schoolgirl's outing, dining at a friend's house with strict parents watching. We ate our fill and were then served tinned fruit and ice cream, neither of which I like, but we were polite and ate it. We then awkwardly excused ourselves to get ready for the evening.

Simonise persuaded me that I had to go to the disco in the centre of the town, even though I felt very tired after the long journey. For her, I mustered up the energy and began to feel better as we met up with Edgar and ambled in the cooling evening towards the ruins of an ancient church. As we walked, there was a slight breeze that took the edge off the day's heat, wafting a refreshing draught across our faces as twilight descended over the town, weaving her magic with glowing red embers flashing across the sinking fireball and spilling flame shadows across the flat rooftops. As the lull of evening settled on the dusty road, mingling with the day's weariness and disappearing into the cracked gullies, the hush descended, pausing before a storm. Music burst and bubbled through the streets, washing away the day's fatigue in a whirlwind of rhythm and lashing the night with a flurry of electric tornado pulses that gurgled up through the ancient gothic spires. The rough, broken stones of the church-yard made our footing uncertain as we made our way through the ruins.

Like entering a film set for *Dracula*, we were lured into the drama as the high church steeples silhouetted against the dark-ening sky appeared like battlements foreboding a mysterious welcome. Half-lit faces catching fragments of light resembled spectres in a macabre masquerade ball as they bobbed in and out of the crumbling remains. There was a makeshift bar erected in the nave of the old church and a laser disco set out in the main aisle with flurries of smaller disco lights hidden on altars off the main entrance. The dancing blazed its own heat, intensifying the rapidly rising pressure in the atmosphere that was brewing toward a grand-scale hurricane. The town had been placed on red alert; the daily news showed the devastation of the latest cyclone whirling across the sea, sweeping its way toward us. People were used to the routine and were well prepared for the onslaught; they partied harder in the face of the imminent attack. Trinidad was in line for a direct hit, yet there was no hint of fear or panic from the community, only prepared acceptance.

Our group gathered at the bar and were entranced by the electric potpourri of surreal images swirling around us. We were seduced into the dance scene, magnetised into the mood of the moment. Balancing my drink in one hand and my handbag in the other, I dodged through the dancers to a corner sanctuary where the shadows performed a fandango of their own, casting patterns over the splintered glass windows. Here the music was not so invasive and I could watch the bizarre charade masking the truth behind the crumbling spoof of decaying religious ritual, where hope was played out on the curious stage of fantasy, while the hurricane world was held at bay. I thought of Saul and how he would have avoided such burlesque bustle.

I shivered as a dark shadow momentarily sealed out the light, as though a secret of something forbidden was teasing and taunting before disappearing behind the show, forecasting something I would never know, but would always imagine of a large athletic man with feminine lips coated in bright red lipstick. Was this a vision of the future warning me fleetingly about someone? I did not dare to hold the image. A tingle of fear, leered a distorted smile, pausing momentarily before vanishing into the crowd which thickened, pushing forwards, showering me with liberating laughter. I pushed the vision away and deliberately erased it, immersing myself in the fiesta fandango.

A voice behind made me turn: "Would you like a drink?"

He was a tall, suave Italian out to party with his male friends who were on a football tour from Italy, and intending to conquer the night.

"Er…," I faltered, not quite knowing how to respond, while I took in his sincere face.

"I think you better have another. I get you what you like?"

"Mojito, please."

He nodded and drew his feet together in an aristocratic bow. I was nervous. I looked for the others but they were lost in the melee. My hands were sweating and I felt guilty. He returned smiling and we talked for a while. Then he drew me into the fracas and we gave our bodies to the pounding music. I told myself I was only dancing and that I was not doing anything wrong. In a quiet pause as we enjoyed another drink he asked me to go to Italy with him and live at his mother's house. I stifled a laugh and couldn't imagine anything worse. He was around forty-five years old, much younger than me, and still living with his mother! I was relieved when I saw Simonise ambling toward me. She said that our group was moving on and I thanked him for the drink and politely left.

As we strode into the night through the muted silence of the dusty streets away from the pulsing electric beat, the low wind began to whistle around corners, sneaking furtive flurries, sniping at awnings and fluttering shutters, warning that harsher lashings waited to be unleashed from across the sea. In the concrete square up the steep incline with the outhouse bar, we retraced our steps to a very different scene. Under the trees that had given welcome shade that afternoon sat myriads of people drinking, smoking, joking, laughing, singing, sighing, feasting, and smooching under numerous silver beacons. In an arena, vying couples competing to win the dance trophy of the week practised their moves. The dance floor was a primitive concrete square set at the top of the steep incline and cordoned off by a thin blue rope. The flair, skill, and ingenuity of the intricate steps were breathtaking. After the couples had danced their first round, it was the turn of set groups sporting the colours of their club, bedecked in sequins, satin, and lip gloss, and polished from top to toe with glam shimmer. They paraded out onto the dance floor like royalty and were applauded likewise by the animated crowd. Steam rose from the dancers like a misty aura as sweat trickled from the performers, dripping and flicking into the crowd as they spun.

Weariness sprang from the shadows and engulfed me, and a sudden longing to be in bed was my only desire. I felt dizzy and apologised to Simonise for being so tired but I had to get back. She and Ed would not allow me to walk back by myself and they accompanied me all the way to the homestead. I was truly grateful for their kind concern, for I doubted my ability to find my way back. Simonise took the key with her since she decided to go back to the party. I turned on the stairway light and quietly made my way up, nearly falling backwards as Margarita poked her head out from behind the flimsy curtain to see who had returned. I offered a rushed, embarrassed goodnight, fumbled with my keys to open the bedroom door, and slipped into the oven-like heat of the tiny bedroom. Being in someone's house was not an ideal situation for either party and again I felt like a schoolgirl returning home late!

I switched on the electric fan that stirred up the hot air like a hairdryer shifting the heat but not cooling it down. I sat on the edge of the bed feeling tired and depressed. I had forgotten to open my note from Saul and I brightened up as I tore open the message:

> I still love you but now I really bloody hate those
> Cubans and anyone else who stands close to you.
> (Grumpy head on today)

> Love, Caveman (with club) x

The note made me smile as he had forbidden me to dance with another man, but it was impossible not to because that was part of the course. He didn't understand that the dance was dance, not a relationship. The heat of the night was unbearable and I lay down in the semi-darkness with the light from the outside seeping through the thin curtains. Knossos invaded my mind and it was difficult to shake off the aftermath of my earlier recall.

I drifted back to my return from Crete and my searching all the available bookshops for information. But there was nothing of substance in any of the shops apart from the usual tourist information; even at the library I drew a blank. As I approached the last small bookshop, I had almost given up hope of finding any clues but when I was strolling down one of the aisles, passing the Ancient History section, I spied a battered red book with a black silhouette of a bull on the spine. I picked it up and the pages fell open at a description of the first excavation of Knossos Palace by Arthur Evans, who wrote that he was overwhelmed by the all-pervading sense of evil which permeated the bricks and essence of the place. It was so intense that he had to rush out of the rubble. When he was able to return to the bowels of the palace, which was where the sensation of evil was most prevalent, he found the skeletons of two young children: the bodies of a young girl aged between nine years and twelve years, and a boy of about four to five years of age. Tests proved that they had been healthy children with no apparent disabilities or signs of malignant disease.

When I read the paragraph, the words jumped out and screamed Izatah and Vangelis. I searched for a place to sit down. A young assistant asked if I wanted a glass of water. I was shocked. I had not expected to find such detail. I tried to argue with myself that it was coincidence, but I knew it wasn't. The book which contained many chapters on ancient places just happened to fall open on the section on Knossos Palace—not only on that chapter, but the very page which explained the discovery of the skeletons deep under the main body of the palace, skeletons that were the exact age of Izatah and Vangelis. The synchronicity was not random. I had a strange feeling of someone looking over my shoulder and I felt compelled to read on, finding that in the room next to the skeletons other bones from children had been excavated, children that appeared to have been healthy with no overt evidence of disease and whose deaths were a mystery. Child sacrifice was intimated, together with perverted sexual rituals.

Izatah's memory reached out to me in the silence of the morning amongst the quiet shelves, and I felt her heart inside mine. I bit back the tears and bought the book. I was certain that my experience had been directed by an unseen force and I phoned several universities to see if I could speak with anyone about it, but when I explained my intent, each time I was fobbed off. I could feel their reaction: I must be a nutcase claiming to have a past life experience of an existence in the palace. No one wanted to know. I couldn't blame them—how could anyone take a fairytale seriously? One professor eventually spoke to me and promised to return my call but he never did. I contacted a friend who was an historian who knew about my psychic abilities and he tried to put a project together, but through lack of funding it was rejected. No one believed my claims and as time rolled from one week to the next, I had to admit that it was too fantastic to swallow.

The summer after Crete was traumatic in many ways. I left my husband and rented a small cottage in an outlying country village twenty-two miles outside York near the ancient castle of Richard the Third. It was difficult because I had to earn my monthly rent and, being a freelance choreographer, dancer, and teacher, I had very little spare time to write and collect my thoughts. When I did, I was exhausted from travelling daily to see the children and working my way through community dance projects. August meandered into September and the first Sunday evening I was free to record Izatah's memory, I felt nervous. It had been a glorious autumn day spent with my two younger children walking in the woods near the castle, watching them run with my little dog, playing hide and seek in the trees, picking blackberries, and collecting kindling for my fire. We had a picnic tea outside in my enclosed garden and then I had driven them back with the sinking Sunday evening feeling of gloom that always descended when I had to leave them.

On returning home I switched on the computer at my desk, which looked out over quivering fields and endless trees that must have witnessed battles, skirmishes, and bloody axe and sword fights on the ancient battleground. My computer began to whir into action as the sky began to darken. There was a tense edginess in the air. I began my first sentence and the beautiful golden evening turned navy blue, with black clouds scudding across the bleak sky. The trees outside my window and across the fields began to shake furiously in a cyclonic wind that came from nowhere. My room was plunged into darkness. I rose quickly from my chair as a streak of blue electric lightning bolted from outside and shot in through the window, exploding across my desk. My computer blew up and crackled in the aftermath and was shrouded in a cloud of grey smoke. My little dog whimpered under the table as thunder boomed over the roof, momentarily shaking the cottage to its foundation. Then the rain came heavy and thick, blotting out the skyline in a whirlpool glaze, thrashing the pan tiles on my roof with whip-crack lashes.

A strange presence stole into my sitting room and waited, watching from the shadows. Determined not to be fazed, I busied myself making a fire out of the freshly-gathered kindling. The twigs crackled and spat, shooting sparks up the chimney. The presence scrutinised me from the far end of the room. It hovered and gloated victory. I steadied my shaking hands and poured a glass of smooth red wine. I sat down on the floor next to the fire with my little dog curled up on my lap. I stared into the roaring blaze as the dry twigs twisted and hissed. A cold fear lodged in my chest. The wine helped to calm my panic and

I fought to steady my breathing. Knossos flooded back through the flames. I felt more than ever that I was fighting an evil force that was hell-bent on preventing me from recording Izatah's story. As I sat there, waves of recognition and understanding began to pound back from my childhood and I wondered whether my early nightmares and visions were part of the Knossos past life. As a small child I had always insisted that there was a lady in my room. I was afraid of her and couldn't sleep. The night when I was found in my cot with the sheets tied around my neck was horrific. Who could have done such a thing? Could a spirit entity be capable of physical force?

Reaching further back, I remembered my birth and the battle for air. Doctors say that it is not a strange phenomenon to be able to remember your birth if it was a particularly traumatic one, as mine was. I was hauled into the world by steel forceps that crushed the lower part of my face. I was not expected to live and my father was sent in the middle of the night to find a priest who would perform a baptism in the hospital. My mother was not allowed to see me for over a week after the painful birth, but when she did she found a sadistic nurse—one who had pumped her breasts until she bled—shaking me like a rag doll. Perhaps she thought it was kinder to kill me as there was not much hope for my survival, or was she coerced by an evil energy to kill me? It all sounded very dramatic and farfetched.

Then there was the occasion when a beautiful dark lady on a black horse, riding in a nearby field dressed in a Victorian riding habit, reached from afar into my head and behind my eyes, sucking out my life force, like a dog with a bone licking out the marrow jelly, making me slump under the tea table in abject terror despite warnings from my parents who could not see anything but the trees in the field. All these thoughts spun inside my head and in truth I was afraid to move, so I sat there pondering all the links, wondering the worst and fearing the next round.

In my Trinidad bedroom I was hot, so hot, feeling the heat of the fire in the autumn rain combined with the heat of the Cuban night cloying my body. I lay in a wet lather with damp hair limp on the pillow. Simonise breezed in. I pretended to be asleep. She quickly threw herself onto the bed, curled up, and went to sleep. She reminded me of my eldest daughter and I was happy to see her peaceful slumber. I couldn't sleep. The electric fan was fine when it blew in my direction for a few seconds, but when it whizzed to other side of the room, the heat gushed back, invading my space until it whooshed away again. My mind turned and rolled, and instead of fighting I allowed my memories space.

The night when I attempted to write Izatah's story my computer blew up in the storm; the electrical surge might have been coincidental but I knew it wasn't. The next morning was the start of heavy rehearsing for a grand show, but I made time to pack the computer and take it to a friend who offered to take a look at it and lend me one of his, as he was a technician at the local sixth form college. He had a workshop at the back of his house. Unburdening me of my broken computer, he promised to take it to college where it would be about three weeks before he could let me have it back. He lifted a model of his own from a shelf and plugged it in. All was fine until he demonstrated the basic mechanism but instead of obeying his commands, it exploded, leaving a pungent smell of burning wire in a black fog of smoke, comically coiling round the blank black screen. Silently, we gazed in shock at the wreckage.

"Well, well, well!" sighed Hugh, dazed. "In all my years working with these things, I've never had that happen before—you've jinxed it!"

His words were not comforting or funny. I couldn't tell him he was probably right and I left in a hurry with my computer in his safe keeping. I did not have any money for repairs or a replacement and bartering was the only way forward, so I agreed to give his wife a few sessions of healing massage in return. The week passed in a rush of nervous energy building towards the final show, but the morning just before I was about to go on stage for our last rehearsal I received an urgent call from the manager's office. It was Hugh on the phone:

"Oh, I'm so, so sorry. I don't know how to tell you this: your computer was in the college storeroom with twelve others and we had a break-in last night. Everything's been stolen. We've had a complete wipe-out! There's nothing left."

I was staggered. There was no insurance to cover it. The college couldn't take responsibility for it, as it wasn't supposed to be there. Hugh didn't have one to lend and I had no money to buy another. It seemed *she* had won another round!

After the performance the buzz, the lights, and the applause faded in the dim corridor where there was nothing left but bits of tickets strewn on the gaudy carpet. My children loved the show but had to return to their father's as it took a long time striking the set and stacking props and costumes. Outside in the cold night air I packed my car then sped back through the bright town lights to the motorway and onto the winding country lanes. The stars were clearly visible once I was away from the city glare. I breathed a sigh of relief. It was great to have success and a large bottle of champagne and scrumptious chocolates but it was lonely not being able to share special moments with someone who cared.

My little dog gave me her usual overwhelming welcome as I stepped inside the hallway and although the night air was sharp, we sat together on my kitchen doorstep, planet-gazing. I opened the wine with a loud pop resounding into the still night while the rest of the village slept behind chintz curtains. There was a light sprinkling of frost on the hard ground like icing sugar on a freshly baked sponge cake and the moon was bright like a stage spotlight. I wanted to dance out in the fray over the meadow and far, far away from the crowds and the pressure and the worries of a lost computer. I didn't feel the cold with my little woolly dog wrapped around my feet and a third glass of champagne warming my empty stomach. From my perch the ancient castle ruins towered up into the night sky, cushioned by grey scudding clouds moodily swirling against a silver screen. The ravens gathered in the turrets silently poised, ready to fly past the moon in a ghostly squadron. Predators of the dark crept around the muddy moat, unchanged in their nightly regime since the jousting and courtly pageants had long paraded into the past.

Too much wine on an empty stomach was not sensible, I told myself as I plunged into a post- production depression. The reality of no finance, no computer, and no partner was bleak. Self-pity stole a slice of reason and I plummeted further into an abyss of despair, wondering how I was going to avenge Izatah's death. I pleaded with the great ones out in the stars to hear my cry, bargaining that if the experience was just my invention then I would agree to draw a veil over the whole affair and forget my promise, but if justice was to take its rightful place and be fulfilled, then please show me a sign. I waited and watched the night sky. There was nothing save the beacon twinkle of pulsing planets. Just as I was about to go indoors I paused, and a funny fizzing in my chest told me to stop. Like the lull before a fireworks display, the sky blinked, then showered the silver-specked curtain with pink sprinkles cascading from a shooting star, falling from one side of the spectrum and arching to nowhere beyond. My sign was beautiful. My sign was magnificent. And with my whole heart I cried, "Thank you, thank you, Universe!"

My sign strengthened my purpose, making me determined to do something to help the memory of the child but what, how, where, or when I had no idea. I could never have dreamt what lay in store.

CHAPTER II

Hurricane!

*Nothing is ever lost in the search for the
perfect dance. Steps which are found and
discarded will lie in wait in the stillness
and when the stillness wakes, the steps
are reborn and the dance is transformed.*

The next morning, after I had snatched a few hours' sleep, I
ate a hearty breakfast with Simonise. We were to have our
first percussion lesson in preparation for cutting our CD. As we
walked in the cool early morning, a truck was sucking up sewage from each house through a huge rubber pipe, leaving a low-
lying haze of noxious fumes choking the air. Across the road a
line of people queued for slices of cheap pizza. We met Edgar,
who was always enthusiastic even though he was dog-tired. In
the shade of shop awnings we strode along to meet the others.
The air was still, with no hint of the impending hurricane. The
newspapers insisted that it was making its way toward us but
probably wouldn't arrive for a few days. In the meantime the
locals were not unduly worried.

As we cut through a main thoroughfare, we passed an
ironmonger's shop reeking heavily of petrol and shoe polish,
a chemist's, and a hardware store before we found our venue,

which was a beautiful open-air bar/restaurant. We entered through an arch of lush green plants and into a large clean arena of tables and chairs set out in front of a stage, where an array of drums on raffia mats were organised in a semicircle. The drums were all different colours, including bright red, black, or white; some were varnished wood. The chairs were neatly arranged behind them, giving the scene a professional and serious overtone. The stage cyclorama was painted turquoise and was dappled with moving bright light, like a glitter ball, as the sun streamed through the leaves of the trees, playfully dancing shadows over our drums.

It was early and only a few members of staff were manning the coffee machine and stocking up bottles. When our entire party had arrived, Carol introduced us to our two teachers, Joseph and Carlos, who were well-known performers and musicians. They escorted us to our places and began tuning the drums. Their expertise was intimidating and we all seemed a little nervous as we took our seats. We were instructed to place our hands on the drum skin and shape our fingers in a particular way. I sat between the Prunesquallors who seemed slightly uncomfortable at having to sit with their legs spread wide, squeezing the drum with their thighs. My drum was black with a shiny metal rim and I began to feel at ease with it after a few minutes of repeating a simple rhythm. I learned how to slide my hand across the skin to make a soft shushing sound, then how to pound the side with my fingers to make a deep resounding note that echoed across the courtyard and up through the glade of trees. There was something hypnotically satisfying about the action when performed in a group, with everyone sliding and thumping in time. Joseph came round to us all in turn and adjusted our fingers. The *djembe* in his hands was powerful and primitive in the way he coaxed sounds from nowhere.

Paddy was not comfortable playing the drum and whether the sound was too harsh first thing in the morning or whether he felt inadequate, I wasn't sure, but he was given a cowbell to ding at specific times. Unfortunately his timing was not good and his ding was often a dong in the wrong place. We didn't mind, but he became frustrated and preferred to sit and watch us, listening to our basic beats whilst drinking a cool beer. After about an hour we had a short break by which time the café had begun to fill up with people breakfasting or taking a mid-morning snack. I loved the space. It was an open-air theatre bursting with life and performance energy. Silver hearts and stars bejewelled the back wall and a thicket of tree roots, branches, and a net of lush leaves canopied the top of the stage. Trails of long stems hung down like party streamers, which gently coiled and turned in the occasional breeze.

Our lesson continued while other performers gathered. A troupe of dancers began to limber up and my concentration wandered as I watched the familiar process, envious of their suppleness and flexibility as my own had worn thin with my disability. By the time we finished our lesson I felt more confident about drumming and was happy that we were to perform two pieces. Joseph had been such a good teacher and Carlos a great leader that the whole group felt a flush of accomplishment as we left for lunch. I wasn't very hungry after the hefty breakfast and was looking forward to my first salsa lesson with new teachers, which was scheduled for the early afternoon in Carol's homestead.

Back in my own lodgings, Margarita returned my passport like a prison guard party to confidential information. She regarded me with suspicion as she handed it over, and I tried to be courteous and deflect her dislike of me with smiles and compliments but she was unmoved. I did not know why she was so negative; perhaps she was envious of my freedom and lifestyle. I excused myself and went upstairs to sit on the bed to read Saul's note:

Baby, it's really starting to hurt now,
I love you very much,

Love,
Saul x

I was a little disappointed that it was so short, feeling that what started out to be a good idea had become a bit of a chore for him, or perhaps I was just having a down reaction after the third-degree scrutiny downstairs. I consoled myself with the thought that Saul had asked me to marry him in a text and I had accepted. He was the man with whom I wanted to spend the autumn and winter of my life. It was my final chance to make a good marriage and settle down; I hoped it was going to be third time lucky, and although we were both so different and completely opposite in our interests, we were both sure we could make it together. I wondered what he was doing and wanted to text but I was afraid he was still sleeping.

Outside, the usual tropical rainclouds gathered, warning of a torrential downpour, and I decided to lie down for a short while and catch up on some sleep before my dance lesson. Closing my eyes, I allowed my mind to drift back to ponder the beauty of the shooting star the evening when I had asked for a sign for help to continue my quest to lay Izatah's past to rest. The night sky had been sprinkled in pink dust and like a Disney wish upon a star, my wish had come true the following day.

It was Monday morning and at nine sharp all my enthusiastic senior citizens bounded into the studio for their dance and fitness class despite all their ailments, their aching bones, and their arthritis. I loved teaching them as they smiled and laughed throughout the lesson, exerting one hundred and ten percent with every step they danced. That morning a new pupil arrived. I loved her immediately, finding in her all the qualities I admired. She shone like a shooting star among a sea of jaded memories. She disguised her hurt, sadness, and loneliness in a stream of jollity, gracefully dancing with flair and even sauciness for her seventy-two years of age. Anne was like the mother I would have loved to love. When she told me where she lived I was surprised, as it was the very house one Christmas eve two years previously that I had blindly run to in deep hurt and distress, seeking asylum in a beacon of light. For no reason other than impulse I had stood outside her gate wondering what I was doing and why. I wanted desperately to knock on her door but what could I say, how could I explain myself? The street was full of Christmas lights and exciting decorations with brightly-lit candles hailing the dawn of Christmas day. I was in emotional shreds, sobbing outside a stranger's house with no idea what had driven me there. I was out of time with time, not realizing that two years later the house and its owner would mean so much to me! Somehow I had drawn strength from her doorstep but never ventured inside; I had gone back to decorate a lonely Christmas tree.

After a few lessons together, Anne invited me to her house and we became firm friends. I found refuge in her company, and shared my personal problems and divulged my secret psychic work. She even opened her house for some special healing and together we were able to help people. One Saturday evening I was invited to go to a nightclub with my eldest daughter and her boyfriend but I had first promised to see Anne. As we sat and chatted, a strong spirit came through unexpectedly. It was her deceased husband. They spoke for a long time and as usual I did not retain any of the conversation as it was private. I was only used as a channel but I do remember a phrase which stuck in my brain: her husband had dictated, "Look after the little bird." Anne took the message to heart and surprised me with two tickets to Crete. She was my shooting star wish come true. She was going to help me revisit Knossos to find some answers to my experience and to give the little princess a loving funeral and bring closure to her troubled life.

It was nearly Easter, just three months after we had first met, and my affinity with Anne grew. It was as though we had shared the same footpath along a lonely road, both of us walking towards the light under the shade of the stars, making solitary footprints searching for each other. Lost mother and daughter hanging in limbo through lifetimes. The universe had answered my plea and whispered, "Onwards—every mile is testimony to the child's rescue and tomorrow is Easter, tomorrow is never too late." My tomorrow was to be September when the visit to Crete was scheduled and I replied to the universe, "I will wait for tomorrow. I am glad I waited for my footprints to reach Anne's door while hope was waiting in the shadows."

Lost in the past, time raced as the afternoon clouds scudded over Trinidad. I got up and hurried to get to Carol's homestead before the torrent lashed the streets. Inside the house, I could see it was much bigger than mine, with an open courtyard leading to outhouses and bedrooms. I was taken into a cool sitting room with a colourful tiled floor of bright pink flowers and green shrubs on a black border. A young girl asked me if I wished to purchase a coconut milk. I was surprised when she brought me a large coconut with a pink straw peeping through a hole in the middle. The milk was refreshing and I smiled as I placed the coconut shell on the gaudy floor, thinking it made a change from the usual Fanta bottles. I took a photograph of it. When the young girl returned with my change she handed me a note from Joseph, our teacher, enquiring if I was going to the main dance that evening. I was surprised and didn't send a reply. At that moment the young Australian couple came panting through the door, "That was awesome," laughed Eric, "but it's way too hot to dance!"

The air was growing heavier and the humidity denser as I entered the open dining area and met my two lovely teachers. Angelica was small with a pale complexion and dark Spanish eyes that glinted a welcome. Her long dyed-blonde hair was tied up in a chignon at the back, ready for action. Her husband Enrico was petite but well-muscled, with shiny ebony skin and laughing black eyes. They had both been dancers at the famous Havana Tropicana night club but on questioning them about it, I sensed some discontent surrounding their experience and I didn't press them further to explain. Instead we began to tentatively mark through the first steps which I quickly grasped and they realized from my style that I was a dancer. From the first patterns we quickly progressed to more intricate rhythms. Together they demonstrated nippy, entwined arm moves and then I repeated them with Enrico. I allowed him to manipulate me like a puppeteer and we whizzed into action as the music spurred us on in torrid syncopation, while the heat beat into us, stealing air and stifling the moment, but the dance was all. The more I learnt, the more I wanted to learn and the more they wanted to teach me, despite the rising wind in the corners of the courtyard, despite the rattling doors, despite the harsh rainfall which cooled the air momentarily. Briefly we paused. I was racing through the styles and they said they had never got through so many different sections in one session. I was pleased. Our bodies buzzed in the glow of the sweltering humidity and we wiped our arms and hands, ready for the next round, but the air became angry and the wind rose up outraged and filled our dance space with electric invisible flames, as the first stage of the hurricane began to spark.

Angelica and Enrico were impervious to the brewing storm and continued our lesson with renewed fervour, pulling, pushing, sliding, gliding, clicking, and flicking me into the Cubanismo soul. I loved every moment sweating in the fiery atmosphere, lost in the salacious salsa while the storm rose in a crescendo, crashing and lashing the tropical trees in the courtyard. My body was alive in the thrill and pulsing with rhythm, yet electrified with a fear of the raging torrent invading our space. All too soon the lesson was over and I tipped them well for their wonderful expertise. Hilary was next and I stayed for a while watching as she too was able to pick up the steps easily. Because she was light, Enrico was able to throw her over his shoulders and under his legs. Even in the dense humidity he worked hard to execute the steps with pizzazz. Women in the house ran to secure the rattling doors in the courtyard and lock down the window shutters. They said it was not the real hurricane, that we were only feeling aspects of the storm, and that it was in God's hands whether the cyclone would hit the island.

They were right. By the time I walked into the street the storm had abated, leaving gurgling streams bubbling down the drains, gushing through exits and potholes in the broken road. For a while the storm had bypassed us and the air was clear once more. Children played in the street ringing their bicycle bells, kicking footballs, calling to each other in a diatribe of relief, happy to have escaped the oppressive assault. I decided to walk to the bar where we had our percussion lessons as I was thirsty after the exertion of the dancing. Tables and chairs dripped from the downpour, shining like Aladdin's cave with sparkling minute jewels as the sun broke through the soaking foliage. A waiter ran to a table and wiped everything down for me so that I could sit in comfort and enjoy my tropical fruit drink. Not long after, a dance troupe arrived to rehearse and I was entertained by their wonderful routines, secretly wishing to choreograph some of the dancers, imagining a piece I could create with their lithe, shiny bodies and their beautiful, graceful arms. The storm had refreshed the earth and the air was flooded with the smell of fresh flowers and wet soil. I took photographs of the dancers and revelled in the joy of their performance, allowing my mind to relax and remember the arrival of that special September when Anne and I flew to Crete.

We landed in Heraklion airport on a balmy September evening as the sun was beginning to set beyond the mountains. Our taxi wove in and out of small villages until we turned down a white, dusty path towards the sea where our hotel was lodged near the beach. It was elegant, grandly set in white stone against the purple and navy sky which was slowly dwindling into a black velvet curtain. After placing our luggage in our rooms, we were hungry and went in search of the dining room. We followed our noses toward a magnificent spread set out on a terrace. We took two plates and piled them high with appetizing dishes. Just as we were about to find two seats at one of the lovely tables set out in pristine white clothes and pretty table decorations, the manager came up to us dressed in his tuxedo and announced that we were not invited guests at the wedding party, that we had attacked the wedding feast, and please would we return our plates to the table. We were terribly embarrassed and apologised profusely. Red-faced, we placed our plates back on the main table and made a swift departure, hurriedly searching for the dining room which we eventually found after a few more mistakes wandering into reserved areas. This was our first journey together and our embarrassing comic mishap was to be the forerunner of many humorous blunders on numerous future trips.

We had a wonderful meal in the restaurant accompanied by a bottle of fruity red wine. Just as we were leaving, a waitress came running up to us saying, "Please, madam. You have not paid for your wine!"

Again, we were mortified by our mistake as we had presumed the wine would be charged to our room but, as the waitress explained, it was their policy to pay for the wine after every meal. We laughed at our innocent mistake as we bought drinks outside in the garden where accomplished Greek musicians were entertaining the audience not only with their music but with amazing feats such as lifting up tables and chairs and clambering over pyramids of stools piled high, teetering precariously in the night breeze. As the balalaikas strummed and sounded chords out across the deep, dark sea, the twinkling lights from two large ocean liners shone like a string of white pearls hanging across a black satin dress. Little multicoloured Christmas lights began to swing gently as we seemed to stir up a new breeze on our way to our seats on a wooden parapet near the garden. The lights began to swing at first from side to side, then were flung into an uncontrollable spin as the wind whiplashed the quivering wires. They spluttered and sent fingers of electric blue currents sparking into the night, where the lightning flashes fizzled and faded into blackness. They spluttered then went out. Anne shot me a questioning glance. Next, the lights around the dance floor and stage followed suit like a house of cards falling one after the other, causing a momentary blackout while the management sought to find alternative small lamps which were quickly issued to each table.

"Goodness me!" sighed Anne. "What do you make of that?"

I wasn't sure, and I tried to push what I really thought to the back of my mind but the thoughts returned, rippling back in tiny waves. My presence seemed to have stirred up dark emissaries from the past. Messengers from an evil force combined to menace our arrival. It was curious how before we arrived everything had been tranquil and buzzing with jovial laughter, but as soon as we sat down a wind lashed and whined in the trees like a disgruntled Siamese cat. The moment we took our seats, all the lights—not just at our table, but the whole of the ground floor—went out. Perhaps it was a coincidence, but it was only the beginning!

The low howling in the trees grew into the roaring of great wildcats ready to pounce, tearing at anything in their way.

Tables were overturned; plastic chairs were hurtled across the stage. The warm gentle breeze turned icy and wild, attacking the stage awning and ripping it from its posts, hurling it across the dance floor. Chairs flew into the swimming pool. The musicians scrambled to unplug their instruments and pack away before the eye of the storm damaged their equipment. People scurried indoors, leaving a wreckage of broken bottles and glasses strewn over the ground. Waiters attempted to untangle the tiny lights in the trees and gather them in like an unripe harvest. The delicate hibiscus bushes shook until the frail heads of the flowers were strewn over the pathways in a carpet of pink and red. There was nothing left of the party, only debris. Anne and I retired to the bar where the locals were shocked by the untimely storm—it had not been forecast and seemed to spring from nowhere. Everyone was dismayed and the wedding party was stunned. As we sat down in the noisy bar sipping our wine, we exchanged knowing glances.

"It seems they know we are here!" added Anne scornfully. I nodded. "Do you think they will try to prevent us from succeeding in our quest?" she queried in her quaint, very English voice.

"I'm not sure," I whispered. I was tired and needed to sleep. The surprise attack was totally unexpected and had knocked my confidence. Fear of something lurking in the shadows preyed in my dreamscape and I wandered through lost nightmares sleeping fitfully. Only when the first streaks of pink dispelled the murky gloom did I relax and sleep peacefully, realizing that I needed my strength if our mission was to succeed.

I was rudely knocked out of my memory by Joseph standing at my table, beaming a wide grin and laughing. "You asleep wide awake!" he jibed.

"I'm sorry—I was daydreaming!"

"No, don't be sorry, it's good to have dreams. We would be nothing without them."

I returned his smile and motioned him to sit down. The sun streaked across our eyes and I was glad to hide mine behind my sunglasses and away from his stare.

"Are you going to the dance tonight?"

"Yes, we all are—we mostly do things together in our group," I replied.

"That is good then. I will see you there." He rose politely and sailed across the arena, gliding like a little boat with freshly puffed-out sails billowing in the wind.

It was late afternoon and time to meander back to the homestead to get ready for the evening. Simonise, Ed, and I had agreed to meet for dinner in a special restaurant they had found called "The Sun" which was reputed to be the best in town. Back at the homestead I felt like an intruder walking in on the family television scene where they were all glued to the set watching a popular Cuban soap. I asked them if there was any news of the hurricane and they pointed to a little sign on the top of the screen which indicated the hurricane alert. It wasn't yet imminent but was growling in the distance. Upstairs, Simonise was almost ready and looked refreshed and eager to get out. We both found the family difficult to live with, especially Margarita, but we weren't complainers and besides, it wasn't anything specific that we could explain. We glided back through the family gathering, disregarding Margarita's suspicious glare.

Edgar's house was not too far away but when we reached it the door was wide open and there was a commotion inside. Edgar came out anxiously and explained that they had been visited by the police—there had been a raid next door. It seemed that his neighbours had more than their quota of visitors and had been reported to the police. In Cuba neighbours were encouraged to spy upon neighbours. The daughter of Edgar's household came out and explained the situation. She said that Cubans had to live off rations and oftentimes the rations didn't appear in the shops until late and if they didn't collect their portion at the allotted time, they lost it. Cubans were not allowed to eat what the visitors ate, especially things like lobsters, which were for tourists only. If by any chance they acquired a lobster, the remains had to be concealed in a bag to be buried in the forest where the evidence could not be found. There were very strict rules about entertaining paying guests and they could house only so many per year. Everything had to be logged and checked by the police. Our passports had to be verified at the police station and everything that we ate or drank had to be recorded in a book that had to be ready for inspection at all times. Neighbours spied on neighbours to ensure no one cheated the system. The young girl told Edgar he mustn't be upset—it was a regular occurrence. The neighbours had broken many of the rules, including eating things that were forbidden. We thanked her for her explanation and felt sorry for her situation.

As we walked away we began to appreciate the reality of living under such strict rules. I felt guilty at eating so well at the hotel in Havana. But as Simonise pointed out, my infusion of money into the economy gave people jobs and that was a good thing. Eventually we found The Sun, which was a converted house. The front room had beautifully polished bare floorboards with antique furniture and gold ornate mirrors. The restaurant was already full but the waiter managed to find us a table. We waited for almost an hour before our food arrived but we drank wine and ate bread and chatted, listening to the families' conversations around us, and feeling drawn into the bosom of the town. Around nine o'clock we meandered down the main street to meet the others. It was early for the dance and easy to get a drink at the outhouse on the hill. We whiled away the time drinking and exchanging stories of our homesteads until the night enclosed the dance arena in a thick, dark blanket and the disco lights blinked and winked different colours that bounced through the gathering crowd. The music began and the dancing took off as everyone swarmed onto the dance floor. The trees swayed to our beat as the dancers swirled in unison to popular songs that the people sang, blending their bodies with the rhythm. Our group joined the throng and experimented with our new steps.

Amongst the masses of faces I spied Joseph watching from afar. He nodded to me and I smiled a response. He joined our group and began to dance with me. A little black face at the edge of the crowd followed his every move. Joseph saw me gazing at the child and told me that she was his daughter. It made me feel uncomfortable, as did his interest in me—I had no wish to be anything other than just friends, as I had promised Saul to always be faithful. I would never break my promise. We had a couple of dances together then I sat out with Paddy who had received treatment from a local dentist and felt much better. Together we enjoyed the spectacle of the dancers gyrating and swinging under the starlit canopy. I didn't stay long at the dance and managed to slip away before Joseph found me again. Not wishing to disturb the others, I left a message with Paddy to say that I had gone home.

There was no sign of the hurricane and all seemed at peace. I knew my way and it was early enough not to be in any danger, not that I would have been at risk since there were so many police around and it was a peaceful town. Back at the homestead all was quiet and I tried to surreptitiously unlock my room, but Margarita was like a boxer watchdog. She prowled behind me and made sure I went to my bedroom and didn't lurk around downstairs. I flopped onto the bed and thought of Saul; he seemed very far away. His note for the day read:

> Hello Baby,
> I hope that you have been faithful and thought about me every day. I have written to you daily but I understand the post can be slow in Cuba.
> I love you,
> Really love you,
> I know this because I did before you left and absence makes the heart grow fonder,
> Love, Saul

I read it and reread it, feeling happy and secure in our love and relieved that I had left the dance early. I began to paint a rosy picture in my mind of our new life together and I thought of all the wonderful things we had planned, but the more I tried to landscape my wishes for the future, the more I was dragged back to the past. My subconscious demanded to complete the memories of my visit to Knossos with Anne and our mission to give Izatah a loving funeral.

CHAPTER 12

A Funeral for Izatah

"Don't leave the ending till the end, you must prepare for it and you must prepare your audience for it, for it is the last image they will have of the dance." (Doris Humphrey)

I slipped effortlessly into the memory of my visit to Crete with Anne, returning to the Sunday morning we were scheduled to visit Knossos. I woke very early, hoping to conjure a special line of energy by blending the sun and moon together to form a shield of strength against the evil force which was intent on preventing Anne and I in our quest to give Izatah a loving funeral. It was around five, just before dawn, that I planned to go down to the swimming pool before anyone was around and slide into the water in a baptismal ceremony, spiritually cleansing myself, whilst aligning my mind and body to the great orbs in the sky. The thought of getting up in the dark was daunting, even more the idea of getting into a cold swimming pool. I argued with myself until I dared myself to get up despite my fear of the water—I was not a swimmer and I hated the cold. I put on my swimming costume, wrapped up warm in a long towel, and tip-toed out into the empty corridor.

I ran barefoot down the stairs into the dark. The freak storm had worn itself out. Stray cats played hide and seek in the bushes and kittens fought amongst themselves for scraps of food left near the tables. A cool breeze blowing inland from the sea rippled the water. The only sound was the gentle lap, lap as the waves hit the sides of the pool. The surface was littered with bits of leaves and twigs that had been hurled into the pool by the torrent, plus dead bugs and half-alive insects with their legs still struggling in the air to keep afloat. I was afraid to get into the water and wanted to run back upstairs. I looked up into the sky. It was a smooth aubergine night with stars curtaining the cosmos. I had to do it! I couldn't turn away. I had to get in the murky water.

Placing my towel on an empty chair, I took a deep breath and lowered myself into the pool. The sharp, icy cold cut through every nerve and numbed all my senses. My breath disappeared into my ribs and rendered me immobile for a few seconds until I struggled to regain it, grabbing quick short, sharp intakes until I was able to breathe regularly through the heavy weight of the mass of water on my chest. I heaved myself up and down and began to swim as fast as I could. At first it hurt, but then I got into a rhythm and warmth flooded back into my veins and my body. I tried to ignore the debris lying on the surface. Birds swooped and dived around me, feeding off the insects, attacking like flying torpedoes, but I swam on, becoming warmer and more confident and enjoying the thrill of the dare. More cats came out to play from under the bushes and kittens devised games of "king of the castle" trying to knock each other off the sun beds.

I managed to swim two lengths, pausing in the middle of the pool where my feet touched the bottom and I could stand comfortably surveying the sky. On my right the moon and stars kept vigil, but to my left streaks of pink and gold tinged with orange bled away the night as the sun appeared in a halo of white. Dual jewels in the cosmos shone, exchanging rays. I was privileged to witness this intercourse of the magical orbs: sun and moon holding court; king and queen of the universe giving birth to a new day; the light keeper and the night watcher in harmony with the universe. Together they formed the light and the life of our planet and I asked for strength to keep both Anne and I safe in our trial. After a while the water grew icy and I swam, watching the day sweep away the blackness with a flourish of blues chasing white clouds across a bright sun. When the moon vanished, I knew I was ready to face the day's ordeal. It was Sunday morning and I needed to prepare for breakfast and take a shower.

I called for Anne and she informed me that the storm was the main topic on the local news. As we passed into the dining room conversation sparked from each table echoing the storm's devilment, as people exchanged stories of how equipment had been wrecked and how terrible it was that the wedding celebrations had been spoilt. The strange thing was that the hotel was the only area that had been targeted. The attack was localised— farther along the coastline there had not been one element of disturbance, not even a chilly wind! The locals said they had never known anything like it. The more we heard the more we were convinced that it was not just coincidence, and yet it was so hard to believe that our presence had stirred up such turmoil.

We sat down in the shade to eat breakfast as the sun shone on the white flagstones that had by then been swept clean of the storm's debris. The sea, undulating softly in a myriad of deep blues and dark greens, was as tranquil as the Sunday peace that hovered over the hotel and curled around the village. Sunday calm oozed into the fabric of the day as the Greek Orthodox mass filled the air, relayed through loudspeakers in the garden. The blood-red hibiscus flowers renewed afresh from the previous night's plunder held their delicate heads upward, revealing pollen-stained stamens. As I gazed into their rosy world, my own tumbled around and around, swirling out of control. I pulled myself back, focussing on the dazzling patterns whirling across the swimming pool like spinning tops across emerald green ice, but the pull from beyond was too strong, especially when the soft pad of sandaled feet echoed across the white slabs.

Flip, flop—plump toes padded in the early morning haze. The servant's hair was swept away from her face and garlanded

159

in pink hibiscus flowers. She carried rose petal water in a pot jar on her shoulder, passing through hibiscus bushes that waved cheerily as she went about her daily chores obeying the spider queen's bidding. It was a scene I knew so well somewhere in my head. The vision was as clear as reality. In a whirl of hibiscus petals I viewed her world through floral-tinted lenses, following her as she slipped her sandals from her feet without spilling any water as she entered the queen's chambers. Queen's chambers? Reason defied the apparition. Anne watched thoughtfully as I returned to the present. I explained the phantom scene of the servant girl from the palace appearing like a Polynesian maid from one of Gauguin's paintings. Anne nodded; she had come to recognise when I was in a trance and accepted it as normal.

Fear coiled like a spring waiting to pounce and I began to shake as we made our way through the dining room. Cold sweat dripped down my back. I needed to get away from the eyes, the stares, the glares of the diners. We had two hours to wait before the taxi was due at eleven o'clock and I wanted to meditate and quietly prepare for the ordeal ahead. I knew something was going to happen and I was nervous, scared that Anne might get hurt. The evil force had demonstrated its presence in untold ways and it was inevitable that a battle of wills would ensue. When I met Anne in the foyer later, she was serene, smiling in her eccentric English manner, determined to stride forth with a smile and a song in a Vera Lynn, "Sweetheart of the Forces" fashion.

I was subdued as we climbed into the taxi. The Greek Orthodox service was being chanted over the radio and the driver was silent as he put the car into gear. He was listening to the congregation's responses whilst miming his own. With the blessing and hymn relayed over the radio our funeral service had already begun. Anne and I reverently listened and didn't attempt to speak; it was as though the service had been prearranged. Our taxi meandered gently up and down the mountains with breathtaking views at every angle; on one side there was the vast expanse of azure-blue sea cupped by majestic jagged rocks and on the other, miles of meadows strewn with wildflowers and delicate grasses quivering in the gentle breeze. The ride was an ascent into heavenly realms, with just Anne and me and no other cars or traffic to mar our perfect journey. We flew along tiny coastal roads then soared into craggy caverns above, until we neared the outskirts of the palace.

It was as before: a sacrilegious shock to see the rows of silly trinket stores and souvenir stands lining the main street with scores of buses parked in rows in the coach station. Our taxi driver dropped us off and on receiving a hefty tip wished us a happy day. There were not as many people packing the entrance as on my first visit when it was a scorching hot August, so Anne and I began to wander around like ordinary tourists, preferring not to be accompanied by a guide. We picked our way down toward the great hall where memories of the little princess were stored and came to life when I spied the huge pots, the honey jars, and the grain stores with the smell of the goat grease torches. I saw the child lying in a dark corner coiled under a sack. Simultaneously I felt her pain. A lump formed in my throat and I found it hard to swallow. Anne handed me a tissue and was silent while I wiped away the welling tears. The image, the gut reaction, and the panic rose from nowhere unbidden. My sadness was so deeply rooted that I was overwhelmed. I steadied myself in the corridor, the dark corridor, the corridor where she fled every night in her filthy torn shirt with her matted cropped hair like a farm boy. Images of her haunted me everywhere.

We didn't stay very long in the great store hall as the memories were too shocking and oppressive, so we ambled out where the calm blue sky was a perfect canopy to what was once a world set apart from the world. Anne led the way and began to saunter through rubble and climb up steps without any handrails, her elegant silver curls bobbing in the breeze, while I trailed behind her, fearful she might slip at any moment. Unaware of any danger, she tip-toed in and around gaping holes, stepping confidently over jutting out rocks, striding up stairs without help along crusty ledges, while I, like a nagging nanny, hovered behind her.

"Are you alright?" she queried.

"Err…yes!" I affirmed, afraid to explain that I was overcome with nervous apprehension in case an evil energy might send her reeling headlong down a hole, or make her stumble down the stairs, or push her crashing over a ledge. I didn't want to alarm her and I tried to hide my rising fears by steering her back to the main body of the palace.

The wall paintings peered shamefully down at us. They were once so vibrant, so alive and powerful. The faded, jaded remnants of their erstwhile forms were pitiful, rendered impotent by the weight of years. Being an artist, Anne loved them but she didn't apprehend their power that I had remembered experiencing the paintings through Izatah's eyes. As we stood in the great hall, the memory of the wedding ceremony's crushing atmosphere gushed back in waves. I remembered the heat from all the candles and the cloying, sticky-sweet smell of the incense that had nauseated me. Izatah's tiny body, bedecked in gold and jewels and weighted down in a heavy ancient costume, was distressing to witness again as she stood obediently waiting with her baby brother and his nurse amidst the banging and crashing of cymbals, with long horn rallies resounding and bounding through the grand hall. She looked so small, so vulnerable, so innocent. Her reaction when she saw Chryanaida was that of a child's truthful observation, like the child's innocent voice through the crowd in the story of the King's Magic Clothes, when he was the only one who dared to scream out the truth. I swallowed back the words gripping my throat and the sounds tearing from my mouth: "The painted bitch on heat is a spider!" The ceremony was cut dead. In the ensuing silence it was almost funny, especially when little Vangelis repeated the words in a nursery rhyme twang. I had to go outside and get some air. The flashback was too strong and distressing.

I sat down on a boulder outside and viewed the panoramic vista, noting where the sloping shrubs met the forest and the forest defined the crops and the crops yielded to the rocks and the rocks framed the mountains and through the valley beyond, on a fine day, you could just spy the sea. Her memories were still with me. I retained her knowledge. From there we viewed the throne room with its single throne looking out to the world, with its large pot standing ready at its feet.

"Do you think the king had his feet washed in that, like Jesus?" enquired Anne in her quaint way.

I laughed. "The high priest screed there!" I replied without thinking, without knowing what I was really saying.

"What does that mean?"

"Well, screeing is a skill where you can see things across the water in the pot. They appear like visions in a crystal ball. Some people scree by the light of the moon or under the strong rays of the sun, or you can screw your eyes up like this and gaze out at the sky and see all kinds of weird shapes and forms!"

My vision from seeing the large vessel filled me with disgust. A deceitful high priest had given the king a false divination. He lied about Chryanaida, painting her to be saint-like and a wonderful mother substitute for his dead wife. The priest was in her pay and part of a long-term plan for her and her entourage to take over the reign. My vision faded as we moved on to the queen's bathroom. I remembered it well! The bathroom with its china blue patterns. Laying in the dust were fragments of the pottery. Anne picked up a few pieces, exclaiming, "My goodness, these are your dresses!"

"What?"

"The dresses you designed and created for your dance performance at Wembley Stadium for the World of Dance. You remember: the ones we could have sold at the exhibition, time and time again. Well, look—these are the very designs in the same colours!"

I was flabbergasted. I took the pieces from her hand and examined them closely. She was right. I had spent hours, days, designing nine dresses for our special performance at Wembley Stadium, creating unusual patterns which were lodged in my subconscious. The dresses were unusual and we had many offers from strangers to buy them, but they were not for sale. I marvelled at how the intricate detail on the tiles was the same as my dresses. Anne was not surprised—the evidence was clear that I held a latent recollection of the motifs from the queen's bathroom tiles. It was extraordinary how the shapes and colours were identical. I traced the remaining patterns on the walls with my finger, visualizing my dresses. I knew these shapes.

We walked out into the morning brightness and were both silent. The proof of Izatah's existence and my experience with her was certainly substantiated by the bathroom designs. I could not have invented the exact patterns without intimate prior knowledge. I pondered the evidence as we walked along to other parts of the palace that I remembered with sadness. I had no idea why I had been taken back to witness her death or whether she was me and the eternal grievance lying suspended in the fabric of the bricks, in the dust, in the rubble had to be unearthed, brought out into the open, and laid to rest. Sensing an image of Izatah's final resting place, I led Anne toward where I thought it might be. Somewhere on the outskirts of the main buildings, away from the thoroughfare and hubbub of the daily palace, I knew it existed. After wandering for a while down toward the edge of the main ruins, through boulders and over piles of bricks, I spied it. A huge boulder lay across the entrance to a small chamber. I recognised it. A sign near the doorway explained that an unusual freak electric storm had caused the boulder to be dislodged and roll in front of the chamber where it had remained untouched ever since. I knew it immediately. I saw it all again and felt everything as though I were she...

In the half light, Xabin stood guard by the door. The air was thick with the smell of the goat's grease lamp as it flickered and spat like an angry cat. My legs hurt. They were bound tightly together with a long piece of rough cloth with my right foot tied over my left. My body was wet, my clothes were soaking. The bed was rough and damp. I coughed a hoarse cry to Xabin. He dared to venture close and, kneeling beside the bed, wiped my brow. His eyes were full of tears. Burning sharp pains like needles jabbing into my bones shot up my legs. A presence hovered near the door and the smell of animal musk and frankincense invaded the tiny space. The queen oozed sparkling jewels from head to toe. Firestones dripped from her ears and her neck was ablaze with yellow and crimson nuggets glinting in the glow of the flaming lamp. Like a viper she slowly reared her head with deliberate pleasure to gloat. Pausing above me she extended her neck upwards, cobra-like, waiting in stillness before striking. The lamp spat, the lamp flickered, the lamp marked time like an executioner waiting in the wings. Who will pay the hooded shadow lurking in the corner? Who will pay the ferryman?

Her presence faded. I could not see. She left but her smell remained. I turned my head sideways to smile at Xabin. He was crying. Through the final haze a dancer softly trod. She floated toward me like fairy dust on dandelion seeds, blown from the winds of time, drifting from the future. She curled and spun, wearing a dress designed with china blue patterns like the sea motifs I knew so well. She danced for me. She held my hand. Her green eyes shone with joy and her hair the colour of autumn corn curtained across my face and felt soft as she lifted me up. I knew her, she knew me. We were one in past, present, and future. She cradled me in her arms like a baby and listened to my story. Suddenly the room was alive with children smiling, laughing, singing, dancing under bright lights, twirling and swirling together in harmony. I was one with them. We were a family. My legs were free at last. There was no pain. We danced out together as the sky cracked the earth beneath our feet with bolts of pink lightning in a magnificent finale. Nature in her anger finally sealed the door.

As I came out of the trance I was distraught, yet happy and relieved. Was I the dancer from the future who appeared to her? Or was I both? Was Izatah me, and did an extension of myself appear from the future to take her away? I didn't know. I didn't have any answers; I only felt what happened from both sides. Anne didn't have to speak. She shared my grief and my release. As we walked away from the tomb, the womb of Izatah's last breath, the silence surrounded us, lassoing us into an isolated corral of stillness. All the tourists faded away, leaving just the two of us marooned in a dry desert of dust and decay. Time stopped and the sky obeyed. Clouds were motionless and grew grey shrouds as darkness descended.

I held Anne's hand and above a sudden rising wind I shouted to her to stay still. The air disappeared. It was hard to breathe— we were stranded in a bleak sandstorm. I clutched Anne's hand harder as an unknown force struck me hard on the forehead and I momentarily dropped down. Anne began shrieking and cursing against the force but I told her to stop and think only good thoughts, embrace only good energy. As we looked up, we saw that something from the top of the hill was rolling toward us. Through the dust pool we could make out a large circle like a boulder of tumbleweed picking up speed as it hurtled towards us. I mustered up every single ounce of inner energy and wrapped it around us like a shield. I visualized a glowing white wall protecting us, and recited, "We are perfect children of the universe. Nothing and no one can harm us!"

The sphere of evil bounding toward us struck but passed through our bodies, disintegrating in a pile of dust behind us. At that moment the sun shot out from behind the clouds, illuminating a scene of two women clutching each other on an ordinary pathway, while an ordinary day in an ordinary way was unravelling time with ordinary tourists performing ordinary tourist activities, scrambling over the rocks, laughing, calling to each other and drinking bottles of water.

From our extraordinary happening we returned to a very ordinary, everyday scene. We stood gridlocked, unable to move forwards or backwards, unable to comprehend what had happened to us. We both experienced the same, so it wasn't one of my visions. When we could speak, we both described what we had witnessed in order to consolidate our evidence. We both had been attacked by the unseen force and Anne had been horrified when it struck me on the forehead. What we both found hard to understand was how we could have slipped time and been isolated from the busy tourists in a sandstorm that obviously didn't exist for anyone else, and how could we have been attacked without anyone seeing it or coming to our aid. It was a mystery and we were both traumatized. I knew something was going to happen but I hadn't envisaged anything as dramatic or sinister.

After a short while, we were able to walk. We agreed that we needed a drink.

"It's over. We've done it! You've laid her memory to rest and defeated the enemy!" Anne made it sound like a Saint George and the Dragon story. She was right—we had succeeded, but the story was not over. Izatah's memory had been laid to rest, but I needed to track down more evidence of what she had shown me. I had to find verification and authentication of the king's ring with the Minotaur seal. It was so real to me that I had no doubts about its existence. I also needed to learn more about Chryanaida and the terrible reign of fear and torture in the palace. I needed to know what happened to her.

As we sat in shock with two large gin and tonics, I explained my intentions. Anne nodded, also believing in the artefact's existence. Our unbelievable experience together was something neither of us would ever forget, and it united us in an even deeper bond. The success of our mission gave us glorious, victorious satisfaction and I loved Anne for believing in me and for giving Izatah the funeral. We made plans to visit Athens on our way home and go to the great museum to investigate the Minotaur ring.

After our incredible experience at Knossos, things became calmer and we settled into enjoying a wonderful break away from all the stresses and strains in England. Our visit to Athens was exciting and I wished desperately to see the ring I had seen through Izatah's eyes. We were not able to see the curator of the museum, but a young assistant listened to my wish to search out the ring. She escorted us to many glass cases of objects found at the Knossos site and left us alone to wander through the maze of objects on display. We saw many pots, utensils, and jewellery all inscribed with Minoan detail but there was nothing that vaguely matched the ring.

Disappointed, we sat under the shade of a cluster of trees above the museum and watched the city at work. Stray cats came to our table to beg and as both Anne and I love cats we indulged their needs by feeding them leftover scraps. Just as I was venting my frustration at not finding the ring, music drifted across the rooftops and echoed around the small courtyard. English lyrics bounced in disco rhythms:

> Children of the world unite,
> stand up and fight for what is right,
> Don't give up your search
> for love,
> Let your guiding star
> above
> Reach out and touch the world
> Unite.

"Well, that's your message then," said Anne defiantly.

"I know," I replied. "I am not going to give up now, not after what we've been through. I know the ring exists and I will find it. I will prove what she showed me exists!"

CHAPTER 13

Chan Chan

"The rhythm of life is a powerful beat..."
(The Rhythm of Life)

Our time in Cuba de Trinidad was racing by. Our exciting drumming lessons had become part of our daily ritual, with practice in the morning and dance lessons in the afternoon. We were learning two songs to sing and play for our recording. Paddy occasionally played the cow bell even though he wasn't comfortable with it. He never hit it on cue; sometimes he dinged it twice by mistake in the wrong place, or dropped it, making an embarrassing clanging across the stage. Ed also struggled at times but managed a few secure sections, whereas most of us were reasonably competent at the basic rhythms, often practicing on each other's hands whilst waiting for drinks or food in restaurants.

One of the songs we were learning was "Chan Chan." It has a popular, recognisable melody with a strong drum rhythm that made exact timing imperative. Joseph was very patient, coaxing us with his gentle touch, taking our hands and placing them on the drum skins with the right amount of pressure applied by altering the shape of our fingers. As we played, I felt connected to the roots of Cuban music: the African folk beat was preserved in the ethnic associations, the *cabildos*, that sustained the African slaves brought to the island. *Cabildos* held the African traditions together even after the Emancipation in 1886 when they were forced to unite with the Catholic Church, but their true religious convictions came to life in the *Santería* movement with its voodoo overtones and strong influence in popular music of Cuba today.

Hilary and I were forging ahead with our dance lessons and enjoyed much praise from our teachers. What we learnt during the day we were able to put into practice in the evening. I never for one moment let the pain in my knee and leg prevent me from giving my body and soul fully to the dance. Always on the island there was a celebration of music somewhere, somehow, taking shape in many different forms under a myriad of influences but whatever the style, the heart and the passion of the music was the people's soul—the true life blood, the force of their being. We were so privileged to be part of the zeal and zest of their life. The colours, the taste, the craze and obsession of the marriage between the dance and the music were total and will be forever immortalised in the essence of the communities' perpetual ritual, handed down through the ages. Every night we were soaked to our bones with raw emotion of the magic and motion, of fixation and contamination of the real Cuban beat. We were hooked, infected, injected with the all-embracing core of the island. Our days passed bound by the internal beat and the heat of the moment, and with the hurricane threat always in the background we savoured every moment of our stay, but on our last day the hurricane had changed its course and was making for a direct hit to our coastline. The television and radio stations alerted everyone to the new threat, whipping up renewed apprehension.

It was early afternoon on our last day in Trinidad de Cuba when our group decided after our drumming lesson to go to the beach. I am not a sunbathing beach person—being fair-skinned I have to be very careful as I burn easily and most of the time have to hide under towels—but I agreed to go with the party. If anything, I could be useful watching their belongings whilst they swam. The beach was beautiful, with long white stretches of Caribbean sand tipped with azure blue inlets of water curling inland, speckled with palms and luscious exotic fruit trees. Under a pile of clothes with a tee shirt on my head and towels over my body, I lay on the beach mummified against the raging heat, while the others blissfully lay out half-naked under the broiling sun or lashed about in the warm sea while local families and visitors enjoyed a barbecued beach lunch. The smell of sizzling onions, fresh fried hamburgers, and seafood was tantalizing.

Simonise persuaded me to have a dip in the sea but I was self-conscious of my plump white body and smothered myself in another layer of sun cream before gingerly immersing myself in the surf. Once in, I enjoyed it, but being a wimp in the sea, I was afraid of my feet touching something lurking below, or a jellyfish floating in my direction, or anything which lay on the surface. After a few feeble attempts at swimming I slumped back on the sand and covered myself up again, afraid of burning. Suddenly a warning bell sounded down the length of the beach. It was a hurricane warning. People acted swiftly to pack away and within minutes the crowded beach was deserted, leaving a few stray visitors awkwardly piling away their belongings, bewildered and nervous in their attempts to evacuate the place. My group was among the stragglers.

My phone rang. It was Saul. He had seen on the television that the cyclone was heading in our direction. He expressed his love for me, pleading, "Please, please come home to me safely! I need you!" I was equally upset and needed him more than ever in that fearful moment. I understood how lovers in wartime craved each other. We could only snatch a few brief words forcing us to say more in our anxiety, proclaiming our love through urgency. His voice crackled over the airwaves and disappeared as our party switched gears and moved swiftly into waiting cars eager to race us back to our homesteads. Simonise and I, sun-kissed, windswept, and sand-blasted, rushed into the house where the family were once again gathered around the television.

"We just heard the news!" said Simonise nervously.

"Oh, nothing to worry about. It may not strike, and anyhow it's not that ferocious. We've had much worse!" stated Alfonse nonchalantly.

We climbed the stairs to shower, eager to prepare for our final round of events. It was our last day and we were scheduled to cut our disc and I needed to take my last dance lesson to complete my course. After a leisurely existence, time was running out and it seemed we had so much to finish within a brief period, plus the hurricane threat meant pressure rising from every level. I changed into one of my best dresses—burnt orange with designer beads strung around the neck—and hurried down the main street. Uneasiness hovered in the empty stillness; I was overpowered by a sense of watchfulness behind barricaded shutters. Inside the house where I had my lesson the family were adding extra protection to the outside windows. My teachers were ready for my final lesson which was joyful, as I managed to fit all the different sections together in a sequence, but sad because I knew we would never have the chance to meet again. The hour passed too quickly in the sweltering humidity and I was tearful when I left Angelica and Enrico. We had forged a firm friendship and I would never forget the uniqueness of being taught salsa with a raging storm beating a cyclonic pulse alongside the sound of razor-sharp trumpets blasting through the rain and the wind.

Saddened, and with fond farewells echoing, I made my way to our drumming bar where we were to cut our disc. After all the practice I was a little nervous because Joseph and Carlos were to make their final choices of who was going to play what, where, and how and who was going to sing. As I entered the spacious arena, the bar that I had come to love and know so well as the home of our percussion lessons was fresh with afternoon rain glistening from the trees and floral canopies. Extra instruments were set out on the stage alongside our drums and I felt a knot of excitement as I spied the electric piano. Dancing and playing the piano has been my life's passion and I suddenly yearned to place my fingers on the keys. The group had no idea that I played and I itched to spring into action.

As we all gathered around the wet tables drying in the sun, our music technician introduced himself while Carol stood by to check that all was going according to plan. I asked the technician if I could just run my fingers over the board while everyone prepared for the session. He didn't mind and switched it on for me. The others at first didn't take any notice but after the first few notes strayed out into the arena, they stopped and listened. Carlos jumped to his drums, adding his own distinctive style. We filled the auditorium with a live improvisation taking leads from each other. I immersed myself into the soul of the keyboard, having been in a drought of playing for some time since the journey began. I let my fingers drink their fill, striking melodies and chords, riding up and down chromatics, and gliding through arpeggios while Carlos kept the pulse, inventing rich riffs to enhance the performance. At the end, the group burst into spontaneous applause and even wanted us to put the piece onto the disc. Joseph came up to me and led me off the stage kissing my fingers, saying, "I did not know you were so talented!"

Once the technicians were ready we practised our pieces. Joseph and Carlos were fair in their final decision, giving us all a chance to sing and play. Paddy was not confident with his cowbell but had a go and, strictly conducted by Joseph, he managed to ding in the right places. The session was fun and we were thrilled to have had the chance to make the disc which would be ready for our departure the next day. For our CD cover, Ed suggested that we take a photograph of everyone rushing toward the gate as though we were on the run escaping. We all thought it was a good idea and after rushing at the gate a few times we managed to get the right shot. It was late afternoon and the group were invited to a special performance by Carlos and Joseph in the bar in the early evening. Just as I was leaving, Joseph came up to me and invited me to take coffee with him. I accepted. We talked about music and his family and our combined interests. Then he looked at me with a serious gaze.

"The first time I saw you, my heart go…," and he beat a perfect rhythm across his chest. "

I smiled. I wasn't sure what to say or how to react. My Spanish was not very fluent and although I understood much more than I could express, it was difficult to relay my feelings without hurting his. I told him I had enjoyed the lessons very much, that he was a good teacher, and that I was looking forward to watching him perform but I could not return his passion. He sighed and kissed my hand. I excused myself and walked out of the bar as the wind began to whine around the tables with a low-pitched warning.

A couple of hours raced by and all too soon we were gathered again in the bar for the instructors' special performance. Carlos used his amazing percussion skills to blend in with Joseph's dance, mime, acting, and percussion talent. The performance began with a blessing of lit candles and lanterns which set a mysterious tone to the magical atmosphere sweeping through the twilight haze of early evening, especially as the pre-cyclonic pressure in the air began to rise. I was totally wrapped in Joseph's spell and I was taken to realms beyond, as his eyes guided me through emotion wrapped in song and mime. He whipped me up into his landscape like a baby in his arms and rocked me gently in a soft lullaby of love. By the end of the performance I was captured in a charm and hated to be brought back down to earth with the crash of applause. I rose to thank Carlos and Joseph for an amazing performance, and Joseph kissed me on the cheek and asked me if I was going to the dance in the cave that evening but I wasn't sure, as the group had organised our last dinner together and I did not know what they intended afterwards. I followed the group out into the darkening street feeling sad; it was like leaving a new-found family.

Our last meal together in Trinidad was jolly and lighthearted with everyone contented that we had completed our recording session. We ate heartily and whiled away the night exchanging funny stories about each other. After the meal, the gang wanted to go and experience dancing in the cave, which was a high spot of the location. It was a massive cavern high in the mountains which had been transformed into a nightclub with disco lights and bars. I didn't feel I could face it. I was so tired and I knew that Joseph would be there. Not wanting to encourage his feelings, I returned alone to the homestead. The house was in darkness and Margarita and Alfonse were in bed behind the flimsy curtain next to our room.

Safely inside the bedroom, I sat on the bed in the broiling heat, glad that it was our last night. I checked my phone and Saul had left a message: "Please hurry home safely. I miss you more than I can say. You are the love of my life." I sent a message back reiterating my love for him and how I was longing to see him and start our new life together. I began to pack and prepare my luggage for the journey the next day. We were to make an early morning start before the hurricane was due to strike. It was so hot in the bedroom and no amount of air from the open window or electric fan gave any relief. I lay down on the bed, glad that it was my last night in the house. I closed my eyes and relived the intensity of the amazing performance we had witnessed. It was more than just an act: it was a religious ritual conjured up from slave heritage, paying homage to a lost homeland, spiced with touches of longing and love, soaked in mystery and magic, hinting at spirits and unspoken rites of the dead. Rites of the dead? I remembered Izatah and how Anne and I had given her a loving funeral in our hearts and how we fought the presence of evil together in a frozen moment outside the palace and how I had tried to trace the king's golden ring with the embossed bull's head.

After the museum in Athens had yielded nothing, I spent time back in England researching other sources but had no luck, yet I was not deterred from my investigation. I was determined that the ring existed and that I would find it. Unfortunately, ordinary everyday living exerted a stranglehold over my time and it was difficult to focus on the task, especially as Anne and I had successfully completed our special mission. Time dragged on and I had not managed to write Izatah's story—I had not the money to buy a computer nor the wherewithal to borrow one. Five years lapsed and I had moved back into York to give my son a sound basis for his final year at college before he went to university. During that time I secured an amazing post as Director of Performing Arts for a travel company based in London which spanned tuition across four different countries. I spent a great deal of time travelling backwards and forwards between York and Greece, Spain, Italy and France. One evening back home, I watched a television programme which had been filmed by my first boyfriend and learnt that he had made a name for himself filming television documentaries. For some reason I was compelled to contact him.

It was great to talk to him again after not seeing him for thirty years and we agreed to meet in London. He had made a film featuring the British Museum's new roof and he suggested that I spend an afternoon exploring it as he had some work to do in the studio. Having not been to the museum for many years, it was a great joy for me to see the innovative architecture and marvel at the structure of the massive glass roof. A thought tingled teasingly into being as I climbed the stairs: perhaps I would find the king's ring or some information leading to it. I rushed through the different antiquities sections until I came to a quiet region where stone artefacts gazed down from great perches and gigantic glass cabinets housed the past in congeries of reverent piles. I carefully scrutinised case after case, letting myself be led by my inner eyes and guided by vibrations from lost time, until I stood in front of a large display of jewellery.

I knew it was there but was almost afraid to look. Amidst the noise and the crowds of the vast museum, I suddenly stood alone. No one was around. In an eerie stillness I gazed at the ring. It was the very one I had seen through Izatah's eyes. A huge gold ring embossed with a bull's face and long horns curling upwards. I had found it! It existed for anyone and everyone to see! My long search was over. It was the last piece of evidence I needed to add to all the overriding data that my experience had been real. Apart from knowing Chryanaida's demise, I had all the missing parts to the story. I stood in awe for a long time in front of the case longing to touch it, seeing it again through Izatah's eyes as it glinted in the goat's grease torchlight the evening when Vangelis was born. Eventually I had to tear myself away as Izatah's memories began swirling, returning vividly.

I decided to go for a cup of coffee but when I got there the queue was enormous, so I left to browse through the shop. As I passed down a long line of souvenirs and tea towels, a book slipped off the shelf into my hands. It was a lovely picture book on ancient civilisations. I placed the book back without opening it and walked around to the other side of the shelf where the same-titled book slipped down as I walked past, nearly knocking over some pot hedgehogs. Amused, I picked up the book and placed it back again. Walking down another aisle I saw the same set of books displayed on a higher shelf and, again, the book jumped out and landed at my feet. This time the coincidence was too great, so I picked it up. The book fell open to a shocking picture.

It was her! Her eyes, her face, her mouth. Her! I froze. A mixture of emotions erupted, blowing like a sleeping volcano blasting into action. My hands shook. Chryanaida was alive on the page. Flushed with guilt for enjoying a vengeful thought, my eyes feasted on the picture greedily. Ashamed, I nonetheless revelled in just and glorious revenge as I witnessed the last moments of her execution at the hand of Mother Nature, whose fiery tongue licked and swallowed everything in her path. I delighted in her gaping cruel mouth prized wide in a defiant scream as the pillars of the temple crashed upon her. She writhed with bulging spider eyes agog in disbelief as the palace fell about her, destroying her empire, while her feeble spider mate tumbled helpless into the flames. It was a fitting end for her, to be incinerated in her own temple with her vile lover.

The picture depicted a rolling ball of fire gushing through the palace, destroying everything in its wake. The last horrific detail was the sight of a child lying on an altar, strapped down and anchored with arms and legs tethered with rough rope, while Chryanaida loomed over him with a sharp blade poised, ready to strike. The final detail cut into my heart, tearing me apart with disgust and horror of a bloody spider's mouth, chewing a twitching heart gouged from a small boy's chest; a tiny chest; an innocent body crushed and smashed down a flight of steps. She pushed him to his death—Vangelis, the little prince, the baby brother Izatah loved who was murdered, his body defiled like the child in the picture who was saved from her knife by the flames.

I did not know how the artist came to create the picture, but I do know that he was inspired by a source beyond this realm. The artist had tapped into the truth and captured her with shocking precision. The sight of her was overwhelming. Not only had I found the ring but I was shown the awful demise of the evil spider woman together with her contemptible spider mate.

I dropped the book, repulsed by the picture and the memories that were flooding back. I wanted to be alone and cry out the crazy stir-fried emotion sizzling in my head. I ran to the lavatories and locked the door. I was angry, sad, relieved, and happy that justice had taken a hand in her death. Everything made sense from a maze of disconnected events. Finally I had the full picture. My search and mission was complete—or was it?

CHAPTER 14

Che

Even when the dance is a solo, there is always a fleeting glimpse of an invisible partner and even when we think we are alone, there is always a presence closer than the air we breathe.

Early the next morning Simonise and I prepared to pack everything for our long journey back. We were glad it was our last breakfast in the house, having paid over the odds for our meals, but we didn't complain as Margarita gleefully took our money and bid us goodbye with an insincere farewell. As we trundled our bags along the hushed streets a cool breeze began to whip up the dust and we knew that the town would not side-step the attack; they were making ready for a direct strike. At Carol's homestead the packing, pulling, pushing, and squashing of bags into our little WaWa bus had begun and our driver was in a hurry to get us out of town. Simonise told me that Joseph had been looking for me at the cave and when I saw the others they relayed the same message. I handed over my bags to the driver and turned around to see Joseph standing behind me holding a small bunch of wildflowers carefully wrapped in pink tissue. He was like a schoolboy with cap in hand and bowed head giving the teacher a prized possession. I watched standing outside myself in the surreal scene, wearing a white locally handcrafted blouse and a long skirt that flapped in the wind around my legs. I felt strangely removed from my actions. The others discreetly disappeared as we walked into the cool front room of the homestead.

"Tranquillo, tranquillo!" he whispered. He hugged me and I began to cry. I had no idea why I was crying but the emotion of the moment beat me into submission. We didn't say anything, we just held each other briefly before Carol hurriedly ushered us all into the bus. Joseph stood by the side of the bus blowing kisses. His face was the sunshine drenched in fresh rain. The wind behind him gathered momentum. The bushes waved furiously as our bus cracked into action and nipped along the streets. I waved back at the man clutching his heart but I held Saul's ring and knew that I must not allow myself to be swayed by the tug of sentiment.

As our little bus beat along the outskirts of Trinidad, buzzing like a tormented bee escaping the ensuing rain, I had a flush of happy memories to save for later on a bleak day. I remembered all our happy times and the rush of raw excitement as I discovered the bartering market with Simonise and Hilary where you could exchange clothes for goods. I thought it was a great idea as my method of travelling light was to discard all clothes I didn't need and leave them for the staff or maids to find, gradually dwindling all the things in my backpack until I had enough room to take back souvenirs. One day, I collected tee shirts and shorts I no longer needed and bundled them up to take the primitive market. I wandered around for a while until I spied a black bead necklace and bangle. A tall African woman behind the rickety wooden stall took my clutch of clothes and inspected them. They were not washed but they were not filthy. She tried not to display any enthusiasm for the designer tee shirts and the up-to-date style of shorts. She said she could not let me have the jewellery, but when I wanted my clothes back she relented and gave me the beads, unable to disguise the glee in her eyes as she hung up my clothes with pride. Simonise and Hilary had not taken part in the exciting exercise and were happy to watch me, like a small child with a birthday present, almost skip along the potholed street carrying my prizes to a beautiful restaurant for lunch.

The sun was high in the sky that afternoon and fear of the impending hurricane had diminished, leaving a sleepy sigh descending over the laid back community. I never tired of peering into people's houses as we sauntered past, noting how the different cultures set out their living patterns in so many differing styles. It was intriguing to take a taste of their intimate ways back home. Always, everywhere in Cuba, the community celebrates their life with music. The soul of mambo, guaracha, cha-cha-cha, afro, canción, guaguancó, bolero, rumba, conga, and salsa—to name but a few genres—are an integral part of life's rhythm, as much as the ticking of the clock. Every wonderful experience is lived through melody and the beat of the drum. Our unforgettable lunch that day was sealed with the memory of magical music.

The Sexteto Ache played in the doorway of the restaurant with white crumbling cement flat roofs and decaying brickwork for their backdrop. The street outside was subdued in the midday heat. Symbolic of the roots of the people with their struggles of daily life uplifted by music, a single, bright red shiny door stood out against the damp, decomposing wooden window frames and shutters of our restaurant. The musicians, all dressed in navy, black, and white check shirts, were amazing. The group consisted mostly of old men who had spent a lifetime playing and entertaining the tourists. The sound of the muted trumpet sexily, soulfully stole into the soup and into the bread as the soft slosh of the maracas mixed with the chile sauce, inciting taste buds to cool in the minty fusion of the mojito. The accordion melted into the cheese, seasoning the occasion with the unforgettable flavour of raw Cuba.

Carol interrupted my flow of Trinidad memories by handing out our CDs. Everyone received our treasured trophies with rising apprehension as she played the results over the decrepit radio system. I was embarrassed by the offbeat rhythms and out of time sections, but nonetheless we had fused together and made an almost acceptable rendering of two of Cuba's favourite songs. It was something I would keep to play quietly to myself on a cold winter morning in England. Then Carol handed me a special medal my dance teachers had awarded to me for showing great flair and learning so many steps. They also awarded one to Hilary, as we had made the most progress in the short time we had to learn all the various intricate moves. I was thrilled to receive it and settled back in my seat to contemplate the incredible journey. That morning in the early half light in our homestead with Simonise peacefully dreaming, sleep swirled and curled in circles around my head. I drifted, submerged in a void of nothing, but rose to the surface on the edge of consciousness to hear a voice. I struggled to listen. The words were jumbled but a few remained, sustained in the front lobe of memory, so that when I fully awoke I retrieved them, listening to the recorded message in my brain: *"I was born living to fight and you were born fighting to live."*

I recognised the message and knew it could have sprung from only one source. He had spent his lifetime fighting a cause he wholeheartedly believed in, yet I think that by the time his energy was running out in Bolivia he had begun to see things in a different light. I am sure he did not regret anything connected with Cuba, but Bolivia had not responded to his expertise nor given him the backing he had been promised. On my travels throughout Cuba, I found him immortalised in the hearts, souls, and minds of the people. His memory would never be destroyed. Che was the hero I expected to find and I had not been disappointed. I was not sure that I knew the meaning of the message which had initiated my trip to Cuba, but I had found the soul of a man I had always admired and loved living on in the hearts and minds of the people. His wife and children must have found his lifestyle unforgivable at times, but I know from scrutinising his Bolivian diaries that he never forgot his children's birthdays or ever abandoned his love for them. Sometimes it is hard to separate dreams and imagination from what we think is reality. I did not dismiss his words but stored them in my memory bank.

The bus grumbled on and we listened to the radio. Two hours out of Trinidad we heard that the hurricane had struck the town.

We had missed it by a hair's breadth but were not yet out of the danger zone. I thought of Joseph and everyone we knew in the town and hoped they were all safe. I recalled my dance lessons in the stormy afternoons and how I had won all the steps through sheer determination and undiluted concentration. I thought of Saul and longed to be back safe with him, ploughing a new furrow together through our stress-worn world. Things never seem so bad when two people "face the music" and I knew he would be there to help me fight my tax investigation, which still hung over me like a burning sword, hovering, ready to chop my life in two. But I pushed that to the back of my mind and enjoyed the lush scenery of wild forests and scrub jungle.

We climbed high into the mountains and approached a small village about midday. The landscape reminded me of pictures I had seen of the wilderness in Bolivia where Che had made his hideout. The small farmhouses were similar to the one shown us where he had made contact with a farmer who provided him and his men with some food. It is recorded that Che healed the farmer's son whose eye was swollen and oozing with pus. He had performed a minor operation on him and given the boy medicine to clear the infection and within a short time the boy could see again. When I read the account I was moved to think that even in the desperate sieges of war, Che had time to be a doctor. His words returned: *"A true revolutionary's weapon is love!"*

Our little bus struggled up the steep slope to the village and came to a halt in an archaic square, cobbled with uneven round stones. Strung from one end of the village to the other was a huge washing line flapping with white linen. At first I thought it was wash day, but then I realised it was the women's way of displaying their craftwork. Lace, hand-woven cotton of all shapes and sizes, beautiful embroidered blouses and bed linen billowed in the breeze like huge sails on a shifting sea. At the far end of the undulating, rolling surf was an ancient tower, crumbling after centuries of neglect but still standing, leaning a little to one side like the leaning tower of Pisa. As we sailed out amongst the local women we were swamped by their calls; everyone invited us to inspect their goods for sale. Not wanting to be sucked into their clutches, I walked up the hill to a wonderful hotel perched in the middle of the scrub jungle, surrounded by amazing trees that I had never seen before. Their roots grew in entanglements of enormous knots, with spiky claws reaching skyward. I spent some time photographing them before making my way to the bar to order a fruit juice. Inside the foyer wonderful paintings were on display portraying the life of the slave worker in the fields. It was a strong statement against an unjust way of life that had been destroyed, leaving remnants of open scars in faraway places.

Somehow I felt close to Che in that lonely village where time hung still, caught in a web of tradition. The hotel spanned two worlds. The world outside its bricks and mortar thrashed around in a diurnal round of seasonal battering, while inside a serene scene painted in a civilised veneer kept the reality outside at bay. I meandered onto a veranda and found a wealth of huge posters of Che set out for inspection. Most of the photographs I had seen before but I found one which was the best photograph ever. The sepia portrait depicted a lighter, playful aspect of Che's nature, as he thumbed his nose to the photographer and, with a glint in his eye, stared upward towards someone with whom he was sharing a joke. The lighting around his head swathed him in an angelic halo, despite his schoolboy's mischievous look. I was alone on the balcony and snatched a quick photograph of the photograph.

The ramshackle huts and stone houses around the hotel were quiet because the women in the village were elsewhere chasing business. I wandered into the square and was swamped by a swarm of them pushing their wares under my nose. I protested that I didn't want to buy any linen but I saw a woman holding out strings of beads. She had about a hundred strung across her arms. She said she would sell me the whole lot for a small price. The beads were made out of pumpkin and fruit seeds and were uniquely designed. She had crafted them beautifully, varnishing each seed, creating lovely earthy jewellery. I decided they would make beautiful gifts for friends, so I bought all of them. She was thrilled and delighted and jumped up and down with glee, waving the money in the air. She wrapped some around my neck and draped the rest over both arms. Overwhelmed with garlands of beads, I boarded the bus and everyone cheered, laughing as I jangled into my seat.

Our next destination was Santa Clara which was founded in 1689 by the Spanish. It was the first city, in December 1958, to be liberated by the Revolutionary Forces. Eighteen men under Che's command fought against four hundred heavily armed government troops and commandeered an important armoured train in a strategic move toward bringing down the Batista government. I was looking forward to seeing the huge statue of Che erected to commemorate the twentieth anniversary of his murder in Bolivia, and to visiting where his last remains were buried.

In the bright sunshine we parked our little WaWa bus and made our way to the museum entrance. My stomach tumbled. I had not expected to feel so emotional. It seemed I had waited all my life to meet a man I would never meet. In the forefront of my mind I remembered the first glimpse of him. The picture on the tee shirt loomed toward me, calling out to the busy London pavement, while under the dim lights his face was illumined by soft shadows. I had gazed at his eyes and fell in love. It was a silly crush, but it has never left me. Sometimes there is a presence in our psyche which remains a part of our being, even through lifetimes and decades it survives. Oftentimes the pull draws the two forces together and for a brief lifetime they exist, but then are forced apart to travel destiny's path alone, one searching for the other with a distant memory clinging to the core of life until they meet again.

One day not long after her father and I divorced my youngest daughter, unprompted, said, "You know, Mummy, it might be that the person you really love is dead and that you will never find him in this lifetime!"

I was shocked by her words but listened as she had an uncanny gift of making strange statements out of the blue, which were forged from another dimension. I didn't want to accept it—it was too sad—but a string in my heart snapped as I pushed the thought away. It was important to live in the present and I couldn't accept anything else. I couldn't bear the thought of half a harmony forever waiting to find its symphony.

The monument to Che stood boldly at the top of a flight of white stone steps where he victoriously dares the world to challenge his purpose, proudly saluting the revolution. His final letter to Fidel proclaimed his unstoppable support to the cause and I was sad that he left his family's future in the government's hands, without directly providing for them. There was an unusual, respectful silence around Che's bronze figure, like in cemeteries lovingly tended for soldiers killed in the First and Second World Wars, where people walk slowly with care on the white gravel path and speak in close whispers. As I entered the museum a sombre note echoed down the hallway of a distant abbey and lingered by a headstone. Somehow it seemed all my life I had been waiting for this moment. Somewhere in the maze of glass cabinets and rows of ammunition Che's body lay in rest.

I followed the others and read the information hanging over each display. I looked at the photographs and soaked up the revolutionary enthusiasm that had burnt holes in lives and purged ways of living into the stranglehold of communism. I followed Che's skirmishes with the establishment and his victories shared with Fidel. I traced his rise to fame and examined the pictures of his famous interviews. I hurried along to gaze at the photograph of him on the morning before he was shot. I saw the picture of the schoolhouse where he spent the night in pain after being shot in his lower leg. Suddenly I had a connection: a vision of his face as he sat with his back against a crumbling wall with his matted, tangled hair frizzing out like candyfloss on a stick. The light from outside cast gentle shadows over his eyes. I saw the soldier on watch keeping guard with his loaded gun poised, ready for action. Che accepted his fate but did not believe at that point he would be murdered. It was peculiar how my first sight of Che blended with the picture of the old schoolhouse. A cold tremor tingled across my heart.

In the morning before his execution, Che stood outside in the bright sunshine, his face wracked with pain, but he allowed his photograph to be taken. The faraway look in his eyes hinted his acceptance of impending death yet still he did not believe he would be shot—he said, "I am worth more to you alive than dead." The soldiers around him—who half-eyed him with awe since he had slipped their traps and ambushes many times—did not believe either that Che would be killed, for although he was a heroic bandit, to them he was dangerous and unpredictable, needing to be stopped whatever the cost; so the soldiers waited obediently for orders. The air was not heavy with looming death but bright and victorious, for they had captured a rare prize. The commander nursed a personal vendetta against Che and was hell-bent on wreaking revenge. He waited while the news of Che's capture was relayed and relayed again across the nations. Che was certain that he would be rescued. The seconds, minutes, hours ticked by until the news came through that he must be shot. When the moment finally came the officer hesitated, but Che said, "Shoot, you coward—you're only killing a man."

The photograph of his dead body lying on an old wooden trestle table was shocking, and the sight of a Bolivian officer standing over him pressing his index finger into the bullet hole near his heart was disgusting, yet in Che's face there was only peace and victory. The nuns who cleaned up his body at Vallegrande said he looked like a modern-day Jesus. The army did not wish to have the creation of a saint on their hands or encourage pilgrimages to Che's grave, so they agreed to have his body secretly thrown into a hole near the landing strip at Vallegrande. Eventually pressure was put on General Hernan Aguilera to reveal where Che was buried and by July 1997 it was announced that the body had been identified. His hands were chopped off and preserved in formaldehyde to assert his identity. His hands returned to Cuba long before the rest of his body. The words "his hands were chopped off" cut into my heart. I read the words innocently yet they stabbed into my vulnerability. "His hands" echoed around and around in my brain.

In the quiet of the moment, tears welled and I felt silly trying to hide my emotions from the rest of the group. I needed to be alone, and made for a sign indicating Che's burial parlour. With streaming eyes I entered the sanctified mausoleum. It hadn't occurred to me just how unusual it was that in the large museum with so many visitors, suddenly I was totally alone. Just Che and me! I approached the grave and watched the tiny, red tea light flickering. I had wanted to speak to him and meet him ever since I first saw his face. I stood shaking, peering at the foliage around the gravel laid out by his resting place. He was not there. His presence had long left the earth, but in the tranquillity, in the reaching beyond the knowing, we were able to communicate through a vibration quivering closer to me than the air I breathed. The minutes spent alone with him were intense and powerful, spiritually fired yet so natural.

I left humbled and honoured. I passed the others filing in. I bent my head as I didn't want them to see me crying. I hid by a glass case and regained my composure. When I left the museum everyone had already escaped into the bus. A torrential rainstorm thrashed and crashed, angrily blasting away the lovely, calm sunshine—the tail end of the hurricane had followed us. Like jumping into a swimming pool fully clothed, I dashed out into the fray and was immediately drenched. When I reached the bus I was dripping from head to toe. Everyone was aboard and I laughed as I squelched to my seat, wringing out my blouse.

"You know, man, you're cool! Everyone came on the bus differently showing their true characters and you came on the bus laughing. Man, you laughed—that's cool!" shouted Eric from the back of the bus. I hadn't been aware of my reaction, preferring to laugh rather than cry at my predicament.

Luckily we were heading away from the whiplash of the hurricane and after a few hours the sun returned as we came to a town where lunch had been prepared for us in a small house down a side street. Those of us who still had wet bottoms were given pieces of plastic to sit on, and we all helped ourselves to fruit juice, an assortment of cold meats and cheeses, with bread and cakes. Our party was tired and we were not as hungry as perhaps we might have been as we were nearing the end of our great journey. We were slowly shaking off the remaining shackles of travelling on our WaWa bus and feeling uncomfortable from our soaking, but looking forward to returning to Havana and experiencing a night in the famous Tropicana nightclub, where we could celebrate our final party together. We still had a few hours' bus ride back to Havana and most of us slept, drying out in our wet clothes in the heat of the bus. As we meandered in and out of dense forests, fatigue wrapped me in a comfort shawl and I succumbed to the lull of the rolling bus, rocking in and out of the rough terrain.

I slept for a while but woke when we hit another pocket of angry rain. It was too hot to close the windows but the cool spray was welcome, even though my clothes had only just dried. The dull monotony forced my mind to trace the events concerning Knossos, and how during the years after the amazing experience things were revealed to me, but there was one final surprise. I remembered how it all began at my friend's house in her kitchen. She had employed a wonderful artist and designer, Esther, to decorate her lovely regency house by the river, restoring it to its former glory. My friend Vanessa was explaining to Esther about my ability to help people but Esther had huge doubts about the process even though she was seeking help herself. I stood opposite Esther understanding her confusion, and used my energy to "zap" her. (Zapping is a method whereby the healer injects a force of good energy into the recipient.)

Esther froze. Her eyes glazed and her whole body rippled as the tremor passed through her. Vanessa watched knowingly. As Esther regained control she was amazed and shaken; she had never experienced anything like that before. She later confided that the energy had enabled her to whiz around in a cyclonic fury all week, just when she needed the energy the most. From that time Esther was converted and we have remained friends over the years. In fact, she unwittingly became the instigator of the final episode relating to Izatah.

Esther relates that she was collecting her daughter who had been away on a school trip. While waiting at the pickup spot, which was the York racecourse, she began a polite conversation with a man who was also waiting for his child. Esther said, "It was strange really, because there must have been loads of parents waiting, but all I saw was him and we seemed to be alone in that odd moment when he described his daughter's terrible condition. No one knew what was wrong with her and the doctors were baffled by her illness. Lisal had been a wonderful swimmer and possessed a great artistic gift, but she had deteriorated into such a state that she could only lie in bed. Well, of course I thought of you, and told him how you had zapped me and gave me renewed energy so that I could cope with my life."

A short time later Lisal's mother phoned me and I arranged to meet them at my friend Anne's house, where we had helped many other people. Lisal was frail, with her pale face shrouded by long blonde hair and cloudy blue eyes peering at me. She was sixteen years old and her time was sifting away like sand in an egg timer. Her voice came from outside her body; she was only able to whisper in short breaths. My heart went out to her and I felt a strange connection with her. Within three sessions she was fully healed. I used regression therapy and other techniques which best suited her ailment. Lisal took up further education, gaining a degree and then obtaining an M.A. in art, which was an amazing feat. We have continued to maintain a bond, one which will never be severed. My house lives her artwork and I am proud to show off her paintings.

In search of artistic inspiration, Lisal went to Crete to take time to meditate and paint. While she was there she had visions and insights to other times and beings. When she returned home we spent time discussing her encounters. One in particular, which shocked us both, occurred when she visited Knossos. She told me that she had wandered down to a certain part of the palace and was overcome with a deep depression and sadness. A feeling of "being lost" invaded her person. She could see that she was small, a young boy, dressed in a princely tunic. She was near some steps and was waiting for someone when an evil energy pushed her/him down the steps where she tumbled into oblivion!

Lisal did not know my story of Vangelis and Izatah and on hearing her vision I showed her the manuscript. We were both dumbfounded to think that perhaps she had been Izatah's little brother. Sometimes during a lifetime we meet people who have been close to us in another lifetime and we either form close friendships or become members of the same family, regaining a former bond. Equally, if we have unfinished business with an enemy, we may meet them again in order to even out the score in a karmic manner.

As the bus neared Havana our party grew restless, eager to get off the bus and stretch our legs. I thought of my encounter at Che's graveside and was grateful to have opened and closed a door on a personal search which I thought had reached a beautiful conclusion—but I had no idea of what was later to be revealed.

CHAPTER 15

Tropical Tropicana

*There are songs which span the length and
breadth of time, melodiously ringing in the
hearts of those who take time to listen for they
will hear the vibration of the universe.*

We arrived back in Havana in the late afternoon and
unloaded our gear from our little WaWa bus into the
dim porch of the hotel where our journey began, feeling like
old friends rather than strangers. We waved goodbye to our bus
driver and quaint little van and as I watched it screech up the
hill a new wave of anticipation flared, as the final section of
the trip was all that was left to complete our amazing time in
Cuba. Hilary was nervous and excited because she was going
to be reunited with the Cuban boyfriend she had met a few
days before we had set off. She had arranged to meet him at the
Tropicana, Havana's famous hotspot. As a dancer, performer,
and choreographer, I was particularly interested to visit the icon
of the cabaret world that had been featured in countless films of
a long-forgotten era of men like Cary Grant with slicked-back
hair and stylish tuxedoes.

We were relieved to discard our travelling clothes and get
ready for a night of fun. We arranged to have our last meal in a

special restaurant before going to the Tropicana. It was lovely to see all the ladies in glam evening dresses and the men in their best suits. The little restaurant was in a house and was fantastically set out with antique furniture and original paintings spread across the walls and even the ceilings. The menu was exotic and I chose a medley of my favourite seafood dishes. After the meal we were raring to party. Having shaken off our travel weariness, all were set for a night of entertainment and merriment. As we drove out toward a part of the city where the bankers and film stars used to live, we passed magnificent Hollywood mansions that hinted at presidential opulence and Ginger Rogers haute couture elegance. I wondered who owned them under the communist regime.

When we turned into the nightclub drive the bright lights set amongst the tropical trees and palms were dazzling. The Tropicana exuded Hollywood glamour and was every inch the hotspot I imagined it to be. Cars drove up to the entrance, engines purring, where stylish clientele were met by sophisticated men in black who welcomed everyone with modest smiles. The hurricane which we had escaped was travelling across Cuba, but its energy was diluted in Havana and the tropical palm branches were merely ruffled by a veil of warm rain. The poor weather meant that we couldn't experience the extravaganza outside under the stars but I was glad to be inside as I usually got fiercely bitten by mosquitoes at night. Inside was like a 1950s film set ornamented with extravagant mirrors and an elaborate décor emblazoned with gold geometric designs. It was a thrill to be where the greatest performers in the world, such as Nat King Cole, Maurice Chevalier, Bing Crosby, Frank Sinatra, and many, many others had entertained the privileged echelons of society. Just being where all the amazing stars hung out was a great feeling and to experience a show that has remained unchanged since 1939 was going to be exciting.

As we were shown into the grand auditorium I felt I was walking into a Humphrey Bogart film. I half expected the scene to metamorphose into a black and white cinematic haze. I followed the others, mouth agog at the glittering throats of the ladies at the tables who dripped sparkling jewels that twinkled in the dark. We were shown to our table at the back but we had a fine, panoramic view of everything, including the audience and the massive stage throbbing with two hundred dancers bejewelled in diamante frocks, feathers, and fresh floral garlands in their hair. The spectacular milieu was breathtaking and the lyric, raucously sung by Shirley MacLaine from the film *Sweet Charity*, "If my friends could see me now, they'd never believe me!" resounded in my head as the champagne popped and the tawny rum overflowed.

Tables were waited upon by beautiful girls who glided through the audience, professionally balancing trays of ice buckets, bottles, and assorted snacks, making sure that no table ran dry of Havana rum. At first we were awed by the club's overpowering lavishness and we drank our champagne shyly, not daring to speak, but then after a few drinks and several scene and costume changes, I noted a slight indifference creeping into our group. A few went outside to smoke, while others went to the lavatory, leaving Simonise and myself watching the cabaret. I didn't want to miss anything and it was true that I had never seen so many elaborate and extravagant costumes in such a myriad of colours, designs, and fabrics, but the dancing and music was not Cuban. Our group had thrived on the raw ingredients of the pulse, the rippling rhythm of the people, which had cradled us from the moment we woke to the time we went to sleep. It had been pure, electric, *Cuban* music. The nightclub strains were a sophisticated, semi-classical cardboard imitation of the real Cubanismo beat. Twee ballet excerpts with perfect arabesques expertly delivered, and beautiful pirouettes performed without a trace of a wobble, were outlined with outstanding symmetry of pattern and brilliant body control. It was lovely, but it was all executed without soul, without feeling, without personality. It was lacklustre, dead, missing the spirit of the real dance which our group had come to know and love and dance every night.

I was disappointed, and I secretly think the rest of the group were too. Moreover, I was shocked by a certain piece of choreography that was allowed to remain in the show. It was an insult to the Africans and I squirmed inside as I watched the titillation unfold, which exposed a raw nerve inflamed since the time of slavery and second class citizenship. The story was about a young, beautiful white girl who was being chased in the jungle by a group of African warriors who mimed violating her. Unable to contain my disgust, I chose that moment to visit the lavatory. Perhaps I was overly sensitive but the style, the message, the genre, and the music, in my opinion, were better left in a dusty cupboard to rot in the humidity.

As our group gradually returned to the table, the rum bottles were replaced and we went another round of sampling Havana's glorious tipple. Maybe fatigue was hitting us after our long haul, because many became disinterested in the show of swirling fans and ostrich feathers beating teasingly, hiding half-clad girls. We stayed until the end, and when the lights came up on the debris spread across all the tables, the seedy sequinned waitress costumes, and the litter cast carelessly in the aisles, I knew we had broken the spell of the magic. It was time to say goodbye. The curtain came down on the trip and, like all last nights where the players are eager to strike the set and flee, we all departed back to our various quarters.

In the morning at breakfast I caught up with the group and exchanged addresses but, as always, it's a token gesture and one we feel obligated to make. We mostly fold back into our own worlds once we return home, leaving the memory holding the treasures of the journey. I arranged to spend another night in the hotel as I had not calculated the dates correctly and expected to arrive back in Havana a day later. The thought of whiling away the day and night alone in that basic hotel was not very exciting and, especially as I hadn't much money to entertain myself, it was purely a question of killing time before moving across town. The view from seventeen floors up in the post-hurricane humidity was obscured by a foggy veil, but I could still make out the massive, sprawling city decked with splashes of brightly coloured classic cars strung out like a festival string of flags. I decided to sort out my clothes, choosing which to leave for the maids, and catch up with my washing. An hour later I sat on the bed wondering what to do next. I sent Saul a message wishing I was back with him as the next few days were time-wasters before my new life with him would begin!

It was hard coming back to reality after chasing the dance across Cuba, and time seemed to hang drearily in the impersonal hotel room. I needed some air, albeit hot and sticky air. I wandered out of the hotel to discover what lay beyond the traffic lights at the bottom of the hill. After the expedition and having the group's support, it was strange not to have a set time to meet everyone or look forward to an evening meal together. The aloneness of the moment was frightening. Suddenly I was in a strange city without friends and I had no idea where I was walking. No one would be wondering where I was or care what I was doing; my anchor had disappeared.

I didn't know I was walking in the direction of Havana's most famous hotel, Hotel Nacional. Only after I trudged up the hill and glanced to my right did I spy an amazing array of classic vintage cars snuggled in the vast grounds of the great hotel. I walked inside the park gates and two guards smiled. I soaked up the multitude of rainbow colours of every car sitting pretty in the lush grounds. I took time to photograph the showroom display but I was drawn to an unusual picture. I spied a young bride alone in a brick alcove by the side of the magnificent hotel entrance. She looked doubtful, even jaded, with her hand perched on her hip and her disinterested body leaning against the wall. Her pained expression and ungainly posture screamed outrageously against the beautiful Cinderella wedding dress delicately traced and edged with fine lace and pearls. The fragile white flowers in her hair were partly squashed as her head rested against the dusty bricks. Her thin, dark arms looked frail in her long silk white gloves. I sneaked photographs of her.

A bridesmaid rolled out of the revolving door, her large frame rippling in layers of bright pink frills and with a twinkling tiara perched on top of her black curls. Her pink and white bodice flounced with silky pink trimmings and pearls and squashed her ample breasts to overspill. She too carried an air of ungraceful boredom. Side by side the lacklustre bride and the comic bridesmaid brightened my mood. I stole a few shots while they were not looking and sauntered into the plush hotel cocooned in history like a vast cathedral, with its high wooden doors, huge ceilings, and quiet, respectful air.

I didn't have much money but I had enough to buy a mojito and longed to pretend I was part of the hotel. A gentle band strummed on the balcony but played a "whitened up" version of *son* music, holding back, as though they did not want to disturb the visitors or excite the moment with the real flavour of Cuba. The genteel sounds were dressed down and underplayed, which was disappointing, so I took my drink out toward the sea view. I unexpectedly saw the bride and bridesmaid out in the grounds and took a quick snapshot of the oversized bridesmaid with her hooped skirt caught in the breeze and lifted high at the back. It was a naughty shot and as the wind played havoc with the gown, the bridesmaid grimaced and screwed up her face in a most unsightly manner, quite incongruous with her formal attire. I entertained myself taking sneaky photos but when the official photographer attended by his team took over the scene, I realized that the two girls were modelling for a fashion magazine and I dissolved into the foliage, glad that the young girl was not actually getting married, merely posing.

I meandered down toward the view of the vast ocean, remembering that it was only hours before that our little group had hurriedly abandoned the beautiful Trinidad beach in the alarm of a hurricane alert. Time rolls onward and within each moment the instant is lost forever. Everything is in constant flux, forever changing, moving in circles, and somehow we expect that it shouldn't and are surprised when it does. The friends I made on the journey were already a part of the past and the memory of our journey together would be a lovely record to play at will. Rocking with the wind and looking at the turbulent ocean with its dark pools and swirling undercurrents, I realized that it is sharing in the turbulence of our experience that binds people together either for good or bad. The contribution of each person links the scene to the soul of the memory. I missed the group and our camaraderie but I had Saul and our new life together to look forward to.

I dwindled away an hour at the hotel and wandered back through the heat and the bustling street to my dingy hotel room where the silence was overwhelming. I attempted to bring my diary up to date but Saul kept creeping into my thoughts and I was restless, imagining what our first few moments would be like together. I wondered whether to telegraph him on my telepathy wavelength but thought perhaps I shouldn't, as he wasn't open to that kind of empathetic energy. I was certain that, given time, he might become less antagonistic toward my paranormal gifts. I would have to slowly and carefully share my life and knowledge with him.

Telepathic communication and prophecy was normal for me and even though I accepted it, I never ceased to be amazed and surprised when it happened. I remembered one night before I was due to drive my weekly long trek down to London to study for my M.A., where in the morning I spent time in the library and danced in the afternoon, then had to rush back to teach early the next morning. Every Friday was the same: I would leave my house around four o'clock in the early hours of the morning to arrive in London about nine o'clock, in time for breakfast. It was late Thursday evening and I stood in front of my dressing table mirror. I suddenly knew that the next day I would have a terrible car accident. I calmly examined the thought and took off all my precious rings, necklace, and jewellery and placed them on the dressing table for my children to find if I didn't return. My thoughts rushed to my little girl living with her father and I wrapped her essence in a pink shawl and drew her to me in thought. I told her, "I love you darling. Tomorrow I am going to London, and…." I faltered. I did not want to say that I might not come back. Instead I just told her that I needed her to know that I loved her.

Suddenly the phone rang and her little distressed voice squeaked through the air waves:

"Mummy, Mummy—I can hear your voice inside my head! Daddy said I couldn't ring you because it's late but Mummy, I know you're talking to me!"

Calmly I assured her that all was well and yes, I had been talking to her in my mind just to let her know I loved her. She was happy with that explanation and promised to go to sleep. In the quiet of my bedroom the premonition returned.

It was wonderful to know that my daughter had heard my thoughts, but also scary. She had heard my voice loud and clear through the universe, proving the strength of a mother's love, but it had sharpened my doubts about travelling the next day. I tried to sleep but the premonition kept returning. Just before dawn I got up and stood in the hallway wondering whether to heed the prophecy about the car crash. I knew I could not live my life as a coward and shy away from danger every time I was afraid to do something, so I looked at my little dog who normally came with me on the long journey and explained that I couldn't take her with me. She cocked her head to one side, listening, and she whined as I closed the door behind me. I was not sure whether I would come back. I placed my life in the hands of the great ones.

As usual I stopped just after dawn at a petrol station which was halfway on the journey. For some reason I was tempted to buy a CD of Eric Clapton's to play in the car. As I entered the dreaded M25 I thought that I must have been silly to believe the warning, as nothing had happened and I hadn't long to go before I reached my turnoff for the university. It was still quite early and the traffic had not built up into the stifling long morning queues dredging toward London. Signs warned road works ahead and traffic began to slow down. I noted a huge DAT lorry swinging in beside me on my left as we turned into a diverted part of the road. The music slowed to a rhythmic pulse and the words sang, "Knock, knock, knocking on heaven's door, It's getting too dark to see, Take this badge off of me, I'm knock, knock, knocking on heaven's door." A terrific bang jolted the steering wheel out of my hands. "Knock, knock, knocking on heaven's door." In front all I could see were the gigantic wheels of the lorry. I was going under the massive tyres. I was not afraid. I only thought of my children and accepted what was fated.

"Knock, knock, knocking on heaven's door" pulsed on and somehow the lorry slowed down so that I didn't go under its wheels but my car bounced off the front of the right wheel spinning me onto the left, then I whizzed across the oncoming traffic, smashing through a police barrier, spiralling up an embankment on the other side of the motorway, landing upside down as the long grass whipped around my wheels like a lassoed rope anchoring me to the bank. I was grateful to the council for making a meadow out of the long grass because the impact had turned the straw-like strands into strong threads that held the car in place and prevented me from rolling into a steel barrier only an inch away! I will never forget the sound and the feel of the quick whiplash of the grass. Zip! Zip! Zip! "Knock, knock, knocking on heaven's door." The windows had smashed, flashing sharp shards of glass inside the cabin like a blizzard. A snowstorm of dangerous particles flew everywhere, landing in my pockets, in my shoes, in my underwear, in my ears.

I climbed out of the car. "Knock, knock, knocking on heaven's door" still echoed through the debris and hung in the air through the smashed windows. There was not one scratch on my body although I did sustain other injuries which were not visible. In the sunshine I stood in a lonely haze. Cars stopped and people rushed to stand and stare at me. They stayed behind the barrier as I stood, embarrassed and shaking, on the other side. The people continued to stare and the music blared on. I had knocked on heaven's door but they didn't let me in!

Police and ambulance sirens screamed and screeched to a halt where the crowd had gathered. I felt like an alien that had just landed on earth. As the police slowly made their way toward me, a young girl held out her hand and stroked me. I was in shock and when the paramedics saw I was alright, they left me to the police. I was led to their car. I was questioned. On their police television the crash had been spectacular. I did not know what had happened. I thought I had hit a grease patch on the road, but the policeman was angry, saying, "Those bloody French lorries! They don't know how to drive here. He smashed into the side of your car because he couldn't see you. How could he, bloody driving on the wrong side? He can't see you from where he is sitting. You're the fifth person this week to have an accident and you're lucky—the rest are dead! Whenever I see one of those damn lorries, I steer clear of them. I hope you get good compensation."

I don't remember the rest of the conversation. I remember the Frenchman vaguely speaking to me but I was not fully inside my body. I was still drifting above myself halfway to heaven's door, still knocking, but I am glad I was turned away!

A knock at the hotel door made me jump and I leapt toward it with surprise as Simonise stood outside with her bags. "Can I come in?" she smiled. "I need somewhere to stay for the night." I was really pleased to see her and happy for her to share the room. It was like old times in Trinidad. It was lovely to have company and to share an evening meal chatting over our trip and discussing her amazing plans for her world tour. The next morning we hugged as I bid her goodbye, giving her the address of my luxurious hotel where I was going to spend two nights before returning home. I was relieved to re-enter the deluxe, lavish hotel and glad to revel in a beautiful bathroom and soak in fabulous fragrant bath foam. I needed to wash off the travel grime and dust, and relax in the aftermath of the success of the trip.

My final days in Havana were pure time-wasters—I was ready to go home and impatient to see Saul. After settling into my luxury room, I meandered down to the dock in the oppressive heat, the kind that stings eyes and dries the throat the instant you walk outside, after which the long trek and the basic, home-cooked food was gastronomic heaven. I indulged in five-star gourmet dishes, sampling a cornucopia of strong flavours blending into an excess of variety of fish, meat, and poultry. Even a simple food like eggs was served in ten different ways: fried, boiled, poached, caked, baked, omeletted, sauced, beaten, battered, and souffléd. I carried my camera and purse in a little plastic bag because I didn't want to be burdened with my large handbag that was cumbersome in the raging heat. I took a side turning down a narrow street and spotted a large, dark room on the ground floor of a building with open windows, full of children occupied in a government-sponsored art class which kept them off the streets.

Women lazily gossiped outside the main doors to their flats while oversized mothers in undersized jeans with their hair in curlers watched me closely. The windows on the street were barred, and once-fine filigree ironwork gates belonging to a long-gone era of opulence blocked the entrances to decaying dwellings. Matriarchs hung over balconies or smoked a cigarette whilst hanging out their washing on double lines that spanned across each other's windows. I was an intruder in their community but I was interested to see what the children were doing.

I ventured to look at the startling models they had made out of papier-mâché as I leaned inside the open window. When the children saw me they attacked like vultures—pecking, poking, lashing and pelting me with bread in a greedy, furious hailstorm. All ages and sizes leapt on me, demanding sweets and goodies, hitting me and shouting abuse. The shirtless boys tugged on my arms and the girls in their rainbow dresses scratched like kittens. I struggled to show them that inside my plastic bag there was nothing, but they persisted like hounds after a fox. I had never been afraid of children, but in that moment they struck like wildcats, scratching and clawing. The teacher was shocked and called to them to stop but they didn't heed him. It was the mothers who shouted and came to my rescue, quickly abandoning their perches to clap ears and haul away kids by their collars. I was relieved when the noise and the fracas died away as quickly as it had risen. Once they settled down to resume their work, I was able to admire the statues and masks they had made, but inwardly I was shaking from the onslaught. I didn't stay long and waved goodbye, leaving amidst friendly smiles. It was hard to believe their unwarranted savage attack.

Near the dock, people flocked to admire the castle and photograph the fortress and portcullis. Just as I was stepping backward off the pavement, a familiar voice from behind startled me. "Hello, great lady!" Orlando beamed a welcome. I remembered his winsome smile from my first day in Havana when he accompanied me to the sparsely stocked market. His friendly greeting was appreciated after the children's frenzied assault. "Would you like me to show you around?"

"No, thank you. I was er…just going back to my hotel." I couldn't think of another excuse.

"I will walk that way with you," he proclaimed proudly.

I nodded, and turned around, walking in the direction from where I had just been harassed.

"Look, I have to see my grandmother. Would you like to come? I live with her, just there."

I looked at the ancient buildings and his open, honest eyes. He was telling the truth. He led the way toward a block of ancient buildings and unlocked a medieval, creaky wooden door that revealed a noble remnant of past craftsmanship. The sight beyond was both shocking and incredible. It was as though I were stepping back in time into a Shakespeare play with the scent of doublet and hose just a sniff away, with chickens and livestock roaming in the courtyard and slop and sewage rotting in the gutter. The present was alarming with crumbling masonry decaying in the humid air, reeking of stale bodies. The wooden slats in the walls and roof lay bare and open in places, like an unfinished building site, except that the beams were withering. It was a Romeo and Juliet stairwell winding up to another landing where the floor was in a terrible state of disrepair, where walls were left half-finished or half-falling down. Orlando knocked on a door that might have belonged to Fagin and his beggar boys.

A sweet old lady opened the door. I studied her face. It embodied the face of slavery, the soul of Africa. I had a fleeting vision of her as a very young girl—quite beautiful with wide, prominent cheekbones and a high, gracious forehead. The vision cleared and before me was a ninety-three-year-old black lady with a toothless grin that was all-embracing. She loved her grandson and her adoration of him shone through her care-worn eyes. Her body was still strong although her movements were restricted. On her head she wore a white turban and her long neck gave her an air of lost nobility. She lived in the little room which was adequate for her needs. Her gods had pride of place on her sideboard together with her plastic fruit and empty lemonade bottles. Her gentleness flowed through her every movement and I loved her for her life and her struggles and her fears and her dead dreams. As she embraced me, her energy connected me momentarily with history and a life I could only imagine with horror.

As we left she clung precariously to her table and Orlando gave her a kiss. His room was opposite hers in the shoddy broken remnants of the building rubble. There was a single rusty tap near the landing, which I guessed served as their bathroom. I was glad to have witnessed their living quarters but it made me feel guilty for living in splendour.

"Come, I will show you where my friend lives. He is also a student. Come."

I obeyed him, walking slowly in the draining heat. He led me through small streets where visitors hardly strayed and up through a winding alley where a row of tiny houses were squashed together like fishermen's cottages in Cornwall. Orlando knocked and we were shown inside by his friend who cordially welcomed us. Inside was the strangest architecture I had ever seen. The little downstairs room was round, with the pebbled walls painted white, reminiscent of the tiny Cornish cottages I had once visited. The stairs wound round in a circular fashion with the walls bubbling with the round pebbles. Everything was painted white and extremely clean and tidy. I felt uncomfortable and uneasy being left alone with two male strangers, and said I had to leave despite their offer of a cold drink. Orlando was swift to see me out and to accompany me the rest of the way back to the hotel. I was thankful to him for his short tour and he offered to take me out that evening to a special salsa bar but I declined graciously. Instead I invited him inside the hotel to buy him a drink at the bar.

Inside the air was cool and the plush décor a different world to the one I had just witnessed. The men in black did not like Orlando being there—he was black and not a guest of the hotel—so I could not buy him a drink, which embarrassed me. I had no idea that the rules about drinking at the bar were so stringent. I apologised to Orlando but he didn't seem to mind or take offence and I watched him disappear back into the sizzling heat. At the desk Simonise had left a message that she would visit, so I hung around in the lobby waiting for her to appear. Around me rich businessmen were talking in hushed tones, drinking their coffee, and signing papers. I couldn't help thinking about Orlando's grandmother and how her dreams must have been shattered when she was abducted from her African village. Her story is not unique, for everyone has a story, each story has a dream, and each dream carries us through our story's journey. But danger lurks if we lose our dreaming, for then our story withers and dies. From the spark in her eyes, I guessed the grandmother never lost her dream, and I hope she is still dreaming.

When Simonise sailed through the revolving doors she was accompanied by a black boyfriend. They both smiled as I greeted them. The men in black watched from afar. My friends were dressed in shorts and tee shirts, quite acceptable for day wear, but the men in black would not allow them to go to my room because he was black. Instead, they agreed, I could buy them both a drink at the bar. Simonise said they had a great deal of trouble walking along the streets together as they had been stopped several times for Santos to have his papers inspected. For us the policing was great, making us feel very safe, but others like Santos were continually hounded and their presence made accountable to the state.

I recounted what Hilary had told me when I saw her for the last time at the dingy hotel when she had called by to collect her bags, saying that her boyfriend's family were wonderful, but they all had to work so hard to maintain a living. She was surprised at how little they earned and how huge the household bills were and how they mostly relied on the black market to sustain themselves. She said that most people hated being held back technologically by the communist regime and that petty pilfering was rife; theft from large companies was almost taken for granted. Most members of the family she was living with had at least two jobs and worked shifts to make ends meet. She was hoping to get her boyfriend to go to England but that was in the lap of the gods.

That evening I entertained Simonise for dinner at the hotel and we had a lovely time reminiscing. She promised to look me up when she visited England and I wished her all the best for her world tour, hiding my maternal fears and trying not to fuss like a clucking hen. The next morning I took my last walk through the parts of the city I knew well, taking final shots of classic cars and hidden portraits of Che down secluded alleys where dead dogs lay in the gloom and strays hid in the dust from the heat. Che was everywhere, and somehow a ray of hope still shone in the hearts of the people, even believing that, like Christ, he would come again and save them from the regime that was once Che's ideal.

I wandered through the Caribbean quarter with its bright blue wooden balconies and shutters. I sat for a while in the shade with a tropical fruit drink, the kind that I had loved so much on the island on my previous expedition, where I was poisoned by a jealous girl who thought I was stealing her Masai boyfriend. That trip to the Land of Colour seemed forever away, when I danced with blue feet in the rainforest and heard the whisper of ancient voices in the temples in the jungle and traced the face of death along the wall of skulls at Palenque; when I was nearly run over by a white van zooming around the corner of a main road when I thought I was about to enter a wooden building, only to find it was a vision from the past. All those memories flashed by as I sipped white rum, coconut milk, and fresh pineapple. I savoured the sharp taste of the present.

The journey through Cuba had been an amazing adventure seeking the music and the dance to take back home and introduce in my school. The unique blends of Spanish and African cultures melting into one Cubanismo style would remain forever intoxicating and enthralling, always thrilling me with the sensual percussion that was the backbone to all Cuban music.

As I walked back through the busy streets to begin packing, I saw a man selling pets on the pavement. I was horrified at the caged animals unable to move in the sweltering heat. It was cruelty personified and I wanted to scream and stop people and have the man arrested but everyone walked by without a care. Two little Husky puppies with thick, russet matted fur huddled together in a tiny cage and were unable to shift their position or even turn as they struggled to breathe in the airless prison. I was so incensed that I hung about near the cage looking for a chance to let them out, but it was impossible and I had to drag myself away, biting my tongue with disgust. Havana had revealed a primitive aspect of her nature with the attack of the children, the accepted cruelty to animals on the streets, and the decay and deterioration of the buildings. As I made my way toward the hotel I watched an old lady, barely able to move, waddling with her walking stick amidst the dust and rubble over-spilling from a skip. She stooped to inspect the skip, poking and prodding with her stick to find something of value which she hoped she might discover, while half-houses tumbled around her and the message "Fidel Is a Country" daubed in blue paint on the walls of a broken dwelling.

Back inside the secure world of the privileged, under the gaze of the men in black, I ordered my final mojito. Fumbling in my bag to find my purse I came across four white plastic drinks stirrers in the shape of ballet dancers with the name of the Tropicana nightclub embossed across the top. I smiled to know that the next time I would use them would be back home where the tropical Tropicana would be a hazy memory.

CHAPTER 16

Endings and Beginnings

*Dance while you have life in you
and while you have life, live!*

It is said that the traveller travels in order to travel home. I was glad to be going back and my journey was made sweeter by the fact that I had someone waiting for me. The thought of seeing Saul again made me impatient. In the airport I whiled away the time by looking around the shops and I succumbed to purchasing two tee shirts of Che. His face commanded triumph and I pondered the initial message I was made to remember: *"My head is as heavy as a revolution."* It had given me the clue to chase the dance and music across Cuba, tracing Che's major victories and giving me the chance to visit his final resting place.

The second message came to mind: *"My body is as weak as a soldier's bayonet after battle."* It was a vision given to me of Che at Santa Clara, where on the night before his execution, I saw his face in the half light, weak and weary after battle. Finally, the third: *"I am as strong as the person I am inside."* It is a message to everyone, as his image remains in their hearts and will never die.

My journey had fulfilled a restless yearning and I felt I had found some answers. I also realized that to spend time dreaming about the past does not leave much space to think about the future and to think too much about the future steals time from the present. The now is all we own and no matter how deep our past cuts into our living, every minute is testimony to our being and we cannot sidestep it; we cannot "drink mandragora, to sleep out the time." Even when bleak is the colour of our comfort zone, the tide will always turn.

I boarded the plane with a strong sense of destiny. People say that love is like a warm glow inside but for me it was not just a glowing ember, it was hot. Hot like the scorching sun; hot like smouldering lava; hot like salt tears flowing in the empty desert. I needed to share my hungry love with Saul and hoped we could find a sweet oasis. I ached to live a normal life, well…almost. As I sat back I folded up the memories of the journey, thinking how different the adventure was from the previous one across Central America, where I had been plagued by terrors of night insects, day creatures, stomach bugs and sickness, filthy accommodations, financial worries, and self doubts on many levels. This adventure had been simpler, with fewer anxieties, and I had support from a loved one back home. The group had been wonderful, without a hint of complaining, and we had all loved the dancing and music which became part of our existence. Life without raw rhythm was going to be bland but I planned to put all my recent moves into practice in my school and pass on my newfound knowledge to my students.

The journey back to my cottage was ordinary, with the usual pulling and pushing of luggage on and off trains and buses but, eventually, in the light of the late afternoon sunshine I was standing in my front garden with the lawn a mini meadow and the shrubs a weed forest. I was not afraid of letters in the post and resolved to meet whatever lay in wait. "I had a love of my own again; I had a love of my own!" I sang in the shower, washing my hair repeatedly, rinsing out the travel grime. I was in a hurry to get ready and look good for Saul. I dressed in a long, flowing, cool dress to show off my tan and when I heard his footsteps in the hall I flew downstairs and rushed into his arms. He kissed me and stood back to look into my eyes to ascertain my faithfulness. I knew his thoughts and felt a little hurt that he scrutinised me, but I shrugged it off—we were happy. To celebrate, he wanted to take me to the hotel where we first met, and we ordered champagne.

"Do you remember when you asked if I had chicken legs?"

I laughed, embarrassed by my daring to ask such a question and feel his legs on our first meeting. It must have been the numerous glasses of champagne that I had imbibed that gave me courage. I was not able to drink very much on that evening of my homecoming, as the lovely bubbly was much more intoxicating than the mojitos I had become accustomed to drinking. Saul was in a merry mood and ordered another bottle which he drank by himself.

As we sauntered back home, the pain in my leg jabbed like sharp needles but I hobbled along feeling happy and admiring the sky as mysterious Miss Twilight, her glorious nature deceptive, descended over the cottages as she secretly protected the dying day, streaking the sky in her magnificent array of gold, orange, and lilac. She waited like a cat for the moment when the sun dipped low to reveal her sovereignty. As Miss Magical wove her enchanting spell I was on the edge of excitement. I had the feeling that no one could tell if heaven or hell waited ready to pounce, or if any battle would be lost or won, or if the night held fear or fun, or if we were all going to fall off the edge of the universe never to rise in dawn's surprise. It was the glorious rise of anticipation as we walked through the groaning gate while Miss Twilight, in her last magnificent bid for supremacy, heralded a new beginning.

When we got inside, the dark of the cottage was a comfort. We decided to sit in the conservatory and watch the light play through the trees. Paul wanted another drink but after pouring it for him I found him fast asleep, his head lolling against the back of the sofa. I sat next to him. He was tired after a hard day defending criminals. I sat as Miss Twilight faded into shades of night and stars sprang like dew in the dawn through a hole in the universe. Some stars fell into jars of black dust, catching promises and wishes like primroses in May that unveil yellow hope for summer, but summer would soon be over. Miss Twilight had vanished, leaving the lights of the factory teasing shadows across Saul's face. I had not expected the evening to end this way.

Suddenly a light flashed across the glass in front and I peered to see from where it had sprung, but there was no source—only a blank wall and trees. I stared at the picture forming and could not believe what unfolded. Che's face stared at me, emblazoned across two large panes of glass. I blinked away the image but it remained. I thought that because I had seen Che's face everywhere on the journey, I was mustering up the image from an imaginary door that I tried to force shut. The image persisted and became even bolder. Che was smiling and I didn't know what to do. I looked at Saul who was in a deep slumber, snoring. I couldn't wake him. Che filled my soul with the lightness of hope and the joy of an unexpected visit. I tried again and again to push away the image, doubting what was before me, but he was there. His face was real and for two hours he remained. The picture never faltered or altered and I became lost in a sense of eternity.

Eventually I helped Saul upstairs and we crashed into bed. I couldn't believe the image which had inexplicably appeared, totally baffling me, but the wind outside my window whined and clung to corner of the garden whispering:

I am the breath of the wind,
The call of the sea,
The warmth of the sun,
The life-giving rain,
The guiding moon,
I am the silent pulse,
I am the tick of the clock when time is broken,
I have spoken,
That is all,
I have answered your call.

I tried to assimilate what had happened and sought to explain it in my mind, but then I wondered how scientists knew that there are three hundred million black holes in the night sky and how they know that electrons can be in two places at the same time. My own out-of-body experiences had taught me that being in two places at one time is possible. On one occasion I had helped a distressed dance student who had major problems and I had told her that if she needed help I would be with her, even if it was in the dead of night. Later she was relaying events to one of her friends who was amazed how I knew about the incident in Costa Brava and asked, "But how do you know all this?" The student replied, "Because she was there, dummy!" when, in fact, I was in bed at the time.

Sleep seemed to elude me, or perhaps I was on Cuban time, or perhaps my body missed the sweltering heat and the sound of a fan whizzing during the night, but I couldn't latch onto the freeway sleep zone. I thought of Aldous Huxley's famous line, "Happiness is never grand." And in that moment neither was mine, but I was content to be back with Saul, hoping our happiness would grow.

Our time passed in a newfound routine and we adapted to our working days with Saul travelling many miles to work and struggling with the journey back so that we could be together. He said my cooking was worth it, and he enjoyed dishes he had never experienced before and I loved unwinding through cooking. I still had to battle with school during the day and teaching in my own school in the evening but I was used to it and Saul didn't want to disturb my work schedule. My leg worsened and the pain increased. Saul persuaded me to go to a specialist and have a small operation; he promised that many of his sporting friends had benefited from the same and were up, out, and about within a few days. I agreed and arranged to have it done. Perhaps I expected too much too soon of everything and became dismayed when the operation did not alleviate my pain. In fact, it grew worse and I was afraid to tell Saul how much it hurt. I limped in silence and never complained. The summer passed into autumn and as the leaves turned in their dying splendour, I ached to be back in Spain for my end-of-season performances.

For ten years I had celebrated the end of summer teaching specialist choreography to groups so that they could take the material back to England to perform in their own schools. I was used to soaking up the lazy heat in the damp sand, laughing, singing by the sea with the students, watching the moon sink over the horizon, working hard in the studio, rehearsing until we were exhausted, and carousing into the early hours. I had a room which the hotel kept for me on my visits where I had a view of the Pyrenees Mountains on my right and on my left a wonderful vista of the ocean and white sandy beach. The staff nicknamed me "the ballerina" and they adopted me as part of the hotel family.

Many teachers and tutors gathered together from all over the world to complete our season's work and make friendships which also were seasonal. One football tutor I remember who was an Eddy Murphy lookalike had been teaching for our company for a while and on our last season had brought his wife who expecting their first child. I hoped to see all three on our final visit but was shocked to discover that he had been killed—run over by a car—and never saw his baby son. I was extremely sad because he had been a wonderful man, full of life and fun, and although his relationship at times with his girlfriend had been volatile, they had eventually calmed down with the expected birth. I had enjoyed many interesting conversations with him on the veranda about paranormal happenings and although he had no personal experience, he was willing to believe in an afterlife.

I remembered the first night back in Spain when I went to bed back in the familiar surroundings of my Spanish hotel room, I was woken in the early hours of the morning by a wind blowing through my window, which I had shut, but it had strangely blown open. The zephyr hovered over my face, gently blowing a cool breeze over my eyes and in my ears, playfully waking me. I was terribly tired and buried my head in the pillow feeling a little annoyed but also slightly unnerved, as it was an unnatural draught arising from nowhere and in all my years of staying in that room I had never known anything quite like it. I didn't pay too much heed to it but the next night when I went to bed I made doubly sure that the window was properly closed. In the early hours again, around four o'clock, the same gentle breeze buzzed in and around my face, waking me. It was as though someone were blowing breath over my face. I sat up and had an eerie feeling of a presence in the room but my schedule was tight and I needed to get back to sleep. Each morning was the same: I would be woken by the cool air hovering over my head. I wasn't sure what to make of it and as I sat in the bar yawning, a rotund, middle-aged bus driver for one of the English schools came and sat down beside me, saying, "My, you're tired so early in the day!"

I explained how for some reason I was waking every morning around four a.m. He looked at me, staring deeply into my eyes, and in a hushed voice said, "My grandmother says you know things—you have the gift."

I looked around, stifling a laugh, as it seemed like a comic scene with a spy delivering a coded message. I half expected to reply with: "Is your grandmother having kippers with the count tonight?" But I didn't, and looked blank.

"My grandmother—God rest her soul—was fey, you know? She often sits on my shoulder and tells me things. She's just told me that you have the gift." I smiled. "Ah yes, I knew it! You do, don't you? What is your room number?" I didn't know how to answer and was reticent to tell him. "I'm sorry, I know how that must sound, but you see I have had the same experience every morning around four, being woken by something, some kind of energy entering my room!"

I was interested in what he had to say and we discovered that his room was directly under mine. Whatever it was, neither of us was imagining it, and we agreed to keep each other informed. That night and the next and the next, the same thing happened to me as it did to the bus driver, but on the final night the most extraordinary event of all woke me up. It was aubergine dark before the dawn blistered the sky above the mountains when I was woken by the playful breath as it breezed above my head, waffling though my hair. I was tired and in the blackness of my room a vibration of energy buzzed an electric current which burst into flame, exploding in golden glory like the first rays of the morning sun streaking through the shadows, blasting away the night. I slowly sat up, shielding my eyes from the intense beams forming corridors of light from a central orb. Outside it was black but inside it was a festival of swirling electricity sparking in all directions around my room.

The eruption was not frightening or hectic or frantic; it was totally, peacefully, all-consuming in a fire of serenity, blazing stillness, and love and calm and tranquillity beyond understanding. I bathed in the light and let my being be invaded by the harmonious symphony of the magical inferno, burning with an all-consuming passion that was not violent but supremely gentle and tender. I wallowed in the magnificent glow, feeling something beyond the flames communicating a message of all-embracing peace. I drifted into a deep sleep, waking in the ordinary light of early morning dawn. I got up to glance across the sea and stood pondering the fantastic experience. I hurried to find the bus driver at breakfast. Their coach had gone, but he had left a written message at the desk: "It finally came and showed itself. It was magnificent, whoever or whatever it was!"

I was glad he had known it too, and the only feeling I had was that the Eddy Murphy lookalike had a hand in the encounter, wishing to pass a message onto his wife that all was well and that his love for her and his child burned on and would never die.

As the autumn beckoned a dark, sterile winter, with all life forced underground, I missed the sunshine and laughter. I was becoming locked in blocks of routine of get up, shake up the blues, listen to the news and the weather. With warnings of "Keep up with the day, and please stay away from your dreams, don't discuss the psychic scenes, keep it real, don't dare to steal an ounce of fun, because you're becoming a bore and what's more, I'm watching the football at the pub!" I was entering a bleak, lonely, black tunnel. Sweet love, gone, gone too soon. Yesterday was here and we have already spent tomorrow. Watery winter sky, tricky shadow of tomorrow waits, lurks. Please camouflage me in hope and swathe me in promises and I will be the one to rally the day and tread through the quagmire of routine. I will try to be patient through your dark time. Why did we marry? We both sought to resolve our differences and felt we could tackle life together, battling through the vespertine time of our lives. Like the moonflower in India opening only at night to reveal its resplendent scent for the stars, we had hoped that in the lateness of our love it would bloom in the moonlight. But our perfume's dark signature grew faint and nothing bloomed in the sterile night of winter.

My disability was dragging me down. I fought each day to survive and struggled to keep my dance classes going. Everyone was wonderfully understanding and danced even harder to make amends for what I could not do. Eventually I visited a consultant who discovered that the root cause of everything was my hip, which had received a terrible blow in my car accident. The surgeon showed me on the X-ray where the joint was rubbing bone on bone; it was no wonder I was in dire pain all the time. An operation was organised and I lived for the day when I would be relieved of the overriding discomfort of my diseased hip. I watched time slip in and out of coiled knots, increasingly becoming tighter, unable to undo the ravelled emotions which sealed each knot in discontent. I had sold my freedom for the safety of little blue fishes, the kind that yielded golden coins in their mouths to pay the tax man. My life was no longer plagued by the terrible onslaught of a tax investigation since I had found a wonderful accountant who helped me sort out the awful mess I had fallen into. He had been a tax investigator and knew how to handle things fairly. I still paid a large sum, which didn't seem fair under my circumstances, but I had to "render to Caesar what was Caesar's" and my husband helped me with the payment.

One Saturday afternoon after teaching I was standing alone in my dining room, music gently playing in my solitary scene. A harp strummed across the lazy sunbeams, victoriously fighting through the grey day. Grey in my heart, grey in my head. *Give me a mojito to drink, so that I can dream out the lost memories in the dull disquiet of pent-up frustration and anger.* I squeezed a lemon and bits of pithy spray hit the sides of the glass like an eighties pop design, random yet meant. I made a poor substitute of a mojito but the fresh mint from the supermarket gave it an air of authenticity and took me back to the warmth of the group and the heat of the days in Cuba and the sweltering nights dancing and the drums beating. Searing symbols echo, passing through our short vows of marriage; our promise to stay together as the song "You Raise Me Up" lingers long and our love falls apart at the seams. What is the panacea for grief? Let's do the fandango into the unknown, while recalling the screaming of the seagull inland, as the Pyrenees to my left and the Ferris wheel to my right swings high above the trees, and the beat goes on in the disco down the street and the sea rolls in and out in its timeless fashion to soften the blow of reality while the gull cries, "Let's get away, far away."

Weekends had become alone time, drone time, our paths crossing at meal times. We shared nothing but routine. I walked back into the kitchen with my little dog following close at my heels, looking at me sideways and wondering if a treat would pop out of the cupboard as it mostly did when we were alone. He was happy with his biscuit and I ambled back into the dining room. I stopped. Shocked, I took a deep breath. The vision was powerful, totally unexpected. Che stared at me from the same conservatory window as before, but this time his image was different. His visage took up one pane of glass this time instead of two, but his face was bigger and his eyes more serious and deeper. I stood still, blinking away the picture, but it remained. I tested the image by looking away, but it was there. It was real. I was drawn into the depths of his eyes, falling into a tunnel of darkness where I listened to his message. In a moment of truth, I understood everything. It was simple and I had missed the whole point. I had been so stupid. I was embarrassed to the core of my being.

The words that came were soft and gentle, falling in a quiet part of my brain where I could listen undisturbed by intruding sounds. He asked me about the first time I had seen his picture when I was a student. When was it? I thought for a moment and replied, "It was early October, my first term in London." Did

I remember the date? I did because it was my grandmother's birthday. There was a pause. Of course, that date I now recognise—it was the evening before his execution, when I had looked into his eyes and a strange connection had occurred on the streets of London. I thought it was only a silly schoolgirl crush and I never knew about his death until many months later, because as a student I lived in the unreal world of college. I had never connected that evening with his death.

The vision given to me in Cuba of the night in the schoolhouse was vivid and I understood in a twinkling that in his fevered moments where his soul took flight from his body, that his energy had been sucked into the warmth of a beating heart and he had stared into the eyes of a young girl, and in the truth of those seconds he thanked me for the love and the energy I had given him. I marvelled at the revelation. I also felt stupid that I had never realised it was the evening of his death. I still find it hard to believe it happened but I feel relieved to tell it and comforted that somehow after all the years, after chasing Che across Cuba, I understood the intent behind the tapestry.

That afternoon remained with me as the last piece of the jigsaw that needed to be put to rest. I had discovered a treasure like diamond cobwebs nestling in stark, jagged twigs. Frosted grass, like brittle spun sugar, lay over the hard grass as I drove to school the next day with the wintry light in morning hues of powder pink and baby blue promising snow. Banks of white clouds mingled with the low-lying mist, appearing like a lost mountain range from the future. I was counting the months to my operation, looking forward to walking again without pain, and dancing, dancing with my students. The cool, wintry, watery sun ascended majestically through a copse of forked trees. I thought of Che, his face in the sky. I heard the words:

"Think of life as your own personal revolutionary campaign and fight to conquer the unknown territory within. Seek to stamp out the negative force, which can rot the very core of your being. It is, after all, only a short warfare. A lifespan is not a generous time. Remember the true revolutionary's weapon is love!"

The words were not mine. I had not left Che in Cuba. I have learnt that heaven or hell is within and either state is of our own making. Che was right. I have much more of the campaign left to fight and reinvent my inner landscape of my own personal revolution.

A new morning arrived and the radio blared out the news. The car almost drove itself to school. A single black crow glided over the rooftops. It was nearly Christmas and the end of term finally wheezed to a halt.

Outside my kitchen window the world was glorious. My ancient cherry tree was swathed in white and the little glass beads I planted in the branches occasionally twinkled. The bronze fairy Arabella whom I placed under the branches had only a small dusting of white over her stomach and her shapely legs were silhouetted against the shaded lower branches. The day dwindled under a watery sky, opaque before twilight's descent. The eerie silence of the still late afternoon remained unbroken. Not a leaf stirred, or a branch rippled, not a speck of snow sifted through the trees. Even the pigeons perched on high in the stark branches were perfectly statuesque. I rose from my little Italian bistro table to stir the stew simmering in the slow-cooking pot.

My little den in the kitchen is special. I hid away and watched the dull cyclorama sky in the fading light. I switched on my special lights. Behind me stood a lamp in the shape of a tree with silver branches and tiny black leaves protruding upwards. Little lights highlighted the silver polished branches. Two large paintings advertising a hotel in the south of France gave hope for warmer days. The blackness seeped in through the windows and my lights inside were reflected outside. A surreal landscape took shape with little electric lights dangling from trees, and next door's smooth snow rooftop appeared like an iced Christmas cake, making me snug and warm as I prepared fresh coffee from Guatemala. My amazing journey in Guatemala was now but a waking dream. The aroma of the freshly ground beans wafted through the kitchen. I walked to my conservatory where a completely different snow scene had taken shape. The sun was setting low through a stark cluster of trees and streaks of pink flashed through the barren branches. The potted palm tree was coated in a sleek, white glaze, delicately adorned by a festive casing. In the failing light everything was transformed into a unique winter wonder world of stark beauty.

I poured my coffee and couldn't resist a tiny thimbleful of Irish coffee liqueur to perk up my mood—after all, it was nearly Christmas. The hot coffee slid down the back of my throat but the liqueur had to be savoured and sucked through my teeth, swilled around my gums before I swallowed, leaving the tingling aftertaste in my mouth. The light was failing and the glow of my little lights inside became prominent in the silhouette of the trees outside. I loved the quiet of the moment, sipping chocolaty coffee and listening to the bubble of the stew on the stove. But up above my head in the rafters, movement began and a creepy feeling of invasion rippled within me. I felt sick with the thought that rats were infesting my space. It had been unusually cold for a long time, with winter dragging on and on, and the rats had stolen a space to congregate. I hated the sound of the scratching and jumping around in my ceiling. I was afraid to imagine what they looked like and how many were gathering in the dark. I feared they'd come through the roof!

On Christmas Eve I sat alone with my little dog in my lovely kitchen, my power capsule with its black ceramic sink, deep red sparkling granite work surfaces, black cooker, and a plethora of Christmas booze stacked in the corner. Candles flickered in the little black wrought iron stand with three plain glass lanterns, emitting red spices of Christmas fragrance, masking the smell of what I feared was rotting corpses of dead rats. The rat catcher had planted poison in tiny boxes and I dreaded to imagine the scene in the roof.

The night was swept away like coal dust in a dead hearth making way for the thick film of melting vapour, hovering over the frosted stiff earth to disperse into the hedgerows on Christmas Day. We made a friendly show at giving each other presents while a silver half-moon hid, teasingly peeping from behind curling cushions of cotton-wool clouds. In the quiet of the morning's food preparation the rats were rambling again, scratching above my head. They were not dead. I shuddered when I heard them jump and scrabble. I was determined not to listen. I had Christmas dinner to cook.

The day eased into itself and Christmas Day ended with a reverberating jangle, a tangle of conflicting views which you cannot bury even at the break of dawn a warning alarm rings in the circuit of your mind. All was quiet in the garden and no sound of the rats disturbed the morning peace in the kitchen, but I wondered what the carnage was like up through the roof? I dared not think about it.

Another morning's layer was lacy, not a thick white blanket as on most days, and I marvelled that we had continuous snow for three weeks. Flecks of lacy filigree latticework decorated the brick wall and I remembered it was New Year's Day. I sifted through my expedition photos. I seeped into each photo and remembered the feeling. I am lucky to have experienced so much, grateful and thankful to have known different worlds.

Happy New Year! The rats were marching again. *Is there a flotsam of dead bodies rotting above me?* Just when you think that it's quiet, a riotous riot begins with their obnoxious claws scratching and you know they're hatching a new plot. *Are they inside the drain?* You think you're insane. Rats smothered my dreams of nightmare screams of monsters galore, scratching the floor, and I know it's absurd but the rat jungle was creeping, seeping into my home.

A few nights later a friend who makes costumes for my school performances and organises the whole gamut of backstage management came round to help me sort out costumes for the next show. They were stored in cupboards upstairs near the rafters. As she bent down to open the door, a cluster of black rat droppings fell over the beige carpet. At first we didn't pay heed to the mess, thinking it was bits of black paper, but as she unzipped a plastic bag full of beautiful costumes, the smell of rat urine pungently stung the air and she gasped as a dead rat lay unceremoniously among the delicate lace and sequins. I shot up in disgust and was nearly sick in the bathroom. My fear of the rats sneaking into the house was true. Saul arrived at that moment and helped us to throw out thousands of pounds of gorgeous costumes which we could never replace. The sight of the rat disgusted me and I found it hard to exist in the lovely cottage with the thought of the horrendous creatures infiltrating my home.

The rat man came again and more poison was laid. Gradually the sounds stopped and the smell of rotting rodents dissipated. Time meandered to spring and cherry pink blossoms sprouted against a baby blue sky. Last year I was surprised by the spring when it flooded my cottage garden in all its wondrous glory, but this year I watched and waited for the signs after the long dreary winter and rejoiced when white buds of snowdrops pushed through the lingering clumps of snow revealing the black earth below, pushing new shoots up through the dead twigs and mouldy leaves. The blossoms, the daffodils, the tulips radiantly rejoiced in the festival of colour and I looked forward to a new lease on life with my hip operation. Six weeks afterward, I was able to walk and not be afraid of steps and stairs. Time drifted and back in my studio I was able to take my first few tentative steps. To dance again was to be reborn.

Today is Sunday and I am sitting in my kitchen watching a grey world. We have been together for two years and he said, "I don't love you, you don't love me!" He took me for lunch. Last week it was our second wedding anniversary lunch and today was our separating lunch. He said, "For some reason I enjoyed the anniversary meal more than the divorce one." I have so many mixed feelings inside. I am crying for what has died and cannot be resurrected; crying for what might have been, and for the hurt endured; for the short bursts of happiness and laughter. Was there a tender moment? Was there a tender touch? Was there a sigh? I thought we were so in love that we ached to see each other and felt lonely without each other. Was there a time, was there a place, was there a moment which spelt forever? Was it lost in a sigh that never came? Did I wait watching across the murky brown river, the hull docks, with the feeling of never quite hitting the chord right, the feeling of never just being the right one for him? How we can we misplace a jewel? How can it slip out of our hands so easily?

We were married one beautiful, bright sunny morning in February when the whole world was bathed in glorious sunshine, but by late afternoon the dark shadows of stormy clouds gathered, brooding, warning of a cyclonic storm which broke in the bleak black night, leaving a tiny storm cloud hovering in fear. The little storm cloud kept the rain inside her being until one day the first few raindrops fell, splashing into a puddle below on the earth. More and more tears crashed until the puddle formed a lake and then gradually it became a tempestuous sea where the little cloud tried hard to keep afloat, but she struggled and struggled until she was dragged down and down where she lost all sense of cloudness and merged her watery wings into the vast ocean and became a tiny droplet. The droplet grew and rose higher and higher until it became one force with the white horses riding the strong waves. The little cloud who was now a white horse rode and rode until she was washed up on the sandy shore of an island where, little by little, it picked itself up and was carried by the wind through the trees where it grew stronger and became the white bones, caverns, and cages of a being who looked and saw through the eyes of someone who waited by the seashore, and when a rescue boat came she did not board it, but waved goodbye and stayed to face new challenges through the knowledge of the cloud and the rain and the sea and waves and the wind.

Now I am happy to be alone. I am surprised when I am caught off balance as a strain of our wedding song leaks through the radio pawing through the airwaves, "You lift me up so I can climb up mountains...." A renegade tear spills carelessly down my chin. He has taken my little dog, and I miss my little pet so much, but I know that the two of them will have wonderful adventures. We decided it would be for the best as he has more time to look after him and they both have a very special bond. Once again I am left struggling with a hefty mortgage and repayment instalments after giving Saul back the money he gave me to pay off my tax bill. Karma-wise, it is correct. It is strange, but as I write I feel you reading. I sense your presence and I know I am not alone. I am grateful to have shared so much with you and a voice inside says, wait, there is more, much more. The phone rings. It is my son.

"Hello, Mum. I've just seen an amazing price for tickets to India. You know we've always wanted to go back together—let's do it!"

"That would be great, darling but…"

"I've been thinking we can raise some money and visit a school to try to help the children. Of course the accommodations would be very primitive. You know what it's like. The children are mostly disabled, untouchables, and are difficult to teach."

"Oh dear, I don't think I want to, or feel able to…"

I leave the idea hanging in the air. I am afraid to venture out again into the unknown, but as night falls and the moon sheds her silver strands of hope, I catch a shiny thread which lights a dancing beam, probing the darkest hour of the deepest night, stealing a path to the morning light. Where from night 'til day, from dusk 'til dawn, old light is shed and a new radiance is born.

Addendum

Return: *To the Land of Durga* is the third part of the Eden trilogy. In *Durga*, the author goes back to India to retrace steps of a forgotten era of the British Raj, to a time when she lived in a Victorian world ensconced in the Blue Mountains of southern India. Her journey takes us into a maharaja's palace and on safari in the jungle, riding elephants and sleeping in a jungle hut. She describes how she fell in love with an Indian prince, and she recounts her time teaching in a poor school in West Bengal. Other exciting adventures await—we delve into realms beyond reality in our passage through the subcontinent and back to England where the author is haunted by an evil spirit in an eighteenth century farmhouse in North Yorkshire.

Lightning Source UK Ltd.
Milton Keynes UK

171954UK00001B/9/P